Transylvanian
Vampires

Transylvanian Vampires

Folktales of the Living Dead Retold

ADRIANA GROZA

McFarland & Company, Inc., Publishers

Jefferson, North Carolina

LIBRARY OF CONGRESS CATALOGUING-IN-PUBLICATION DATA

Groza, Adriana, 1954–
    Transylvanian vampires : folktales of the living dead retold /
Adriana Groza.
        p.   cm.
    Includes bibliographical references and index.

    ISBN 978-0-7864-7702-9 (softcover : acid free paper) ∞
    ISBN 978-1-4766-1492-2 (ebook)

    1. Vampires—Romania—Transylvania. 2. Folklore—
Romania—Transylvania.   3. Vlad III, Prince of Wallachia,
1430 or 1431–1476 or 1477.   4. Dracula, Count (Fictitious
character) I. Title.
    GR830.V3G76 2014
    398.2109498—dc23   2014004617

BRITISH LIBRARY CATALOGUING DATA ARE AVAILABLE

On the cover: Portrait of Vlad the Impaler (Photos.com/
Thinkstock); background (iStockphoto/Thinkstock)

Printed in the United States of America

McFarland & Company, Inc., Publishers
  Box 611, Jefferson, North Carolina 28640
    www.mcfarlandpub.com

Table of Contents

Acknowledgments

A book of this sort is never the work of a single author. Of the many individuals who helped me along the way, I especially want to express my gratitude to Ligia Mirişan, Katherine Morse and David Drake, Lucian Groza, Vera Csorvasi, Joanne Ferraro, Allison King, Meredith King, Trina King, Glen McClish, Dorina Zaharescu, Mihaela Ghişe, Liviu Pop, Dana Ciorapciu, and Jim Edwards.

I also want to thank the directors and curators of the art museums at Cluj-Napoca, Craiova, and Oradea, as well as the National Art Museum in Bucuresti; the archivists at the Babeş-Bolyai University libraries, at the Biblioteca Academiei in Bucureşti and at its Cluj-Napoca branch; and the archivists at San Diego State University.

Finally, I want to express special gratitude to my husband, Ron King, who read and commented on every page of my manuscript.

Introduction

Adriana Groza with Ronald F. King

Count Dracula—the medieval Transylvanian aristocrat who survived the centuries by feasting on the blood of others, especially young virgins—was in fact born in London in 1897, and his "father" was Bram Stoker, an Irish novelist of horror stories. Transylvanians had never heard of him.

Transylvania, a province of modern Romania, does have a rich folk tradition in which vampires do appear. Usually they go by the names *strigoi* or *moroi*, and they exist alongside demons, werewolves, ghosts, evil spirits, or the devil as creations of the mythological imagination. In the past, Romania was comprised largely of peasant villages. Stories of the evil outsider reinforced moral norms and local integration. They also were a source of entertainment on cold winter nights in an era long before television or radio.

Vlad Țepeș, often known as Dracula, was a real Romanian historical figure. He was briefly prince of Wallachia (although he was born in Transylvania) toward the end of the 15th century and is celebrated for his courage in battle, moral righteousness, and ruthless punishment of enemies, whether domestic or foreign. His fame as a bloodthirsty tyrant is based largely on the propagandistic condemnations found in certain German and Turkish manuscripts of the period. To Romanians, however, he is remembered as national hero, brutal yet fair, who fought to preserve regional independence against imperial invaders.

Romanians, even today, tend to find strange the popular association of Transylvania, vampires, and Dracula. In their folk tradition, stories of vampires never mention Vlad; stories about Vlad Țepeș never contain the least hint that he was a vampire. Romanians smile politely when asked about their fangs and tolerate with good humor the tourists who come to the country on vampire tours. Yet popular image seems more powerful than historical reality. In the last few years, the Romanian state has even jumped on the bandwagon, promoting visits to "Dracula's Castle" and developing plans for a Dracula theme park.

This book, by contrast, remains true to the Romanian folk tradition. At its core are twenty-one village stories in which vampires play a critical role. I learned from extensive research in Romanian libraries and archives that there is no single, authoritative source for such stories. Some exist in continuing oral tradition. A few have been adapted for their own purposes by Romania's nationalist poets and writers. The most common source is the works of cultural historians and amateur anthropologists of the late 19th and early 20th centuries (Șăineanu 1886, 1895; Niculiță-Voronca 1903; Pamfile 1916; Dumitrașcu 1929) who compressed into brief mention, usually a paragraph or two, the long narratives that had been told and retold by village storytellers. My purpose for this volume is to re-expand what has been preserved only by compression, and thereby bring those narratives back to life.

The Romanian vampire stories in this book represent my own personal attempt to restore by re-creation a tradition that is disappearing. Expanding upon the fragments and summaries preserved in existing sources, I have written these tales as they would have been heard in the villages across the centuries. The original versions have often long been lost. The stories in the book are an accurate reflection of the great majority of all vampire themes found in the existing sources, and they are presented in a style authentic to the popular Transylvanian folk narrative. Nevertheless, the prose and the details of story construction are mine. Thus, the main chapters of this book sit somewhere between the innovative and the derivative. It is, after all, what tellers of folk tales have always done, appropriating an essential plot that gets reconstructed at each recounting, thereby providing continuity from past to present.

This volume also contains an interlude, placed mid-way through the stories, listing common vampire traits as found in the village stories. The categories specify who might become a vampire, what vampires do, how vampires can be recognized, and how one can defend oneself against a vampire threat. I have constructed these lists based on the traditions and superstitions that once circulated in Romanian folklore.

Finally, the volume contains seventeen Romanian folk stories about Vlad Țepeș that I translated into English from a compilation put together by Ion Stăvăruş (1993). A number of the historical chronicles written about Vlad—in German, Latin, Turkish, and Russian—have previously been translated (McNally & Florescu 1994; Teptow 2000). Instead, in keeping with my main focus, the stories in this volume are aspects of Romanian national folklore that circulated orally among the villages for centuries. The stories are not inconsistent with the archival history, but they embody the language, interests, and attitudes of common people.

One will not find in these pages romanticized accounts of aristocratic seducers, glamorous apparitions, Victorian damsels in distress, exotic conquerors of new worlds, powerful mystics, or controlling masters. The vampires of Transylvanian village stories come from a more modest—to my mind far more interesting– mythology. Nor will one find accounts of Vlad Țepeș as a predatory cross-generational survivor with hypnotic ability and a predilection toward drinking the blood of innocent virgins.

One of the goals for this volume is to reclaim the vampire story from the deformities imposed by contemporary popular culture. In its modern appearance, the vampire has transformed far beyond even Stoker's wild imagination, shifting from foreign nobility to gothic superhero to romantic teenage idol. In the process, the vampire has lost its individual identity and literary purpose. My opinion is that, in this transformation, the ageless vampire has now truly begun to die. He is being killed more effectively by popular proliferation than by garlic or religious icons or a stake through the heart.

It is important to remember and retell authentic folk vampire stories in a version similar to what once existed in Romanian villages. They teach simple but profound moral lessons and supply deep psychological insight into human desires and frailties, finely attuned to the rhythms of life. They are rooted in a historic European culture experienced in adversity and rich in symbolic representation. Transylvania deserves memory for its own vampire stories, not those artificially created for it by others. Before turning to the stories, however, a bit of background information might be helpful.

The Vampire Literature and Bram Stoker's Vampire

A popular vampire literature existed for more than a century before Bran Stoker's *Dracula* first appeared. Literary historians often begin with the short German poem "The Vampire" by Heinrich Ossenfelder (1748), in which a man whose love was rejected threatens to come nightly to suck the blood of a young maiden. Göethe's *Bride of Corinth* (1797) is similarly based on the living undead, in this case a young woman who leaves the grave in search of her love.

In the summer of 1816, Lord Byron, Percy Bysshe Shelley, Shelley's future wife Mary Wollstonecraft, and Byron's personal physician John Polidori spent a stormy night by Lake Geneva in Switzerland challenging each other to devise the best horror story. (It was the night that Mary Shelley invented Frankenstein.) Bryon had begun work on a vampire story but never completed it. Instead, it was Polidori's short story, "The Vampyre," that became a literary sensation. The main character, Lord Ruthven, was explicitly modeled on Byron. The work was originally published anonymously, and, at first, many attributed it to Byron. Polidori's story was immediately translated into German and French and sparked a new theatrical craze. Soon, there was "no theatre in Paris without its Vampire" (Summers 2001, 303). Alexandre Dumas and Claude Baudelaire wrote vampire stories. The most infamous of the 19th century versions was Sheridan Le Fanu's novella *Carmilla* (1872), with clear lesbian overtones.

Bram Stoker's contribution to the genre was to anchor the vampire legend to a specific person, Dracula, and to a specific region, Transylvania. This was certainly not his initial intent. As Stoker drafted the novel, his main character was called Count Wampyr. His working title was "The Un-Dead." His location was Styria, a region in Austria (the same location selected by Le Fanu). We know this because of the details contained in the book contract that Stoker signed in March 1897 with Archibald Constable and Co. Apparently, the changes in name and location—so critical to contemporary vampire lore—occurred only a little before final publication (McNally & Florescu 1994, 151).

While in London, Stoker sometimes published in a popular magazine, *The Nineteenth Century*. Also published in the magazine was an article by Emily Gerard entitled "Transylvanian Superstitions," which was later incorporated in her comprehensive book about Transylvania, *The Land Beyond the Forest* (1888). Gerard depicts Transylvania dramatically, as a place of fascination, foreboding with the supernatural. She wrote, "The very name of Transylvania tells us that it was formerly regarded as something apart, something out of reach, whose existence even for a time was enveloped in mystery" (Gerard 1888, 3). It is plausibly argued that Stoker was captivated by Gerard's portrayal, enough to change the location of his story.

While working on his novel, Stoker met with Arminius Vambery, a Hungarian professor and frequent visitor to the fashionable salons in London. The professor was the author of a history of Hungary and most likely served as the real-life inspiration for Professor Van Helsing, Dracula's nemesis. It is likely that Stoker learned stories about Vlad Țepeș from conversations with Vambery. There are records that Stoker researched Transylvanian geography and general history at the British Museum. His bibliographic search included William Wilkinson's *An Account of the Principalities of Wallachia and Moldovia* (1820). We also know that, during the 1880s, the British Museum had an exhibition on Eastern Europe and one of the featured exhibits was a manuscript about Vlad's alleged atrocities (McNally & Florescu 1994, 150). Stoker's *Dracula* is quite accurate regarding the Transylvanian region's main geographical landmarks. The characterization of its desolate nature is largely fanciful, as is the portrait of the actual medieval ruler known as The Impaler (Țepeș). Thus, history becomes reinvented through literature.

On the Historical Character of Vlad III, Dracula

Vlad Țepeș—formally Vlad III, and sometimes Dracula or Draculea—is the name of a real historical character who ruled as voivode (usually translated as prince) of Wallachia for seven years during the middle 15th century. He was born in Sighișoara (a city in Transylvania) in 1431. His father, also named Vlad, was a member of the chivalric Order of the Dragons, an organization founded to defend the Catholic Church and fight the Turkish infidels who were threatening to conquer that part of Europe. Old Vlad got his nickname, Dracul, from this affiliation (Treptow 2000, 8).

As Wallachia was contested territory between the Hungarian forces from the west and the Turkish forces from the east, Wallachian rulers, including Vlad Dracul and his son, Vlad Draculea, were compelled to play a complicated balancing game, shifting alliances and allegiances as circumstances dictated. In 1442, in order to rebuke a Hungarian-backed attempt to oust him from power, old Vlad agreed to pay tribute to the Ottomans and to send his two legitimate sons to the sultan's court. It was a common practice imposed upon vassals, used to ensure their fathers' loyalty. Young Vlad was eleven at the time. His younger brother (later called Radu the Handsome) was friendly with the sultan's son (later Mehmed II) and, eventually, became a leader of his Janissary troops. Vlad, instead, allegedly was more defiant and was treated more harshly. By psychological inference, it was here, most probably, he began to develop his famous shrewdness and disregard for human life, his taste for revenge, and hatred of Mehmed II.

In 1447, rebellious boyars linked to the Hunyadi royal family of Hungary rebelled against Vlad II, killing him. His oldest son, Mircea, was later tortured and buried alive. The Turks attempted to place Vlad III on the throne but were unsuccessful. In the resulting instability, Vlad fled, seeking protection during the years when Constantinople finally fell, and the Ottoman army pushed into Europe. Taking advantage of a Christian counter-attack in 1456, he seized the Wallachian throne and held it for the subsequent few years. He repressed squabbling boyars, strengthened the army, and joined with other Christian forces, led by King Matthias Corvinus of Hungary, in the offensive against the Turks.

Vlad III's leadership in battle, strategic skills, and great courage established his fame. He personally led his armies in several battles, including a famous victory over the superior forces of Hamza Pasha. He was praised throughout Europe when the Turkish army temporarily retreated across the Danube in 1462. Vlad also gained the terrible reputation of a cold-blooded killer from the manner in which he dealt with his enemies. His preferred punishment was impaling, resulting in his nickname Ţepeş. Apparently, he killed people eagerly. In a letter addressed to Matthias Corvinus, Vlad confessed to having killed men and women, old and young along the lower Danube. "We killed 23,884 Turks without counting those whom we burned in homes or the Turks whose heads were cut off by our soldiers" (Pop & Buzdugan 2006, 263).

By 1462, continuous battles with the forces led by his brother Radu (funded by the Turks and supported by rebellious boyars) left Vlad desperately in need of assistance. He traveled to Hungary, where he was betrayed by former ally, Matthias Corvinus, and imprisoned for more than ten years (Treptow 2000, 157–8). Eventually, the political climate changed. Radu III died suddenly in 1475, and Corvinus endorsed Vlad's return to power, confirmed by a dynastic marriage to one of his close relatives. Vlad's third reign, however, lasted only a few months before he was assassinated in late 1476.

During the years of his imprisonment, horror stories of Dracula's abject cruelty began to circulate, often written for propagandistic purposes. His victims allegedly ran as high as 80,000. Woodcuts showed him surrounded by stakes implanted in the ground, eating and drinking among those he impaled. The first of the foreign stories most likely resulted from an angry encounter between Vlad and three Benedictine monks proselytizing in his country. One of the monks was impaled, and the other two sought refuge at monasteries in lower Austria, where they entertained their hosts with exaggerated stories of what they had seen and heard. German-language manuscripts about Vlad, filled with accounts of sadistic torture and execution, were quite popular during the late 15th century, spreading with aid from the newly-invented printing press. The most famous was a poem by Michael Beheim, "The Story of a Bloodthirsty Madman Called Dracula of Wallachia"; it was performed in the court of Frederick III, Holy Roman Emperor. Turkish chronicles of the time supported this terrible image of their arch-enemy. Russian chronicles, instead, depicted the Wallachian Prince somewhat more positively, as a strong ruler whose actions were simultaneously "cruel but just" (Florescu & McNally 1989, 206).

Within the Romanian tradition, Dracula does not carry the indelible image of a terrifying monster. Historical accounts praise his skill in war, serving the Christian cause at a critical moment. For example, the Turkish sultan allegedly turned back to Constantinople upon seeing the 20,000 corpses impaled outside of Târgoviște. The Romanian accounts emphasize Vlad's campaign to rid the country of corruption and theft, and his harsh treatment of rich boyars. It was said that he ordered the boyars to build Poenari fortress with their own hands, and that the high standing of priest or boyar would not save an individual from death if he was accused of injustice or other evil. Over time, Vlad became the heroic subject of patriotic poems and symbol of moral rectitude. Every child in Romania can quote Mihail Eminescu's ironic lines (1881), wishing nostalgically that Vlad would return to grab all those responsible for societal decay, separate them into the "lunatics" and the "rogues," put the former in the asylum and the latter in jail, and then set fire to both institutions. This same positive image is captured in the everyday village folk tales about Vlad Țepeș translated as part of the present volume.

About Transylvania

If the real Vlad Țepeș was not the vampire of Stoker's imagination, the real Transylvania is not and has never been a savage wilderness filled with gloomy forests, ominous animal cries, and crumbling ancient castles. Stoker's fantastic novel needed a mythic location situated beyond the boundaries of civilization, designed to be other than sedate and civilized Victorian England. He thus gave Transylvania a reputation that it does not deserve.

The Transylvanian plateau is separated from the rest of Romania by the Carpathian mountain range to the south and east. To the west, it shares a border with Hungary. Using its present-day borders, it comprises nearly 100,000 square kilometers, approximately the size of Portugal or South Korea, of Kentucky or Indiana in the United States.

Anthropological excavations reveal evidence of settlements in the region stretching back to the Neolithic era. Transylvania was a center for Dacian civilization, and the extensive Dacian Kingdom (82 BC–AD 106) had its capital there. The region was discussed favorably in classical works by Herodotus and Ptolemy. The epic battles between the Dacian forces led by Decebal and the Roman forces of Trajan are commemorated on a famous column in Rome. Following the Dacian defeat, Transylvania became the furthest eastern territory of the Roman Empire.

After the Roman legions withdrew in AD 271, the territory was invaded and conquered by several migratory tribes—Avars, Bulgars, Cumans, Gepids, Huns, Magyars, Szekelys, and Visigoths. From the 10th through the 16th centuries, Transylvania was part of the Hungarian Empire, a Christian holding against the invading Ottoman armies. In 1601, Michael the Brave united Transylvania, Wallachia, and Moldova into a proto–Romanian state, but this lasted only one year before he was killed. In the following period of instability, Transylvania was an independent or semi-independent principality, sometimes a vassal of the Ottoman Empire, before firmly becoming incorporated into the Austrian-Hungarian Hapsburg Empire. It was reunited into Romania by the Treaty of Trianon after World War I. Except for a brief period during World War II, Transylvania has constituted one of the main provinces of contemporary Romania, with about one-third of the country's total population and slightly more than one-third of its GDP.

Transylvania is notable within Romania for its cultural, linguistic, and religious diversity. The region consistently has had an ethnic Romanian majority. Yet, despite the xenophobic communist period under Ceaușescu, the province still contains a significant number of Hungarians, Szeklars, Germans, and Roma. The cities are, architecturally, baroque jewels, with ornate theatres and spacious central squares.

Historically, however, the vast majority of ethnic Romanians were peasants, living in small, relatively self-contained villages. Romanian vampire folk stories are stories from these villages. Romanian vampires are, thus, village folk.

Transylvanian villages are places where time moved slowly. Inhabitants hardly ever traveled outside the local area. When they did, it was to regional town fairs to sell produce and buy necessary goods, or to visit relatives on special occasions. Those with knowledge of the wider world were most often former soldiers, young men who had been drafted to fight.

Geography established the relative isolation of the villages and also imposed constraints on the patterns of land use. It dictated the closeness of the village community, along with the jealousies and feuds of those who lived together in proximity. Given the lack of mobility, village local culture and traditions persisted easily across generations.

Households were largely self-sustaining. The family lived on what it could produce, supplemented to only a small degree with what it could secure from trade. Each household would have its own crops, livestock, and handicraft goods. The farm consisted of land that the family unit could work, rarely more. As a child, I spent summers in the village where my grandfather served as teacher and priest. The majority of people wore popular costumes. The elderly wore handmade shoes.

There was little social stratification to the Transylvanian village. Some peasants were more prosperous than others, of course, owning more fertile land or experiencing greater luck, but the sense of integrated community predominated any divisions of hierarchy. The priest was the local person of wisdom and authority. Doctors and lawyers belonged to the strange realm of towns and cities. There were no titles of nobility or rank, and there certainly was no perception that members of one family were by inheritance of name better than members of another.

Village life was predictable, with rhythms corresponding to those of nature. Work in the fields occurred in spring and summer; the fall was for harvest; winter was for indoor activity, especially repairs and weaving. Celebrations largely followed the Church calendar, establishing a regular cycle for community get-togethers and dances.

Peasant existence was largely quiet, peaceful, and stable. Life was difficult but not oppressive. Work was hard but not fruitless. Yet it would be wrong to romanticize the Romanian village. They were repositories of folk wisdom, but equally of folk superstitions. The world outside was often viewed as threatening, to be engaged at one's own peril. The person from outside was a stranger, carrying false promises and unanticipated risks. Even within the village, the random tragedies could spark terrible fears. It was a world of communal identity, but also of gossip, rumor, ignorance, and suspicion.

On Transylvanian Vampire Stories

One should understand Transylvanian vampire stories in this village context. Often in the villages, the unexplained receives explanation by means of the mystical. Stories are told of the strange forces at work in the world, that, at times, would invade and disturb the local order. These stories were also a source of community entertainment, and the expert storyteller was a village celebrity. The stories equally had a moral purpose—teaching correct behavior, reinforcing village norms and traditions, deepening local integration, and preserving the existing social structure against outside influence. All of these features are visible in the folktales of this volume.

The Transylvanian vampire is not a romantic hero. Nor is it the earthly representative of transcendent evil. It is certainly not the master from the underworld. Although it is dead, the vampire does not even fully belong to the "other world." In Romanian mythology, the forest is the symbolic place of uncontrolled nature and the wild beast. The vampire can enter this space, but it does not innately belong there.

In many Transylvanian vampire stories, the creature is someone who came from the village and had lived ordinarily among humans before the transformation and is often referred to by name. In some, the creature still lives in the village, pretending to be an inconspicuous member of the community. On occasion, it is concerned with home and family, and it takes its deadly cravings elsewhere, far from friends and lovers. In other Transylvanian vampire stories, the creature comes from outside the village, but is recognizable by villagers as potentially one of their own, albeit a bit strange in behavior.

No one in these stories chooses to be a vampire. The cause is not found in the self-centered desire for eternal life. This is not an ideal that the Romanian peasant dreams of. Some vampires are selected randomly, some by ill-fated accidents of birth, some as condemnation for wicked acts. Regardless of origin, the Transylvanian vampire does not welcome the experience. Most assuredly, the creature is not in pursuit of a fascinating existence full of endless possibilities and infinite opportunities, like the modern ones (Williamson 2005, 1). It is to be feared and pitied, not admired. There is nothing at all glamorous to the status of non-dead.

Nor is the Transylvanian vampire invincible. Its powers are real, but limited. Some, for example, can change shape into dogs or wolves. Nevertheless, effective countermeasures against vampires exist, and knowledge of these resides within village culture, often preserved by the old women or the wise priest. Romanian peasants are not quick to admit that the living undead has entered their domain, but the eventual realization does not bring shock or panic. Terrible forces exist in the world outside their village, and these, on occasion, intrude to disturb its peace and security. Appropriate remedies then become necessary, usually to be found via special potions, incantations, and religious icons, sometimes aided by the crowing of the cock and the emerging light of dawn. Cleansing the village of the vampire threat does not entail epic battle, but instead is an aspect of recurring struggle, far more common in purpose, to maintain the sanctity of the community against external threat.

The Transylvanian vampire thus does not share much family resemblance to the mysterious count of Bram Stoker's imagination, and even less when examined in contrast to the glitzy special effects and unrealistic fantasylands of the contemporary popular vampire production. The creature of Romanian folklore was embedded in a real, human culture, reflecting the apprehensions and anxieties of common people seeking to make sense of their existence. The fact that it emerged from the rural village community should not mislead us into trivializing the embedded meanings and symbols. Rather, as an expression of the collective unconscious, the folk vampire story reveals systems of attitudes and values inherent to the human condition—instructing moral behavior, reinforcing social unity, helping to cope with the unknown, and profoundly reaffirming the integration of death within the normal cycle of life.

First, regarding moral instruction, vampire stories are often cautionary tales intended to reinforce good behavior and established customs. Therefore, in this volume, there are stories that emphasize the virtues of housekeeping, of loyalty to friends, of kindness toward strangers, of proper religious ritual, of moderation in one's abuses, and of accepting responsibility for one's errors. Most of the stories instruct by means of negative models, warning of the risks entailed by violation, for, otherwise, the vampire might get you. You should not promise things beyond your ability to deliver, for instance, or you tempt the vampire to act on your behalf. You should not be greedy or dishonest in business dealings, for your target might well be a vampire, easily capable of turning the tables on you and taking its revenge. Virginity before marriage, most certainly, is among the virtues promoted; unlike the Victorian romance, however, there are no undertones of repressed sexuality and no fixation with the blood of virgins.

The second theme visible within these stories is the construction of social unity. Evil, most often, does not reside naturally within the village itself, but instead exists on the margin or comes from the outside. It is a permanent threat to the soldier or the traveler who departs the confines of the safe and comfortable community. It is transported inside by uninvited strangers, especially those who seek to purchase confidence but should not be trusted. A common theme is the mysterious suitor for an innocent village girl, whose background is unknown and whose behavior is particularly secretive. Young girls should not blindly follow their hearts; there are dangers when one rejects the familiar and dreams of the exotic.

The vampire story thus promotes the distinction between us-and-other, those who belong and those who do not, those to be encountered with confidence and those with suspicion. The outlook is decidedly parochial and narrow, but it served to reinforce the close communal relationships necessary to the isolated peasant village, and it reminded villagers of the importance of collective security, to work together against common dangers. The terrors of the private domain could eventually spill into the broader, public domain if not promptly addressed and properly disposed of; the afflictions to one family could just as easily descend upon another.

Third, all of the stories in this volume involve death or the ominous presence of death. In this context, the Romanian vampire tale addresses directly two of the inherent uncertainties of the human condition—what happens after death, and why some people die unanticipated deaths (including innocents who do not "deserve" death) without obvious cause or explanation. Regarding the former, the intermediary space between life and death, the space allegedly occupied by vampires, does not exist within the doctrines of Romanian Orthodox Christianity. There is no purgatory or antechamber to the afterlife. For the Orthodox, spirits after death enter either heaven or hell. Vampires, by contrast, are anchored on the axis between life and death, and it is this ambiguous status that awards them some degree of magical power. Yet vampires profane the sacred realm of death and simultaneously bring corrupted mysteries into the secular realm of life. It is the obligation of humans to restore the legitimate separation of the realms, and, in this task, they can find assistance from religious rituals and icons. The underlying lesson is that people must submit to the finality of death, accepting without question or challenge its absolute authority.

Importantly in these stories, although Christianity can help to defeat the vampire, it never succeeds in eliminating the underlying threat. The symbolic implication is that the Romanian vampire tradition arose independently of Christianity and is quite a bit older. This most likely explains the long endurance of the village vampire narrative. Transylvanians customarily describe themselves as "brothers of the forest." No village is far from the forest where the sun barely penetrates, within which, according to pre–Christian mythology, roam magical creatures and fantastic beings. Among them, sometimes, is the vampire. Extraordinary and surprising things happen at random in the forest. Unexpected dangers emerge from it. Venturesome travelers and innocent wanderers alike can be victimized. In a traditional world where death comes unforeseen, the old "mythology of the forest" provides welcome understanding. Enduring and encompassing nature is strange and powerful, containing primeval forces that pre-exist human virtue and vice. They can be resisted only temporarily. The rich, non-transparent realm of paradox and mystery must be recognized as part of fate. Historic village folk culture is filled with lessons of acceptance, bordering on resignation to the unexplained powers that reside in nature.

Thus, most important, the Transylvanian vampire story helps to domesticate death, normalizing the rhythms of life and immunizing us against our ultimate fears. Death is commonplace and not always explicable. People should reject the alternative of immortality and all artificial constructions that promise to extend consciousness beyond its normal borders. There is a legitimate order to things, and one must make peace with the inevitable. Even untimely death, as represented by the vampire attack, visits the community periodically. The vampire, simultaneously, is repelled yet anticipated. There is a famous Romanian ballad in which a young shepherd destined to be murdered in the morning spends the evening not attempting to escape but instead telling his sheep with serenity and dignity that his time to marry death is approaching. These vampire tales, therefore, do not represent the global battle against consuming evil, but instead reduce our fears to a scale that is manageable, promoting harmony and balance with the natural world.

The object of this volume is to take the partial accounts and narrative fragments about Romanian vampires as found in the anthropological literature and to retell them as stories, thereby bringing them back to life. It is not important whether people in the villages actually believed them. Their purpose, across centuries, was to entertain and instruct. They remain today important mechanisms for transmitting traditions, worldviews, and values. The folk story is an enduring vehicle of cultural conversation. Authentic meanings have been removed and are in danger of being forgotten through the radical adaptations of the vampire legend by Bram Stoker and his popular successors. The Romanian vampire story, for its own intrinsic virtues, merits due attention and regard.

PART I

Village Morality and the Danger from Vampires

The Daughter of the Priest

Romanian stories from the villages are often morality tales. They instruct that one should follow established patterns and lead responsible lives, or become a victim of the vampire. We thus begin with a simple and cautionary tale about the virtues of good housekeeping.

My story is developed out of a brief abstract from Pamfile, printed in his Mitologie Românească *(1916/2000, 108–9). The attributed source is a much longer version told to him by N.I. Munteanu, a peasant who lived in the village of Zărneşti-Jorăşti.*

There are a number of similar stories about vampires who kill or eat maidens who fail at their housekeeping. Folk tales often reflect the customs and traditional behaviors embedded in daily village chores. Hard work is praised and rewarded whereas laziness is punished. Some other variants of the basic plot, found throughout the Balkan region, end with a gory description of the murdered woman. This is unusual for the majority of Romanian vampire folk tales merely acknowledge death, yet do not paint a striking visual image.

Once upon a time, there was a priest who lived alone with his daughter, Irina. His wife had died unexpectedly after a very short illness, and the young girl had to take over the management of the household.

Irina and her father lived in a small house, as the priest did not put much value on earthly goods. He believed that they should not live in luxury. He did believe in cleanliness and neatness.

The priest's wife had been a hardworking woman. She had taken much pride in their house, which she kept immaculate. The other women of the village admired her and considered her a role model. They would often come to her for advice, from housekeeping and cooking to very personal issues.

Even now, with the wife dead, the door to the priest's house was

always open. It was common for people to just stop by, both those who needed help and those who offered help.

Fortunately, Irina inherited her mother's good disposition. She was welcoming and did her best to keep the house exactly as it had been when her mother was alive. But she was inexperienced and not quite as meticulous as her mother would have liked.

Her mother had paid special attention to finishing her cleaning by night, leaving the kitchen absolutely spotless. She would say, "The kitchen is the heart of a house. The life and health of a house comes from it. It feeds us, but it can kill us because the vampires can enter the house through it."

Vampires, she insisted, have power over certain objects and can make those objects obey their commands. To prevent this from happening, her mother taught Irina, everything must be neatly back in place by the time a woman left the kitchen in the evening.

Her mother would never put out the candle and leave for the bedroom before double-checking that each dish was in its place and was facing down. She also made sure that the water jug was not empty. Every evening before going to bed, she would fill the jug with fresh water and cover it with a tiny embroidered napkin.

"The angel of the house should always find fresh water to drink in our small abode," she would say.

Despite the loss of the mother, things went relatively well in the priest's household. Irina was careful and conscientious so as not to disappoint her father. One day, however, her father had to go to a ceremony in the neighboring village and planned to stay there overnight. Irina was in charge of the house by herself for the first time. Neighbors came to help with the cow and the garden during the day. But in the evening, after everybody left, she was alone.

After she finished the chores of the day, Irina locked the doors and bolted the windows as advised. She cleaned up in the kitchen after she ate. She washed the few dishes she had used and swept the floor. But she was too tired to double-check that everything was perfectly arranged in its place.

Opposite: Petrecere câmpenească (Pastoral Party), Arthur Verona (1868–1946). **The Romanian vampire comes from the peasant villages. This painting shows the traditional community dancing the *hora* together. The vampire, representing the village "outsider," sometimes comes to prey at such events (courtesy Craiova Art Museum).**

"I am sure everything is fine. It always is. Besides, nobody other than me was inside the house today," she thought to herself. So she blew out the candle and went into her bedroom.

At midnight, a vampire came lurking. He wanted to get inside the house, for he knew that the girl was alone and could not be protected that night by the priest, her father.

He tried to open the doors, but they were locked. So he began asking for help.

"Hey, mugs! Come quickly and open the door for me!" the vampire ordered. "We cannot move," the mugs answered. "We have been placed face down."

"Hey, pots! Come quickly and open the door for me!" the vampire ordered. "We cannot move," the pots replied. "We have been placed face down."

The vampire tried and tried, calling to other objects but with no success. Finally, it was the water jug's turn. "Hey, water jug! Come quickly and open the door for me!" the vampire shouted.

Unfortunately, the jug was empty. Irina had forgotten to fill it with fresh water. The angel of the house had come by earlier, but it did not stay to watch over the house. It had become thirsty and left to go elsewhere because there was no water in the jug to drink.

The empty jug heard the vampire's command and had to obey. Reluctantly, it unlocked the door and let the vampire in.

The next day, when the priest returned home, his daughter was dead.

The Wedding Day

Fear of the unknown is an entrenched and inherent theme in Romanian villages. The outsider is suspect, for he comes from unfamiliar places, carries unfamiliar experiences, and might bring with him concealed dangers. One must always be wary of mysterious strangers, especially if they intend to seduce young virgins. Village girls face grave danger if they choose to stray from traditional paths.

Opposite: Peisaj de vară la țară/În curte (Summer Landscape /In the Court-yard), Theodor Aman (1831–1891). The Romanian traditional village of the 19th century was relatively poor, comprised of simple houses, unpaved roads, and shared wells. This painting shows a woman doing her washing in public and well-dressed man who clearly does not belong (courtesy Craiova Art Museum).

Folk stories that warn against marrying the stranger were relatively common in central and eastern Europe. In this example, the lurking vampire is defeated by supernatural forces. The villagers did not realize the risk and did nothing to deter it. Yet salvation came from above, implying that God is ever watchful in protecting the flock.

My story is developed from a brief comment about religious holidays that Pamfile collected from G.F. Ciauşanu and published in his Mitologie Românească *(1916/2000, 103). Importantly, it features St. Elijah's day, July 20 in the Romanian Orthodox calendar. According to Transylvanian superstition, St. Elijah uses his lightning to rid the world of evil. The saint tends to punish those who work on his day rather than celebrate it. Elijah is especially merciless toward vampires and other malevolent creatures that dare to walk the earth on that day. Senn (1982, 109) cites interviews from Transylvanian peasants who, allegedly, still fear the unforgiving power of St. Elijah's lightning.*

Once upon at time, there was a nice young girl named Veronica. She was loved by everybody, for she was both hardworking and merry. She was always busy around the household. Her laughter and singing would tell you where she was. In the morning, she was in the garden, clearing it of weeds, planting new things, or harvesting vegetables for the day's meals. In the afternoon, she did her chores in the family's small cottage, cleaning and dusting, but she usually made time to visit her friends. They would sit and work on their embroidery, fashioning linen and clothes for their dowry, and talk happily about their future. Sometimes, Veronica would go to work the village fields, together with other members of her family, where she would cheer people up with her songs. At night, she would help her mother prepare the family meal and neaten things afterward.

Veronica was always happy. Her siblings and friends wanted to be in her company. As a result, she always had help with her housework and with her little pranks, too. Last summer, for example, after a big hailstorm, she convinced her sisters and friends to go out and play with the ice in the meadows. Another round of the storm came by, and they all were stranded in the old mill until late that evening.

They all thought it was funny, although Veronica's mother had warned: "Don't go out! Stay close to a shelter! The storm is not done yet. It's St. Elijah's day. There will be more thunder and lightning today."

The villagers believed that St. Elijah used lightning to kill vampires. They also believed it was not wise to go outside on St. Elijah's day because the saint was not a good shot, as he sometimes missed his target. How else could one explain why, sometimes, innocent people were hit by his bolts. The villagers delighted in telling and retelling stories of the bad things that happened on this particular day. Some time ago, the barn at the old mill was struck by lightning and burned down. A few years ago, a traveler resting under a big tree was struck and killed.

Like all young people, Veronica thought she was invulnerable, safe from all danger. Her favorite time of the day was the early evening. Behind her house was a large orchard, which led to the top of a hill. From there, she would feast her eyes on green mountains and valleys. She especially loved to watch the sunset. She would watch the sun go down as often as possible, and she liked to spend this moment by herself. She had a favorite spot at the far end of the orchard, by a tiny spring. It was a remote place, with only an overgrown hedge separating the family property from a big pasture. Often times, she would sit there and sing peaceful tunes to herself while watching the shadows grow darker and swallow the valley below.

"Don't stay out in the dark by yourself," her mother would warn. "Young women should not sit outside all alone at late hours. Only bad things happen at night. This is when vampires and evil spirits look for prey."

But Veronica did not listen to her mother. She loved the view and the fragrances of the orchard. Besides, there was something else that attracted her there.

For a few nights now, a handsome young man had been passing by. She was not quite sure how things started or where he came from. One evening, he was just standing there, on the other side of the thick raspberry hedge. She was humming a song to herself, watching the sun approach the horizon across the valley. She felt his gaze and turned around. He was looking at her with fascination, with an enigmatic smile on his face.

Before she understood what she was doing, she responded to his admiration and smiled back. Everything happened so spontaneously that she did not have time to be afraid. After all, she was alone with a stranger in a relatively remote place. A moment later, she remembered her shyness and ran toward home. But her heart was lighter.

The scene was repeated a few evenings later, and then again. Apparently, he was in no hurry to speak to her, and that reassured her. Later, he politely asked her name, and they started talking, as young people do.

Veronica did not know exactly why, but she felt strongly that she should keep their meetings a secret. She believed that it was his wish, which she understood intuitively. But it was also her wish because the private meetings of the two young people were so delightful. Anyway, she did not tell anybody about the mysterious stranger and their evening conversations at the far end of the orchard.

Nevertheless, she did become curious about the man's identity. "Who is he?" she wondered. She was positive that she knew all the nice young men in the village. He told her that his name was Sandu, but this was while he was merrily teasing her about names, so she was not really sure he had told the truth.

"Could he be Sandu, the teacher's nephew?" she wondered. "Is he the same boy from the far-away city who would spend summer holidays here when we were only nine or ten?" That Sandu had a white puppy that played fetch and sat so well at command. But then she remembered that the boy from her memory had blue eyes, and this stranger's eyes were very dark.

Veronica, increasingly curious, started asking him more direct questions. No, he was not from nearby. No, he did not have relatives in the village. He had some business in the area and had to travel quite a lot. However, he told her, he was planning to settle down in the region. In fact, he was about to buy property in the village—the old mill with all the land surrounding it.

Indeed, she soon learned of rumors that a mysterious stranger wanted to buy the old mill. It was said that a young man appeared at the house of the person who inherited that abandoned property and offered a good price to buy it. "Isn't that lucky!" people said. "The place will be restored and inhabited again." Later, further stories spread. "Guess what! The stranger paid for the mill with gold coins, some rare old ducats that looked like new. I saw some of them with my own eyes."

"I have worries," commented the old blacksmith, one of the wisest men of the village. "The old mill is doomed. One of the millers was killed by a vampire. It was during our grandparents' time, and he, too, became a vampire. The miller and his kin are still haunting that place. Bad things will start happening if anybody disturbs them."

But the younger people of the village laughed at these old tales. Many were pleased that there would soon be a functioning mill close by, and that they would not have to cart their grains several miles away. Moreover, the old blacksmith passed away a few days later. In recent years, he had become quite thin and frail, so nobody noticed that he suddenly appeared to have lost all his blood. It was even a relief not to hear his constant reminders of bad history from times long past.

Veronica was now very happy. She could not wait for evenings to come. Together the couple began talking of the future. When he asked how she might like living at the old mill, she knew he was soon going to propose marriage. A few days later, he did propose, and she accepted joyfully although with one condition. "Yes," she said, "I will marry you, but you will have to meet my parents and formally ask them for my hand. That is the custom in our village. I would not have it any other way."

The stranger agreed and promised that, in one week, he would ask her parents for her hand. It would have to be in the late afternoon because he had to travel on business during the day.

Veronica was delighted, and so was her family. They were eager to meet the man, impressed that he was wealthy enough to buy a nice property. Yet they also held back from too great a show of excitement. They were quiet mountain people, like all Transylvanians, and tended to wait for things to follow their normal course. "We will see how much value we put on him when he shows up," the father said.

On the arranged afternoon, as the sun began to set, the young man came to the family home and politely asked for Veronica's hand in marriage. All went well, and the wedding day was settled for the end of that month. "It will work out just fine," her mother commented. "You will be married on the eve of St. Elijah's day, just as we had married."

As with most girls anticipating their wedding, Veronica was impatient. She had prepared her dowry chest, full of lovely things, many of which she had made herself as the custom required. She had beautifully embroidered towels and sheets and pillows, and she daydreamed about how to arrange them in the big house she would get to occupy. She did not dare to go to the mill on her own, but sent her two younger brothers, 13 and 14, to inspect the place and report back to her.

The boys were more than willing to oblige. They always had been intrigued by the old mill and welcomed the idea of exploring it. Now, they were sent there on a mission. What could be better than that! They even invited some of their friends to share in the fun.

Their report confused everybody. Allegedly, nothing had changed at the mill. There had been no new construction. The place was falling apart. It looked as if not a soul had walked through it in years. Yet people, wanting to believe the best, were forgiving. "He probably did not yet have time to start the renovations," the parents counseled. "He must be traveling a lot."

Veronica's young man somehow knew about the boys' visit. When the lovers next met, he told her directly, "If you want to see my house, just ask me to show it to you. It is soon also going to be yours. Do not send the boys! They don't know how to look at things."

Later that evening, as they took their evening walk together, the man prompted Veronica to talk about her dream house. "I would like it to have enough room for me to display my embroidered pillows; that's for sure. I would also like it to have a nice room for a hand-carved cradle for when, you know..." she told him, blushing. And he answered, "You had better come and see the house with your own eyes."

They decided to meet the next day at the mill. "Come tomorrow at dusk," he instructed. "But you must come alone."

The old mill was on the outskirts of the village, but the walk there was not too long. The house was hidden by old weeping willows although its high, tiled, red roof was visible from miles afar. The young man was waiting for Veronica at the gate.

The girl felt a slight dizziness as she walked over the threshold. The house was chilly as the evening was slowly settling in and the sunlight was disappearing. To her surprise, the rooms were partially but beautifully furnished. There were nice wooden benches waiting for her embroidered cushions and oak chests waiting for her clothes. The windows only needed some curtains, like those she had been working on. In one small corner room, there was a hand-carved cradle. Everything she desired was there, just as she had dreamed.

"Oh, the silly boys," she thought. "One can never trust them. They do not know how to look. Who knows what they actually saw. Maybe by mistake they had explored an old barn somewhere else."

Veronica was counting the days until her wedding. She had grown a little weak lately. A few times, she had almost fainted. But she insisted that there was nothing really wrong. She was just a little tired with all the preparations and emotions.

Her father was more concerned. "Let us all hope that she will be fine. Let us pray that her newly acquired paleness is not a sign of the strange disease that lately has been ravaging the village. Several people have died of it, although they seemed healthy just days before."

Her mother insisted, "She will be fine after the wedding. Women just worry more."

Four days before the ceremony, the local priest came to talk to Veronica's parents. "I come with a suggestion. Why don't you postpone the date for the wedding ceremony so that people can celebrate it fully and with complete pleasure. There will be two funerals on the scheduled day, the eve of St. Elijah's day, and the same villagers will be attending all of these events. This strange and fatal disease that we are fighting is keeping me very busy."

"The reasons make sense," Veronica's father agreed. "We will have the wedding on the following day, on St. Elijah's day, so that people will not have two sad funerals right before the festive wedding. The sad and the happy should not occur together under the same sun." The priest offered to announce the change, so that everybody knew of it.

"What an excellent idea," Veronica's mother said. And she added, with her customary talk, "It will be a double celebration—of the wedding in our family and of they day when St. Elijah uses his lightning to rid the world of vampires. This should bring the couple additional good luck."

On St. Elijah's, the morning promised great weather with a clear sky. Everything was going well. People were gathered at the bride's house, waiting for the wedding ceremony to begin. They anticipated good food and cheer, and looked forward to hours of dancing.

When the groom arrived to meet his bride, however, all eyes set upon him with apprehension. The weather suddenly changed as he walked toward the house. The wind blew angrily, and gray hail clouds hid the sun. Thunder roared in the distance and lightening lit the darkening skies. The bolts struck increasingly nearer, closer and closer in rapid succession. The last spark of lightning hit its target in full, striking the bridegroom as he stopped before the gate. People gasped, one large, common gasp like a wave.

All saw it together. First, the stranger turned into an ugly monster. Then it began to burn. Then the fire extinguished itself with a horrible, unnatural hiss.

In no time, all that was left was a pile of black ashes. Even that did not last long. The black clouds dissipated, and the angry winds hurried away, taking the ashes along with them.

Nothing again was heard of the mysterious man. The old mill remained in ruins. The epidemic of strange deaths ended.

The Mysterious Suitor

This is a somewhat similar story about the dangers that come when young girls reject the familiar and pursue relationships with strangers. One certainly should be warned against "men from the outside world or the other world." The vampire here is cunning and manipulative, yet in the end, the girl is saved. This time, however, the critical intervention comes from a loving human rather than from supernatural forces. A true heart and strong courage are required to overcome the evil outsider and restore village equilibrium.

My story was inspired by an account in Şăineanu (1895, 570) with the title "The Fiancée of the Vampire." Şăineanu only provided a one-paragraph summary, but he also listed a number of variants that he encountered. The differences come primarily from the manner in which the girl escapes from the vampire's clutches. In some, her family intervenes; in others, it is a loyal brother or a rival suitor. Sometimes the girl manages to save herself at the last moment, but, on occasion, deliverance is unavailable, and the girl dies.

This was the second wedding in the family. Cornelia, the middle daughter, was getting married to Radu, a local young man. It was an impressive affair with plenty of food. A huge pig and tens of chickens had kept the butcher very busy the day before. The grassy yard was nicely prepared for the feast. There was a large dining area and a large dancing area. The ten long tables could seat twelve people each, but, still, people would take turns on the wooden benches. In the back, the improvised outdoor kitchen was lit by open cooking fires, as was normal for such occasions.

The midwives of the village, in charge of the food for all big events, had made hundreds of stuffed cabbage leaves (*sarmale*) – everybody likes them and eats at least three in a serving. The women had worked busily all morning boiling the soup and potatoes in big cauldrons. They were used to working together for the occasions when villagers got together, mostly weddings or funerals. In fact, there had been a funeral to prepare just a few days before. Today, however, everybody was happy, chatting merrily about this and that.

Nearly all the villagers were there, as the custom required. Attending were the relatives of the bride and groom, their friends, and their neighbors. These people knew one another very well for they would often get together as part of community life.

As people arrived, they congregated around the big pots, eager to taste the delicious-smelling food. A little farther across the yard, the hosts were pouring generous servings of the homemade plum brandy and red wine. People first would whet their appetite with the strong brandy. Then they would wash the food down with the bloody red wine. All were cheerful and noisy, and they repeatedly toasted the newlyweds.

"Beautiful bride! You are allowed to cry a little today since you are leaving your parents' home, but then smile to your chosen husband and new life!" an old man shouted.

"To the health of the hosts of this party, the happy parents of the bride! Two daughters already married! Only one more to give away!" an uncle said.

"You mean only one more to have taken away from me," the father of the bride yelled back.

The feast was on. A band played music on the lawn, and the youths danced. The old women watched and wondered what new couples were being formed under their eyes. That's what happens at village events, and that's what happened exactly one year before when Maria, the family's older daughter, married the mayor's son. Now, with the two older siblings out of the house, all agreed that it was Zina's turn to choose a husband. In fact, Petru, the groom's younger brother, had eyes only for her and was full of hope.

But Zina was not interested in any of the local lads. She was curious about "men from the outside world or the other world." This is how she teasingly would refer to people who were not from her village.

Toward the evening, a person from "the outside world" did appear at the wedding. Seemingly out of nowhere, a handsome stranger showed up while everyone was dancing. He was thin and pale and wore dark clothes. From the beginning, the man gazed intensely across at Zina, as if he were there especially for her, invited by her thoughts and desires. She noticed him immediately and responded to his gaze. The two young people danced together until late. By the end of the festival, she was entirely under his spell, smitten by his magnetic eyes.

The mysterious stranger reappeared out of nowhere, just like the first time, on several other occasions. He would stand by the fence of the vegetable garden as Zina was picking produce for dinner. He would materialize by the stone well to help her carry the heavy water buckets, lifting them as if they were feathers and leaving them at her doorstep with no visible effort. Soon they started to walk together under the willows by the river or in the shade of the orchard on the outskirts of the village. Each time, their path would take her further away, toward the old cemetery by the forest.

The stranger was not a merry companion. He never laughed. He also never answered her questions about himself, his work, or his background. He valued his privacy, he said. This made Zina ever more intrigued and smitten with him, and so she agreed to keep their relationship secret for a while longer.

One evening, the young man brought Zina a ring and asked her to marry and go away with him. Zina was overjoyed by the proposal and the idea of a life beyond the village. She was especially fascinated by the ring. Once she put it on, she felt as if she belonged to him exclusively. Since she was not supposed to wear the ring in public—only temporarily, he assured her—Zina tied it into her handkerchief and put it in her bosom, close to her heart.

She promised to leave with the man in three weeks. She also promised not to tell anyone about their plans. He was afraid, he told her, that her parents would not consent for her to marry somebody who was not a local. Later on, he explained, once they had traveled to his home and lived amongst his family, they could come back to the village for a visit. They would bring expensive gifts to appease the family, convincing them that her move away was the right thing.

But keeping such a secret was too much for Zina. She wanted to show off her ring and talk about her fiancé. She wanted to share her emotions and anticipation with someone especially dear to her. Of her two older sisters, Zina was closer to the middle one, the recent bride, and so she decided to make Cornelia her confidante.

The sister was surprised at the news. At first, she hesitated but then agreed to support Zina's decision. "Now that I am so happily married," the sister confessed, "it is only fair that I should help you find such joy."

Cornelia, however, knew that her brother-in-law Petru was in love with Zina and hoped to marry her. She and her husband had often talked about how much fun it would be for two brothers to marry two sisters and live nearby to each other and share work on the family land. She did not tell her husband about Zina's plans to elope with a stranger, as she did not wish to betray her sister. But she did let her husband know that Cornelia was in love with somebody other than Petru and advised him to discourage the brother's pursuit of Zina lest he should end up with a broken heart.

Petru, though, was too much in love and would not willingly let anybody take Zina from him. He suspected that he knew his rival, the mysterious stranger who went walking with Zina in the evenings. (As is common with young men in love, Petru quietly watched the girl when she was unaware.) "I do not like this stranger," Petru decided. "He does not belong here. He is not one of us. I am going to find out who he really is, and then try to get rid of him."

He asked around the village, but no one knew who the dark stranger was, or where he lived. In fact, only a few really saw him, and they could barely remember anything about him other than the vaguely chilling memory of a shadow.

At the end of the week, there was a dance for youths in the central square of the village. Petru stood on the margin, waiting for the stranger. He saw Zina arrive and watched her look around as if in search of somebody. Then, suddenly, there he was, standing in shade of the big walnut tree. The stranger had appeared as if by magic. "Where did he come from? How is it that I never noticed him arrive?" Petru wondered.

Zina saw the stranger, too, and walked toward him right away. They talked for a short while and then strolled slowly down a grassy lane toward the entrance of a big orchard that stretched all the way to the fields. Petru followed them secretly and heard her say, "No, not tomorrow. I am not yet ready. Let us leave in two weeks as we initially decided."

Petru could not hear more because he had to hide quickly behind a bush, afraid that he might be caught spying. He waited for a few minutes and then followed again. "Where is he taking her?" he wondered, more disturbed with each step.

The path ran through the orchard, leading to the old cemetery on the outskirts of the village. There was little out here but the road connecting to a village on the other side of the mountain. It was not a commonly traveled road. It rapidly climbed upwards and become rugged and unsafe, especially through the forest. People came this way mainly to reach some distant summer sheepfold or to get lumber for firewood.

Petru hastened to catch up with the couple. The man was leading the way now, as Zina's courage seemed to have deserted her. They had nearly reached the point where the footpath crossed the mountain road. A carriage appeared in the distance, and Zina jumped back with a cry. "My father! He wasn't supposed to be back till tomorrow. He finished his trades with the shepherds earlier than planned. Oh, my God, I have to run home immediately!"

The stranger, however, continued on his way and Petru cautiously followed as the man entered the cemetery and stopped near a grave. It must have been somewhat recently dug because wreaths were still piled on top of it, although they were all now dry.

The shadows were getting longer as the sun set behind the hills. A chilly breeze was blowing and the leaves of the old trees started to shiver. Petru approached slowly, his steps muffled by the grassy path. "It is getting more frightening here by the minute. What is he trying to do?" Petru wondered. He reached for his pocketknife, not sure why, just to have it in hand in case something happened.

He saw the stranger pulling at the wreaths with determination, as if he was trying to open the tomb. The stranger then stopped, sensing the presence of the intruder. He turned around, obviously annoyed at the interruption. His dark eyes sent ominous arrows at Petru. His face started to change, and a savage sneer revealed a set of sparkling fangs. The face looked more like a wolf's than a man's.

Petru was overcome by an unnatural fear. He felt paralyzed and incapable of reacting. The creature walked slowly towards him. It hit him hard in the chest and then threw him effortlessly to the ground. It crouched and prepared to attack him more decisively. The young man was not sure how it had happened, but his pocketknife was in his hand. He slashed upwards, the silver blade catching the attacker's clothes and cutting deeply into its legs. With horror, Petru observed that the stranger's legs were not normal. They were furry and had a curious shape. The harsh truth was thus revealed. "This man is not a human being. He is a vampire, and he is here in our village."

The creature roared in anger and readied itself for the final assault. With the strength that only the fear of dying can generate, Petru jumped to his feet, caught hold of the cross he always wore around his neck, and ran toward safety, never looking back. Fortunately, the creature did not pursue him, God knows why.

Over the following few days, Petru was too weak to walk, but he was unable to rest. The mysterious rival, he now knew, was a vampire. A person who looks a vampire directly in the eyes is condemned to a short life. He would continue to grow weaker and weaker, and soon would die unless somehow he could overcome the creature.

Far more troubling was the recognition that Zina was in mortal danger. There was no way she simply would believe his story. The vampire controlled her thoughts through unnatural powers. But he had to try something, for there was little time before the intended elopement.

In desperation, Petru begged his brother to carry him to Zina's house, saying that he urgently had to see her on a matter of life and death. His behavior was so unusual that the brother consented.

Zina, too, was surprised to see Petru arrive at her doorstep, so pale and infirm. In pity, she agreed to listen to what he had to say. Of course, she did not believe him, but she did not dismiss him harshly. "Poor Petru, he's obviously sick and jealous," she thought. But some seeds of doubt were effectively planted. Zina began to wonder about the extreme secrecy upon which her fiancé strongly insisted. To allay any doubt, she devised a test.

The following evening, when she and the secret fiancé met for their walk together, Zina said she had to leave early in order to visit her aunt's house. Her parents were there, she explained, and had planned for the family to walk home together. This was only a pretense. Zina intended to follow her man without notice, as Petru had begged her to do. He had also given her his pocketknife with the silver blade for protection.

Zina cautiously followed the fiancé as he took the road toward to the old cemetery. She kept her distance and hid in the dark shadows of the walnut trees along the road. She watched the man enter the graveyard and approach a grave exactly in the area that Petru had mentioned in his account. When he reached it, he stopped and—right then and there—transformed into a large black dog, in front of her very eyes. There was no denying the fact. The mysterious fiancé was a horrible vampire whose home was the grave.

Zina was shocked. It happened so quickly that thoughts had no time to form in her head. The creature, however, sensed her presence and turned around. Two fangs sparkled, and two red ferocious eyes fixed on her angrily.

The wind stopped, the long shadows of the evening froze, and a cold silence engulfed everything. The dog opened its mouth, snarling with menacing fangs, ready to jump in her direction. Zina panicked, stepped backwards, and tripped. The special ring fell from its hiding place in her bosom and rolled away into the grass. Somehow, in her hand, was the pocket knife, its blade shining brightly. She never fully understood whether it was the dog that landed on the knife or whether she had actually stabbed it in self-defense. Before she realized what had happened, the dog was dying with a horrible sound. The silver blade was embedded fully in its heart. The body of her attacker then turned to dust, and the dust blew away. Not a trace of the bloody battle or of the strange creature remained for evidence.

Zina stood there in the reddish dusk. A pleasant summer breeze caressed the tall grass, and the crickets were singing themselves to sleep.

It took some time and patience for Zina to regain her tranquility and for Petru to recover his strength. Eventually, the two of them could be seen walking together through village, holding hands and talking quietly. And Zina never again was heard to say that she was curious about men "from the outside world or the other world."

The Promise

A common theme in village stories is the peasant who thinks himself too calculating and clever. He even seeks to cheat his neighbors in business dealings, offering trades that augur windfall profits for apparently little cost. In the end, of course, things turn out badly, and there are penalties to pay. In this case, the intended victim is a vampire, who nearly succeeds in extracting his heavy price.

My version develops from a story collected and summarized by Rădulescu-Codin (1913, 261). At its core is a theme familiar in central and eastern European folklore. The critical character often differs—a dwarf, a gnome, a fairy, a wolf, a dragon, or an old hag—but in all the victim is a conniving peasant who makes a promise that he never intends to keep. Thus, the central lesson is constant across variants. Peasant societies are heavily dependent upon trust. A promise is a binding contract between individuals. Violation of that contract is a threat to social cohesion and must carry fateful penalties.

Once upon a time there was a middle-aged couple. They had been toiling for years, but they were very poor. Somehow, fortune never smiled on them. They lived on the outskirts of the village in an old house with a small garden behind it. Husband and wife had tilled the land diligently, but the previous two winters had been brutal. The previous summers had not been good either, one excessively hot and windy, the other cold and rainy. Some of their crops started growing too late and were not ripe by harvesting time; some simply withered and did not grow at all; some froze before they could be picked.

The poor couple had exhausted their supplies. The white flour, potatoes, apples, salty cheese, lard, and plum marmalade were all gone. The few chickens they had at the beginning of winter had died mysteriously, one after another, the blood sucked out of them. All they had in their baskets were a few onions and a little corn flour for a small polenta. They still had the milk cow, but not for long.

The man was quite desperate. Not only were they almost starving, but his wife of twenty-five years had begun to feel unwell. She had dizzy spells and an unusual weakness, and he was afraid something might be wrong with her.

"I guess we will have to sell the cow," the poor man said. "It is grow-ing old and giving less milk than it used to. Anyway, we don't have any hay left to feed it." The woman agreed. "We really have nothing left. Besides, the vampires of the region, the curse of our village, have been feasting on the animals. I am sure they will eventually get our cow, too."

The couple decided to take their cow to the marketplace as soon as possible. "You lie down and rest," the man advised. "I will go and sell the cow to buy some supplies and, maybe, if we are really lucky, we can purchase a milk goat. That would solve our problems for a while."

"A milk goat and supplies! That would be wonderful," said the wife, merrily. "You are so wise and clever, my husband. I am sure that you will get a good price for the cow, and that we will then have enough in the house to last us until the next harvest. Our luck is about to change. I can feel it in my heart."

The husband had barely arrived at the market when a pale, dark-haired man approached him and asked, "How much do you want for your cow, man?"

"Twenty gold coins," he answered after a moment's hesitation. He had named a high price, considerably above the normal rate for a cow.

"That is a lot of money," said the pale man. He then very slowly took out his purse, opened it, and looked inside as if to count the coins that he had.

The purse was absolutely full of coins. The villager was fascinated by the sight of so much gold. He wanted it desperately. "The cow is a very good one," he lied, trying to persuade the pale man to buy it for his high asking price. "It gives a lot of milk, and is still young and healthy."

The buyer was taking his time. He watched with a strange smile, for he realized that the man had become fascinated with the purse. Tauntingly, he asked, "You really would like to have all of this money, wouldn't you? But then you would have to offer me something in addi-tion to the cow. What else do you have to give me?"

"I don't have anything else," the man answered miserably. "Look how poor I am. The cow is all I have brought to market."

"Maybe you have something at home," the pale man replied with a strange smile. "I'll tell you what. If you promise to give what you hold most dear, I will hand over to you the entire purse and all the coins within it."

The villager now smiled back. The stranger certainly would not be interested in his wife, who was no longer so young and attractive. And there was nothing else of value in the house. They had no important possessions, no extensive forests, no stocks of animals, not even any reserves of food. The stranger, he thought, must be fool. This was the opportunity of a lifetime. The deal could only work to his great advantage. It had to be made quickly, before the stranger realized the mistake and withdrew the offer.

And so, although faking great reluctance, the poor man made the promise. "I will give you what I have most precious at home, in addition to this cow."

"Then here is the purse," the pale stranger said. "I will come and collect my possession later." They shook hands to seal the bargain.

The man hurried away into the crowd, extremely happy. He now had more money than he ever dreamed of, for the purse held more gold coins than he had suspected. But he did not feel guilty at all. "The buyer should have taken better care of his money," he thought to himself. "It was he who came with this idea of a promise. He should have checked to see if I had anything valuable hidden at home to give him. In fact, he left without even asking me where I lived. It's his own fault," the man decided and put the stranger out of his mind.

He soon arrived home with a full load of supplies, and a milk goat, and lots of extra money. Upon arrival, there was a big surprise waiting for him. His wife had not been sick; she had been with child. Although far past the usual age for childbirth, she soon gave birth to a healthy daughter.

For year upon year, the couple's luck did change. The harvests were plentiful. The goat gave good milk. The man gained a reputation for the excellent plum brandy he made. The daughter grew up to be a beautiful young woman. The man never thought of the strange fellow who made him promise to give away what he held most dear. Eventually, it was the girl's time to get married.

The ceremony would be celebrated in the old church of the village. The place looked especially festive since it was late spring and all the lilac trees in the cemetery behind the building were in full bloom. The bride was radiant in her traditional wedding clothes. Family and guests were present to celebrate with the young couple. Among them, near the entrance to the yard, stood a pale, dark-haired stranger.

Hardly had the bride entered the church when she was overcome by a strange weakness and fell to the floor. At first, they thought she had fainted—but the bride was dead.

Commotion was followed by great sadness, as there was nothing to be done. As was customary, the girl's body would be left in the church for three days and three nights before burial. During the day, people would come for the wake. At night, one person would keep watch over the body.

All that day, instead of the wedding feast, the family prepared the girl's body and cried at her coffin. For the night watch, they left behind a trustworthy cousin, a strong young man from the village.

The next morning, when they arrived for the wake, they saw the bride in her coffin and her night guardian lying next to it, dead on the floor. They now had two bodies, both young people who had died mysteriously.

The same thing happened the following night. A second young man lay dead by the coffin, and the people of the village became alarmed. Upon examination, they discovered that the bodies of both guardians did not have a single drop of blood left in them. Suspicions disappeared. It was the work of a vampire.

It was then that the father of the bride recalled the strange trade in the marketplace and the promise he had made long ago, before his daughter was born. It is not a sin to make an advantageous business deal, and so he had never confessed it in church. But now the man was confused. He went to the priest.

"Oh, you silly man," the priest scolded him. "Don't you understand? You sold your daughter to a vampire. On her wedding day, he came to reclaim his property and transformed her into a vampire. In turn, she killed and drank the blood of the two poor souls who guarded her body. Everything is now clear."

Word got out, of course, as always happens in small villages. Everyone found out about the promise. The groom was in shock to discover that his beloved had been doomed since birth to become a vampire. His love was strong, however, and he refused to accept his loss as final.

"Tonight I will guard her coffin," he announced. "I want to see for myself what is happening. Maybe, God willing, I can save her soul."

Although young, the groom was wise for his age. He was aware he was not going to solve the problem by himself, and he knew where to go for advice. Not far from the village, there lived an old monk. People were always going to him for help. He knew which plants could heal the body, and which prayers could soothe the soul. The young man found the monk working in his small garden and told him the story.

"It is too bad that fool father chose to forget about his past dealings," the old monk said. "Had he spoken about it, we would have taught him a long time ago that there are ways to fight against evil."

Fortunately, the monk knew exactly what to do. He gave the youth a silver cross, a Bible with a silver cover, and small bottle of water in which he also put a clove of wild garlic. The water came from a deep and hidden cave where the monk had found an ancient altar. Thus it was holy water, the monk explained, and since it had never been touched by sun, the water had power over the forces of darkness. The monk instructed the young man how to use these gifts and gave to him his blessing.

When night came, the groom went into the church to watch over the coffin of his beloved bride. He did exactly as he had been instructed. "Hide behind the icons; she won't be able to see you there. Do not simply stop behind any icon; find the strong ones—St. George's or the Virgin's. Do not move till midnight, and make sure you do not fall asleep. By all means, do not fall asleep, or you will end up dead."

It was a difficult wait. The silence of the church and the long shadows cast by the candles made him sleepy. There were many moments when he could barely keep his leaden eyelids open, but the young groom remembered the monk's warning, and this helped him to stay awake.

Exactly at midnight, he heard noises from within the coffin. Suddenly, the young man became absolutely alert. The lid opened with a screech. His bride emerged. She looked the same, and at the same time she didn't. Her eyes were much darker and looked about with an empty stare.

"Resist the temptation to answer her," the monk had instructed him. "She will know that some human being is close, but may not be able to see you. The area behind the icons is safe. Remember that she is no longer your bride. She is a vampire, and vampires' eyes cannot look at icons."

The bride sensed the presence of the man, his warm blood throbbing. She searched determinedly, but she did not look toward the altar with its icons. "I know you are here! I can feel it! Come. Let me see you! Do not be afraid," she said as she searched, further and further away from the coffin.

The young man waited for her to reach the far side of the church and turn her back. He then raced across the room and placed the silver cross and the Bible covered in silver in the coffin. The words of the monk were still echoing in his mind: "Place the cross at the head so that its horizontal hand would be across the eyes and place the Holy Bible at the chest where the heart would be."

The groom did exactly as he was told. In perfect silence, he placed the holy objects into the empty coffin and then ran back to hide behind the icons. A short while later, his bride returned to the coffin, frustrated by the failed search. When she saw the cross and the Bible, she jumped back with a hiss. The groom watched her circle around the coffin in great agitation, not knowing what to do. Then he heard the cock's first crow.

She heard the crow too and, as if it were a command, she lay down on the ground near the coffin and closed her eyes. She seemed asleep.

The young man waited one more moment. Then quietly he drew closer and splashed some of the holy water on the young woman's body.

The first rays of sun slowly made their way into the deep darkness of the church. One icon started to sparkle, and then another. The rays ricocheted and reached the silver Bible in the coffin. The metal started warming up, and a burning sound could be heard from it, as if the cross and the Bible had suddenly turned into branding irons.

The young man splashed holy water over his bride's body for a second time and again for a third time. He saw her begin to move and sigh. She opened her eyes and looked at him with a warm, loving smile. They both turned toward the coffin in amazement.

The coffin was now occupied by the body of the pale, dark man— it was the vampire. He had an incandescent silver cross and an incandescent silver-covered Bible burning into his chest.

The young groom did not waste any time. He quickly cut off the vampire's head and poured the remaining the holy water onto it, destroying the evil creature for good.

On that day, the people of the village had both a burial and a wedding to celebrate. Both events were highly cherished. For the first time, a funeral was a happy event.

The Two Girls

Religious rituals are important to Romanian villagers, as both an expression of faith and a means of protection against evil forces. Young girls are warned especially never to neglect customary mystical practices. They face grave risks unless they take necessary precautions to fend off the visitors who come with the night. Disregarding such fundamental rules often comes with high costs. In this example, two young girls are alone in the night, but the wiser one quickly grasps the situation and leads them in a spirited defense.

Pamfile (1916/2000, 125) collected from Romanați county and briefly summarized two variants of the story of two girls. In the first, a priest and his wife leave home on a journey and let their daughter sleep with a girlfriend for the night. The priest's daughter falls asleep immediately, but the friend cannot sleep because she perceives a dead man's hand coming out from under a linen chest, where a vampire was hiding. The demon intended to use the hand to drug the girls, but the spell did not succeed and the wide-awake girl takes measures to defend the house.

In the second Pamfile version, the two heroines are attacked by a vampire, but they manage to cut off the creature's hand. The crippled monster then retreats into the underworld.

What I found most interesting in Pamfile's accounts is the theme that young peasant women are not merely weak and defenseless victims, but instead can be fully capable of standing up against evil and constructing elaborate strategies to defeat it. My account expands considerably on the crude story outline. In particular, I include the idea that knowledge necessary to resist the powers of darkness exists within the community. I also heavily emphasize the inter-connection in village practice of magical, pre–Christian symbols with those that come from the Orthodox religion. Thus, in addition to votive lamps and holy water, the story incorporates the rich Romanian tradition of counter-curses, magical rhymes, and herbal remedies.

Florica was a fifteen-year-old girl. She lived in a small house on the outskirts of the village together with her mother. Her father was dead, and the two women took care of their household by themselves. The girl was famous for her embroidery skills. No other girl had a nicer collection of handmade items in her hope chest—beautifully crafted blouses and pillowcases, lovely towels and tablecloths.

The girls of the village often would get together at someone's house to tell stories and sing songs while doing their handicraft, especially during the long winters when there was less work to be done outside.

Florica's passion for embroidery was so great that often, when she was alone in her room in the evening, no matter how tired she was, she would choose to work a little more. Midnight might find her seated at a corner table near the strong votive oil lamp hanging from the wall, under the icon that she had received as a baptism present. She felt at peace in that corner, warmed by votive light and comforted by the icon. She would stop her work only when her eyes were almost too tired to see. She would extinguish all the lights and go to sleep in absolute darkness.

Her mother would scold her, "Do not blow out the votive light in your room! It is supposed to be lit all the time to protect you from evil. That is what votive lights are for. Besides, icons do not like to be kept in the dark. It is disrespectful. You can blow out the normal candles, but this votive flame must remain."

But Florica liked to sleep in the dark. She found the darkness and chilliness of the night refreshing, so she also slept with the window open.

"Young women should never sleep with their windows open at night," her mother would tell her. "You do not know what terrible things can happen in the dark!" Like many young and willful girls, sometimes Florica listened; sometimes she didn't.

One morning, Florica woke up with a strange sensation. She felt particularly weak and wasted. It was as if she had been working all night long. She thought she had caught a small cold, and she did not pay any mind to the bizarre marks that appeared on her neck. "I don't know where these marks come from. I have no memory of scratching my neck," she said when asked about it, shrugging her shoulders.

"I am tired. I do not feel well," she announced that evening. To the surprise of her family, Florica put away her needlework and went to her room early.

The small room felt stifling, and so she decided to open the window. As she did, an angry gust of wind blew out the light from the votive lamp. A strange weariness descended upon her, and a grey heavy cloud entered her room.

Florica's eyelids were suddenly made of lead, and she lay on her bed quietly. She had no notion that the grey cloud hovered above her for a short while. Then the fog grew denser, and it took the shape of a human silhouette. The dark cloud became a dark man with an ugly, hairy face, thick brows, and red eyes. It was a deadly vampire. The creature leaned over the sleeping girl and bit her on the neck.

Florica was under the vampire's spell. She was lost in a very deep, unhealthy sleep. She would have never woken up if it had not been for her mother who, worried that her daughter was not well, came in to check on her.

"Oh, she left the window open again. That is how my dearest daughter must have caught a cold in the first place." The mother closed the window, lit the votive light, kissed her daughter on the forehead, and made the sign of the cross over her. She did not notice a grey cloud dissipating rapidly, but was relieved to see that Florica was breathing more easily and seemed more relaxed.

A few days later, things happened the same way. Florica went to bed early, as if some stronger power was calling her to the bedroom. The moment she entered her room, the same weakness came over her. She felt compelled to open the window and to extinguish all of the lights. She then lay down in darkness and fell into a deep, heavy sleep. At midnight, the grey cloud appeared, invaded the room, and the vampire again materialized.

But her mother couldn't sleep. As the clock struck twelve, she felt a strange chill overtake the house, and, extremely restless, she went to check on her daughter. "That girl does not learn. I am certain that she again left her window open." On entering her daughter's room, the mother noticed that the votive light had gone out, too. "I guess the wind must have blown it out," she thought to herself. Florica's mother, as before, closed the window, lit the lamp, and made the sign of a cross over her sleeping daughter. The pale blinking oil lamp shone on the icon, which had been swallowed by the dark, and the grey cloud dissipated. Florica moaned, took a deep breath, and went on sleeping—a more relaxed sleep this time.

A few days later, Florica's mother had to go away for a week to attend a funeral of a cousin who had lived in a distant village across the valley. The girl did not like to be alone in the house at night, and so she invited a friend, Lenutza, to sleep over. The house was not big, but the girls were happy to share a room.

As the evening approached, Florica prepared her friend's bed. She used a nicely embroidered pillowcase that she herself had made, and spread a homespun sheet on the bed, a handmade one identical to hers. She had stored the linen in her hope chest where she had also put some dry lavender bunches, intended to keep the moths away. It had been a while since she had opened the chest to let its contents, the treasures of her embroidery, breathed a little fresh air.

As the smell of lavender was now strong in the room, Florica decided to leave the window temporarily open. Things would be better, she decided, by the time they went to bed. Once she closed the door behind her, however, an angry gust of wind came and blew out the votive oil lamp under the icon in the room.

The two girls spent the evening talking and laughing by the fire in the kitchen. Young girls never quite seem to finish their stories, and they kept talking merrily until midnight, when Florica suddenly felt extremely weak and tired. "Oh, my! I had not realized how late it has become," she exclaimed with a yawn. "It's midnight. Let's go quickly to bed."

The bedroom was cold and dark when the two girls entered, and their eyes had not yet adjusted to the lack of light. Thus they did not discern the grey cloud hiding in the corner.

Lenutza watched her friend fall asleep almost immediately, but she could not yet sleep for she was used to saying her prayers every night. She took off the little cross that she wore on a chain around her neck, held it close to her heart, and started a silent chant.

As she lay in the dark, praying silently, she saw the grey cloud and watched it turn into what seemed to be a man. In panic, her heart missed a beat. "This should not be. I know Florica does not have a secret lover. There should be no man in the house this night."

Through her eyelashes, Lenutza saw the silhouette drift toward her hostess's bed and lean over her neck. The man made absolutely no noise. This was no real human being, she realized, but a vampire, the monster of the night. She was afraid that her breathing would make him notice her.

Indeed, the vampire did sense that somebody else was in the room still awake. He stopped and raised his head slowly, turning toward Lenutza. Once his eyes found her through the dark, he snarled at her menacingly, showing sharp fangs like a wolf's. His face was ugly. His eyes were sparkling red and evil.

"Go away you evil spirit!" Lenutza shouted, completely horrified. But her fear alone was not enough to scare away the vampire. Quite the contrary. The creature was about to step towards her. In despair, the girl sat up in bed and threw at him the tiny cross she was holding tightly in her hand.

The cross passed through the silhouette of the vampire and hit the opposite wall with a clatter. Its magic worked, and the vampire turned into a black cat that jumped out through the open window, disappearing into the night.

Lenutza leapt out of bed and quickly closed the window. The noise woke up Florica. She put her hand to her neck and found that there was fresh blood where previously she had seen the unexplained scratch. She watched her friend light the votive lamp under the icon and say a prayer of thankfulness and deliverance.

"My God. What happened to me?" Florica cried, looking in confusion at the blood in her palm.

"You have been attacked by a vampire," Lenutza told her. "An ungodly creature, a *strigoi*, was here in the room. And those signs on your neck, they are vampire bites. I know it for sure. My grandmother taught me about such things."

"A vampire here?" asked Florica in disbelief. "What are we going to do? What if he returns? We are all alone in the house, the two of us."

Lenutza was a little younger than Florica, but on this occasion, she was by far the more courageous one. "We must make sure it will not get into the house. We have to defend ourselves," she announced with determination. "My grandmother taught me how to fight them. Vampires can be kept away with garlic."

The two girls fetched fresh garlic from the kitchen and put it on the windowsill.

Then the girls spread some dry basil in front of the window to erase any trace that the creature might have left behind. When they heard the first crow of the cock, they knew that they were safe for the day. Vampires always disappear at the first crow.

The brave Lenutza also knew what to do about Florica's wound. It had to be washed with holy water. Their priest traditionally gave each family a small bottle of holy water on Easter Sunday. Every household kept the bottle safe for cures and rituals during the year, stored next to some dry basil.

Having finished their labors, the two girls went to bed for a few remaining hours of sleep. "Let us rest now," Lenutza said, "but do not be confident. The vampire will come again, to finish what he has started. You are in extreme danger until your wound heals completely. We will continue tomorrow, for stronger defenses are required."

The next morning, full of sunshine, they woke for a day of big preparations, necessary to fight the vampire and be rid of him, once and for all. After a small breakfast, they paid a visit to Lenutza's grandmother and asked for advice.

"Fortunately," the old woman told them, "you have a couple of days to prepare. Vampires never come to the same house two days in a row after they have been found out." She also gave them elaborate instructions.

"First, you take some old garlic, dry basil, and a speck of incense. Put them into a small jar and cover them with a bit of fresh water. Then carefully pour just three drops of holy water into the jar, saying: 'Water for fire.' Repeat this phrase three times. Then strike a match and drop it into the jar. As the flame goes off hissing, say: 'Ashes into the water.' Repeat the phrase three times. Next, strain the mixture through clean cheesecloth. Drink three small sips of the water, both of you. Pour the remaining liquid into two tiny bottles, one for each.

"Finally, you have to bury the strained dregs of the concoction in the graveyard, north of the church, at noon when the sun shining strongly. After you have buried all the remains, you should throw some extra dirt over them with your right hand, saying: 'May the ashes return into the ground.' Again, repeat the phrase three times, loudly. Now go home and wait, but keep the water bottles that you prepared close at hand."

Nothing happened that night, just as the old woman had predicted. Florica's neck wound was very slow to heal, however, and so she knew that the vampire would return. They then made their preparations exactly as instructed.

Two days later, the girls were still by themselves in the house. Waiting for the vampire to appear, they pretended that they were not afraid. All the time, they kept the tiny bottles with the special concoction close at hand.

They spent the evening in the kitchen, doing handiwork by the fire. When it was almost midnight, the hour when vampires tend to appear, they went into the bedroom. Intentionally, they blew out the votive light, opened the window, and lay down on their beds completely still, with their eyes almost closed. Both held the tiny bottle in their right hands, keeping it covered with their thumbs. In their left hands they had a small bunch of dry basil dipped in holy water. This was the trap they prepared for the ungodly creature. Since they were not trying to scare him away, there was no garlic on the windowsill.

Soon the dark, grey cloud appeared and entered the bedroom through the open window. The room became chilly, and the girls started to shiver. As before, the heavy cloud hovered near Florica, and then a silhouette took shape next to her bed. The girl felt its power and the strong temptation to sleep, but her fear combined with a strong will helped her manage to stay awake. Through her lashes, she watched the creature lean toward her, ready to bite.

Before the vampire reached her neck, Florica splashed the special water from her bottle onto his face and sprinkled holy water on the foggy silhouette with the basil leaves in her left hand.

Lenutza jumped from her bed and joined Florica in the battle, splashing more of the specially prepared water on the vampire. He cringed with a terrible hiss, shrank under their very eyes, and turned into ash. The girls chanted, over and over as instructed, "Water for fire; ashes into water; may the ashes return into the ground."

Soon, nothing remained of the lethal creature. The girls made the sign of the cross over the spot where the vampire had stood, to erase all memory of it. They closed the window, lit the votive oil lamp, and hung a garlic wreath on the window knob.

After that night, for as long as she lived, Florica never failed to keep lit the votive light in her bedroom, and she never went to bed with her window open. No wise girl in her village ever did.

PART II

Vampires Among Us

The Dinner Guest

Village life contains its own dangers and terrors. Tragedies sometimes occur without apparent explanation. When bad things happen to good people, it might very well be that a vampire is involved. The five stories of in this part differ from those of the preceding part because there is no precipitating violation of social custom. It is simply that vampires can live hidden among us, doing their evil deeds within the cover of ordinary society. One should take heed and always be prepared.

The first story makes the point clearly, with regard to an unusual dinner guest.

I heard this story as a child in my grandparents' house in Bratca, a picturesque village in Bihor county. My grandmother, Doamna Preoteasă, the petite wife of the old village priest, would always be joined by other women who helped in the kitchen and with the chores. This story was told by one of the peasants, as if it had happened to one of her relatives. I remember clearly asking the adults whether it might have actually been true, but they never gave me a straight answer. For days afterward, my cousins and I were hesitant to go out after dark, afraid that strange visitors might appear.

A lone traveler once passed near the village of Bratca, on the Crişul Repede river. He had been in the mountains, arranging to purchase some wood to be delivered in the winter.

The traveler had in the village a distant cousin who generously offered a bed for the night. The journey had been long and tiring. The traveler decided to stop at his relative's house to rest and spend the evening.

He found the house quite easily. It was a fine property, resting comfortably between a small stream and a hill covered in tall fir-trees. The cousin, Toma Negru, lived in an imposing building with two parallel staircases in the front and a long veranda. The yard was large and grassy and very neat. There were two more buildings at the back, a barn and a summer kitchen.

The Negru family welcomed the traveler and, as custom dictates, invited him to dine with them. His hostess promised to prepare chicken and dumplings—a traditional dish whenever there were guests. While the women—the wife and two daughters—were working in the kitchen, the men sampled the local plum brandy, accompanied by ewe's milk cheese, smoked bacon, and onions. In no time, the skilled women had the meal ready, and everybody sat merrily at table.

Hardly had they filled their plates, however, than an old man appeared at the doorway. The family exchanged terrified glances. The hostess turned pale while the host, her husband, rose to his feet and invited the old man to eat. "Good evening, Father," Toma said. "Do you want to share some food with us?"

"Thank you, son, but no. I do not want this kind of food," the old man answered. He merely stood there and watched them intently. After a while, he added, "I will rest here for a little and then go."

The good disposition of household vanished. Nobody uttered a word. The company ate their meal in silence, eyes cast into their plates. The guest thought about asking the old man something, to be polite. But all conversation had ended, and he dared not break the silence.

The strange dinner ended soon. The old man got up and left without a word, as abruptly as he had appeared. People retired quickly to different parts of the house, crossing themselves several times.

The traveler had nothing else to do but go to bed right away. The host showed him to his room. The hostess joined them immediately, carrying a wreath of garlic and a votive light. She hooked the wreath on the window knob, placed the votive light in a corner under a cross, and went away without any explanation. "Sleep in peace, and may God protect you," said the host.

The tired traveler fell asleep quickly and arose early the next morning to continue his journey. He did not ask about the old man's visit, and nobody in the household mentioned the subject either. Soon, the traveler was on his way. He enjoyed company on the road, so he joined a group of villagers who were heading in the same direction.

Opposite: Diavoli si strigoi (Demons and Vampires), **details from the Exterior Fresco, Voroneţ Monastery (15th century). Romanian churches sometimes contain frescos combining Christian and pre–Christian symbols of people's hopes and fears. The Monastery at Voroneţ contains a particularly striking set of images, replete with devils, demons, and creatures from the underworld (Doru Munteanu).**

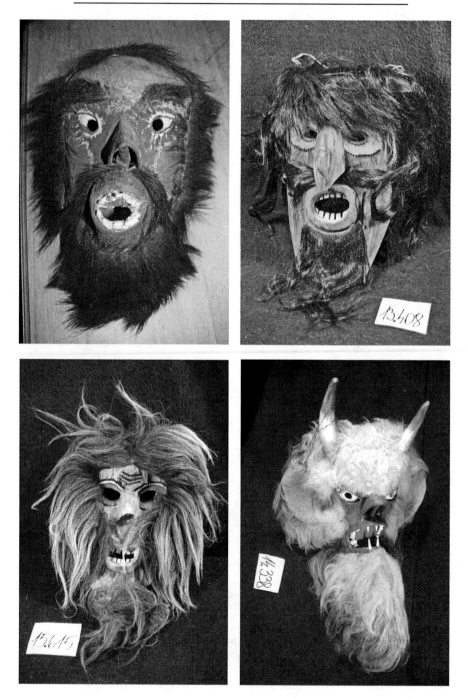

"Have you heard the news?" one of them was saying. "Marin Toader died last night."

"He died? Poor fellow. But he had never been sick a day in his life," someone else replied.

"Yes, he's dead all right. Early this morning they found him cold. There was not a single drop of blood left in him. We must all beware for the cursed *strigoi* is killing again."

"Precautions have to be taken. Once we learn who the vampire is, its family will have to dispose of it."

"The rules are clear. It is the job of the family that buried the creature. Just like the Crisan family did last summer."

"There is no other way to deal with it," somebody else agreed.

"The Toader family are all in danger now. The vampire will surely come back after another member. Once a creature has tasted one member of a family, who knows for what reason, it tends to return until they are all dead."

The traveler was fascinated. He had heard stories of vampires attacking humans, but he had never taken them seriously. They were the kind of tales told by old men with little else to occupy their minds. "What can one do about vampires?" he asked. "How can one fight them? They are creatures of the night. They are not easy to meet, let alone kill."

"Oh, but sometimes they are," the grey-haired man answered. "Most of the time, vampires returning from the grave come after their kin. They start by killing members of their own family. That is why the family must take quick action."

"That's true," a fellow traveler agreed. "The family has to dig all likely suspects out the grave and check the coffins. If the deceased appears to be sleeping, and if there are bloodstains in the coffin or on the face, these are telltale signs. The creature's head must be cut off and the head placed at the other end of the coffin, face downwards. A stake must be driven through the heart. Then the body should be buried again."

"If they fail to do that," the grey-haired man agreed, "they are doomed."

Patru Măşti (Four Ceremonial Masks). Romanian village ceremonies often contain characters dressed up to represent fearsome creatures from the wilderness. Ceremonial masks of the sort depicted here also can reveal the inner soul, displaying the inner ugliness of villains, vampires, and other demons (courtesy Ţării Crişurilor Museum, the Ethnography Collection, Oradea).

The image was not a pleasant one to contemplate. To change the mood, the villagers shifted their attention to the lone traveler. They asked him polite questions about his destination and his business, as is normal with people who share the road. "Where did you spend the night in our village? Do you know anybody there?" somebody asked.

The traveler told them of his cousin and made some positive comments about the fine property on which he lived.

"Yes, it's a very nice property that the old Negru left to his son, one of the nicest in our area. And Toma Negru is lucky that he did not have to divide it with any other heirs."

"What are you talking about?" the traveler asked in confusion.

"We are fond of Toma," was the reply, "and are glad for his good fortune. His father worked hard but was not especially well-liked in the village. Toma has now taken his father's place, as is customary with a sole heir. And we welcome Toma, who is quickly becoming one of the leaders of our village."

"The old man died? Toma's father is dead?" he asked again, in shock.

"Yes. Did you not know? We buried him two months ago. A very sudden death, that was."

"But I saw him, old Negru, last night! He came to join us at dinner," the traveler said.

"Man, you saw a vampire. May God protect you," one of them concluded. The villagers crossed themselves and a deep silence fell over them all. It remained until the lone traveler separated from villagers, taking the road that would lead him toward home.

Over the years, the traveler would repeat this story often, even when he became a very old man. Some never believed him, but others did.

The Pet

Animals are an essential part of any Romanian village. They do much of the labor and provide companionship. Yet it is wrong to believe that humans can fully know the minds of the animals around them. Even man's best friend can turn out to be a vampire.

As a child, I would spend a part of my summer vacation in the village of Bratca. My paternal grandparents and several aunts lived there, and family members from around the country would gather at their house in summer. My aunt, Sabina Negru, would sometimes bring us to the village school where she taught. This is one of the stories I heard her tell her young students.

Radu, a thin, freckled lad, about seventeen years old, sat carving a pipe on the front porch of his home. It was a warm summer afternoon. The sun was slowly beginning to set, and he was trying to finish before the good light disappeared. As he worked, he thought of Ion, his best friend, the one who had taught him how to carve a pipe and play it. Ion had died a few weeks before, God knows why and how. Everything happened so suddenly. Now Radu was missing his companion, playmate, and friend.

As the evening set in, a stray dog entered the courtyard. It wagged its tail contentedly and stood there watching him. Radu noticed this with pleasure. He was fond of dogs, and he immediately thought about keeping this one as a pet. He once had a nice German shepherd that would accompany him everywhere, but it was killed one night when keeping guard outside the house. Nobody knew what happened. They just found the shepherd lying lifeless in front of the entrance door with a small wound in the neck.

"Maybe some lonely wolf attacked him in the night," suggested one of Radu's brothers. But this was unlikely as it was summer, and wolves tended to come this close to human habitation only during exceptionally hard winters when food was difficult to find in the forest.

"Hey, black dog! Hi there!" Radu shouted out. "Come see what I am making. Maybe, if you behave, I'll even play you a little song once I finish carving this pipe."

The dog lay down on the grass and watched him attentively.

"A strange dog you are! You do not have very friendly eyes. But if you don't bite anybody, we will be friends," he promised.

The stray dog stayed around the house. Radu baptized it "Carbunaru" because it was all black except for one of its front paws and one ear that were white. The youth did not know where the dog spent its time during the day, but most evenings, it lay on the grass in the family backyard, watching carefully. The family was a big one, and there was always somebody in the yard doing something. But the dog had its eyes mostly on Radu.

A few days later, one of their sheep was found dead. The stable gate was closed, so it remained a mystery how entry had been achieved. As for how it died, that was an even greater mystery. The sheep lay peacefully with only a small wound in the neck.

"I don't think it could have been a wolf," his father said. "Radu's new dog would have either chased it away or barked in defense. Somehow, it would have alerted us."

Soon, animals suddenly started to die at other farms in the area. At first, this did not appear suspicious, as such things happen sometimes. Yet, almost every other night, the body of a lifeless animal was discovered, Sheep, horses, and cows died, with only a small neck wound. Nobody could afford the loss of such livestock. People began to talk about the presence of a mysterious killer. Several alleged that they saw a black dog prowling around where animals were attacked. Some instead said that they had seen a person shrouded in the darkness. Others claimed to have seen both a man and a dog. The more stories were told, the more confusing the information became.

But one of the details made Radu pay attention. Those who claimed to have seen a dog all repeated a remarkable fact—it was black with a white paw and a white ear. Radu decided to watch his new pet more closely.

That evening, the dog appeared as usual and lay down in the family yard. Radu went out and fed the dog, did his normal chores in the yard, and then turned toward the doorway, as if intending to enter the house for the night. The dog watched him carefully, and it walked away when it believed that Radu was leaving. But the lad was pretending. He did not go inside. Instead, he closed the door noisily but followed the dog away from the family yard.

The animal crossed a dirt lane and purposefully headed straight towards their neighbor's stable. Radu hastened to keep the dog in sight, making sure to stay silent. "Fortunately, the wind is blowing in my direction, and the dog will not smell me," he thought.

Radu reached the stable and cracked the door open slowly, just in time to see the black dog turn into a young man. In horror, Radu realized that it was his dead friend, Ion, the one who used to be as close to him as a brother, the one who taught him to carve musical pipes. He had the exact same white scar on the side of his forehead, which he had received as a small boy when he fell out of a tree.

In shock, Radu saw his friend—now turned vampire—attack a cow tethered in the stable and bite it deeply on the neck. It was too frightening to watch. In panic, Radu turned and bolted toward home and safety.

As Radu lay alone in his bed later that night, his thoughts became clearer. His dead friend was a vampire, and he had returned to haunt his village. He visited the family yard, just as he had done when alive, but now in the shape of a dog attached to Radu more than to the others. Maybe the friend intended to infect him as well, so that they could be together in death. Why else would the mysterious dog spend almost every evening waiting for him? Radu realized that he had to act. He decided that he needed assistance, and that he would share his worries with his older brother, Andrei.

Next evening, the two brothers followed the dog in its hunting. As before, the animal appeared to have a clear destination in mind. It walked down through the back lanes of the village and then hurried across a plum orchard, reaching the side door of the stable owned by a prosperous farmer.

Hidden in the darkness, they watched by moonlight as the mostly-black dog turned into a young man with a white scar on his forehead. The creature opened the stable door and entered. The brothers ran to the stable, arriving to see a most horrifying scene. A vampire was biting into the neck of a stable boy who had been asleep on a haystack.

Instinctively, they intervened. Andrei picked up a rock and threw it at the vampire, disturbing him in his violence. The creature turned toward them and showed its teeth menacingly. The teeth sparkled. The lips were red with fresh blood. There was no doubt—it looked just like Radu's dead friend. The vampire was about to attack them when Radu cried out in despair, "Ion, for God's sake! What are you doing?"

The vampire stopped. It hissed loudly, transformed itself into a dog, and dashed away into the darkness.

The next morning, the two brothers went to visit their grandfather to ask for advice. They explained that they were in mortal danger since a vampire knew that they had discovered its identity. The old wise man told them what to do. He could still remember everything his own father had taught him, many years ago, at the time of a previous vampire attack in the village.

"You must never approach a vampire directly and never at night-time. During the night, they are always more powerful than humans. Do your deed in the afternoon, while the sun is shining brightly. Do not disturb the other dead. That is a great sin, one that may have terrible consequences. They might come after you themselves."

"To find the right grave, take a black horse to the graveyard and try to make it eat fresh food or drink fresh water at the suspected spot. If the animal gets scared and will not accept nourishment, it is, for sure, the grave of a vampire.

"Then open the grave. If you find a person who looks asleep with his face downward, that is a certain sign that he has been out walking."

"Evil creatures can be very deceitful," the old man told them. "Vampires can take any shape they want, and sometimes they may choose to look like some real person. To make sure that it truly is Radu's old friend, Ion, you must look at the creature's face when it is asleep in the grave, with the sunshine upon it."

The brothers were told to arm themselves with a strong spike made of hazelnut wood. They had to cut off a branch from a living tree, at least five years old. They also had to make sure that their pocketknives had been sharpened recently, and that there was no rust on the blades. Last, to protect themselves from evil, they had to carry silver crosses in their belts and several garlic bulbs in their pockets. They also had to wear a white feather and a little basil in their hatbands.

Radu and Andrei prepared everything as they had been taught. They went to their friend's grave early that afternoon when the sun was shining brightly. The dug up and opened the coffin with no difficulty.

Ion was lying face down, just as they expected. He looked as if he were asleep. They turned him over and found fresh blood on his lips. Indeed, Ion had become a vampire.

Without hesitation, the brothers proceeded with their ritual. Radu said a prayer and Andrei drove his spike through the vampire's heart. The creature made a terrible, loud, groaning sound and wriggled in its coffin. Then, with a sigh, it died for good. Its face relaxed and turned ashen. The two brothers then cut off the vampire's head and placed it at the other end of the coffin. No fresh blood appeared at this time. The body looked just like it should, lifeless and dry, as if dead for some time. Radu and Andrei spread basil and garlic into the coffin. They closed it tightly, nailed it shut, and buried it again in the grave.

The two brothers never told of their adventure. The black dog no longer visited their yard. All strange and sudden deaths in their village ended.

The Strange Attraction

It is often said that a young girl should follow her heart. Yet this can have dire consequences—especially when her yearning has been instilled secretly by a vampire who has intentions to ensnare more than merely her heart. In this story, the vampire is relentless, and the young girl is fully bewitched, ultimately choosing the evil outsider over her natural parents.

My story is a variation on a brief narrative collected by Niculiță-Voronca and published in the Transylvanian magazine Familia *(1898, No. 6: 64–66). In that account, a poor orphan of an unknown lineage is rejected by the father of the girl he loves, suffers a violent death, becomes a vampire, but continues to lure her at night. The idea of the vampire as a revengeful lover is common in the Romanian folklore.*

The orphan, in village tales, is often suspect, representing the Other or the evil from afar, and never fully succeeds in being integrated into the community, especially when little is known about his family. In my version, I also emphasized the popular folk theme, that bad influences can exert enormous strength on the innocent, to the extent that the young girl in the story is willing to lie, steal, and cast black magic spells to return the vampire to her side. In the end, she also becomes an outcast, losing all ties to the family and village.

"Innkeeper, I offer to buy a round for everybody here. Good men, listen to me. Drink to the health and fortune of my newborn daughter, Lina!"

The man celebrating was a young farmer, well respected in the village. He was known as hardworking and honest, and his household was plentiful. He had been married for a nearly two years, and today, finally, his wife bore him their first child.

"The best of luck to her and her family," one man said.

"May she be merry and bring you joy!" another one added.

"May she be hardworking, beautiful, and obedient," the innkeeper said.

"The baby girl is fortunate to be born to such nice people," the innkeeper's wife remarked. "Some children are not so lucky. A few days ago, a caravan of gypsies passed by. They had found a small boy along the way. God knows where. Apparently the boy was an orphan, so they took him. Maybe they changed their mind later, or maybe they grew afraid of keeping him. Anyhow, the boy—Viorel is his name—remained here after the caravan left. He is now upstairs at the inn, but I do not know what I am going to do with him, poor soul."

The farmer, full of good cheer, made a critical decision. "I will take him with me. There is enough food for another mouth in my household. He will grow with my child and later will help me with my work."

The farmer took the orphan home and raised him in his household. The boy was never what one would call handsome, and he was always a bit secretive, but he was never any trouble. He did not seem to be friends with the other boys his age. In his spare time, Viorel would disappear for hours into the forest, armed only with his pocketknife. He would go alone, and must have been a skilled hunter judging by the lifeless bodies he brought back.

Viorel was always protective of Lina. As he grew older, his infatuation became obvious to all. He would stand in the corner for hours watching her giggle and gossip with her girlfriends. Lina, despite the teasing from her friends, was polite to Viorel, but certainly not encouraging of anything more.

But the parents nevertheless became concerned. They had in mind a different future for their daughter. And they worried that Viorel had become too attached. The father decided to take immediate measures.

"Listen, Viorel," he told the youth. "You are a young man now. It is time for you to go and find your fortune in this world. Besides, I do not want you to start dreaming about things that cannot happen here. You can make a better future for yourself someplace else. Go away, forget my daughter, and never come back."

"Since you have been a hardworking member of this household," the father added, "I will not let you go empty-handed. Take this purse. You have earned the money in honest work. Use it well, and may you find your luck!"

The youth was shocked. He knew that he was powerless. He had no choice but to leave the village. The money offered did not appease his anger. "Some day, I will return. Lina, herself, will summon me. I will make her my very own, and you will not be able to stop me."

The father thought nothing of the empty boast, and let the boy proceed on his way.

Lina grew up a lovely and hardworking young woman, and there were many young men who were suitors for her hand in marriage. Yet, one after another, they were all rejected. "There must be something wrong with me," she said to her mother. "I am not at all interested in any of these men, although they all seem pleasant and funny and earn a good living."

She did not tell her mother, but increasingly her thoughts were fixed on Viorel. She remembered his great loyalty. She wondered how he was doing. She imagined him as a husband, coming home tired after work, eating dinner together, sharing the same bed. It was as if he haunted her dreams.

Her mother guessed what was wrong. "Forget Viorel. He was not meant for you. He had to leave to seek his own fortune. Turn your eyes away from the distance. Fall in love with a boy from the region."

But two years passed, and nothing had changed. If anything, Lina was more and more captivated by thoughts of Viorel. She was not able to take her mind off him. He had become an obsession. She spent much of her time sewing or weaving yet thinking privately of what might have been.

Finally, her father had enough. He arrived home one evening to declare that he had just concluded arrangements with a prosperous family in the neighboring village. Lina would marry their son, and their heirs would inherit both lands.

Lina was frantic. She begged her father to wait one full month before making the announcement. In desperation, she sought out the old woman, Baba Gaia, who, according to village talk, was a witch.

"Baba Gaia, please bring Viorel back to me. I have been told that you can bring people back, even from death. I am sure you can do it!"

"I can make him appear to you in your dreams," the old woman suggested.

"No. He already occupies my dreams. Bring him back from wherever he is."

"People sometimes change when they go away," the witch asserted. "God only knows what things they have seen or done. It is dangerous to bring somebody back with too little information about them."

"I do not care. Just bring him back! Besides, nobody needs to know," said Lina.

"Maybe I should first try and read his wanderings and his fate in my cards," Baba Gaia suggested.

"Can you do that?" the girl exclaimed. "Please, tell me where he is. Does he think of me as much as I think of him?"

"Bring me an object that belonged to him," said Baba Gaia, "and a silver coin for the cards. My cards are blind without the silver. They need to be paid for their effort."

"I will bring you his flute, a wooden flute that he made. He gave it to me before he left. I hear its tune constantly inside my mind."

The next day, the girl brought the things as promised. The old woman spread her cards on a small table and stared at them for a long time, as if she did not like what she saw.

"I cannot see him well," the witch admitted finally. "There is a lot of blood in my cards. I also see him walking, but he is upside down, and he is facing away from the sun. Maybe we should try reading the cards again on Tuesday. Today, there is too much that is unclear."

"Forget about reading the cards again!" Lina shouted with impatience. "I do not want to wait. Just bring Viorel back from wherever he is. Make a spell."

"Since you insist so strongly, I will do as you wish," the old woman agreed with a sigh. "You will have to bring me some red thread and two feathers from two hens, a white one and a black one. I will also need a long feather from a cock's tail. And bring a golden coin next time, for spells work better in the presence of money."

"A golden coin!" Lina thought to herself. "I might have to steal a coin from mother's special necklace, the layered one that everybody admires and covets. She will believe that one of the coins came loose and was lost."

The very next day, Lina brought the things that Baba Gaia had requested. The old woman dropped the golden coin in a glass, poured some water on it, and told the girl, "Say these lines after me, and take a sip of this enchanted water after every line."

> *Look for him to the right.*
> *Look for him to the left.*
> *Look for him straight ahead.*
> *Look for him in the wide world.*
> *Look for him in the air.*
> *Look for him underground.*
> *And bring my Viorel back to me.*

Baba Gaia then tied the three feathers together with the red thread and poured the water remaining in the glass over them. The golden coin she tucked away.

"Put these feathers under your pillow tonight. Wear one feather next to your breast during the day to lure him back. He will return," Baba Gaia promised the girl, "any time between three days and three weeks."

Viorel appeared at dusk exactly three weeks later. Lina was sewing on the porch when she saw a figure approach from the back of the orchard. At first, she didn't recognize the shadow, dark under the trees. As he drew nearer, she exclaimed with delight, "Viorel, is it really you? You have come back."

He was watching her with intensity. His eyes were pitch black, and he appeared more mature than the youth who had left the village. "I have returned because you called me," he explained stressing every word.

"For many years," he continued, somewhat mysteriously, "I protected your family from the evil that abounds because they were kind to me. They gave me a home, and they allowed me to be near to you. They then sent me away, and I have lived as my kind always does. Now, I have come to take you away with me. I have a place to take you, if you will accompany me."

Lina felt the young man's enchantment more strongly than ever. "I will go with you if you will have me."

Viorel was clear in his instructions. He looked her directly in the eyes and said with determination, "Be ready to leave tomorrow at dusk. Do not tell your parents, or they might try to stop us. Nobody needs to know. Nobody will be able to separate us again."

Lina was excited all the next day. She prepared a small sack with a few of her things and hid it under the porch, to have it at hand for the journey. She then sat down on the bench, pretending to be sewing. She was happy and kept singing a merry tune to herself.

"Finally I see Lina happy again," her mother commented with relief. "I have not heard her sing such a merry tune since Viorel went away." But the mother's mood was soon to change.

The next morning, Lina was gone. Not a single soul had seen or heard anything. At first, her parents suspected robbers or kidnappers. However, when they saw that some of Lena's clothes were also missing, they suspected that she had eloped. A neighbor reported that someone who looked a bit like Viorel had been seen one evening coming out of the forest. There was only one plausible explanation –Viorel had returned and taken Lina away with him. The parents were heartbroken.

One evening, a few weeks later, the parents were sitting sadly and silently by the fire when they heard their dog whine from outside in the yard. It was a strange, terrified sound that ended as if dissolved into air. Before going to bed, the father went out to check on the farm animals, as was his custom. He found the dog lying mysteriously dead on the ground in the middle of the yard.

"I do not understand what happened to our poor dog," he informed his wife. "I did not see an open wound, so I don't think it was attacked by a wolf. Besides, there is no sign of a fight, as there are no bloodstains around him. I am tempted to say that the poor creature lost all its blood."

"Oh, my!" the woman exclaimed. "Who knows what evil creatures lurk in the dark."

On the following night, it was a pig that was found dead. The night after that, it was the cow.

On the night after, as the couple was getting ready for bed, they again heard a tormented whine in their yard. The man armed himself with a knife and was about to go out to check when the door opened, and their daughter entered.

"Good evening, dear mother and father," she said simply.

"Oh, my Lina! Where have you been?" the mother exclaimed in surprise.

"I have been in a wonderful place," the girl gushed with happiness. "And now, I am back because I want to take you both with me."

"But, my girl, you look changed," the father observed. "You are so thin and pale."

"I am just tired from my journey," Lina replied, looking at them with an intense gaze. And she began telling them about enchanted travel through the air, about a magnificent castle in a beautiful forest, about lush green pastures where fabulous birds sang merry songs.

Her parents were skeptical at first, but slowly they warmed to Lina's story. They knew little of the outside world, and they listened with fascination, swept away by the images and absorbing every word of hers.

Whenever Lina tried to halt her storytelling and send the couple to bed, they would beg her, as if they had lost their self-control, to tell them more about this amazing place. They hardly realized how much time had passed, until they heard the cock's first crow.

At this signal, as abruptly as she had appeared earlier that evening, Lina turned and fled outside.

The magic of the evening was broken. The parents rushed after their daughter, trying to grasp what had happened. But Lina had disappeared into the darkness. She was gone, nowhere to be seen. There was only one of the family's horses, lying dead and bloodless in the yard.

With shock, the poor parents now realized that the appearance at their house was no longer their loving daughter. She had been transformed. What remained instead was a dangerous vampire that had tried to lure them into its wicked world. This was Viorel's revenge.

The couple took precautions, with garlic wreaths and holy water, to insure that neither Viorel nor Lina would ever visit them again.

The Parents with Two Sons

Parents everywhere like to take pride in their children. They worry about their future. They try to give them the opportunity for happiness in life and success in their ventures. Yet the situation can be different when the children turn out to be vampires, making the parents responsible for their fate.

The motif that children conceived on certain ill-fated days are doomed to become vampires is well known in Transylvania and can be found in many recorded folk tales. The belief might still be alive in rural villages, for Senn heard such accounts in both Sălaj and Bihor counties during the late 1970s and early 1980s (1982, 94 and 112).

I developed this story based on a strange narrative that haunted my childhood. It was about two brothers conceived on ill-fated days. The boys turned out to be vampires, capable of transforming into wolves and killing people at night. Over the years, I heard different versions of the story, some in which the boys simply left home but also darker ones where the vampires were killed by their parents. The tale bothered me as a child, and I still find the inherent theme fascinating. The dilemma exists in all societies: What is the obligation that parents have toward their children, and to what extent are they responsible for protecting the community from the misdeeds of their children?

Sandu and Silviu were brothers, not twins. The former was eighteen and the latter nineteen, but people often thought of them as twins because they resembled each other almost perfectly. When they were boys, they played only with each other. Now that they were nearly grown, they were inseparable as a team, preferring their own company while shunning the social activities normal among village youths. Both were introverted, in an almost secretive way. They often disappeared for periods of time to wander by themselves through the nearby forests, meadows, or fields.

Along with their looks and personality, brothers also shared the fact that they both had special birthdays—one was born on St. Andrew's Eve and the other on St. George's Eve. There were old people in the village who would cross themselves whenever the boys walked by, commenting that those are days when vampires are born.

The family was a prominent one, with land and cattle. The two youths helped their father on the farm. Sandu and Silviu were not friendly or talkative, but they were hardworking and efficient. Most of the time, they finished their work quickly. It insured time for them to disappear together at the end of a day's work.

Their parents did not know where the brothers wandered, but the two would always return exactly when dinner was ready or when some task needed their contribution. "We have been close by," they would say, never providing details of their whereabouts.

Their mother, like all mothers, worried about them nevertheless. "Husband, I wonder," she would say. "Is it not time that our boys were curious about girls? Soon they will have to take wives and get married. They will have to separate from each other and set up different households. I am bothered that neither has yet taken any interest."

"What are you talking about, wife?" was the husband's reply. "I am glad they are not yet attentive to girls. There is plenty of time for that. For now, it is enough that they are good, hardworking boys who do not get into fights and keep out of trouble."

"I guess you are right, " the mother agreed. "I certainly am grateful that they do not drink at the inn and then scuffle in the street. Think of our neighbors' boys. Just last month, their oldest son was strangely attacked on his way home, badly beaten, and lost so much blood that they thought he was going to die."

"Don't pay too much attention to gossip, woman," the husband dismissed the story. "The foolish boy probably got drunk at the inn, staggered home and fell, and did not want to admit to it."

"It is not gossip, man. His own mother told me. He was attacked and left for dead, but he did not see his attackers. Fortunately, the miller happened to pass by, found him, and carried him home."

"Ha, ha! The miller knows something about getting drunk, himself," the father commented.

"This is serious," the woman insisted. "When the neighbors' boy showed no sign of recovery after three days, they sent for the priest to give him the last rites. The old priest said a special prayer and used holy ointment brought from a monastery on Mount Athos. It saved his life."

"Really! I did not know it was that serious."

"Very serious. It is said in the village said that those responsible for the attack were not ordinary human beings, but vampires, because they left the boy with no will-power at all. He appeared to have lost much of his blood, but not a single drop was seen where the attack took place."

"This is even more reason to be glad that our boys are always together," the father concluded. "Vampires only attack people who are alone. They are afraid of groups. Our boys take good care of each other." And indeed, nothing bad threatened the two youths, although strange things increasingly happened in their village.

One day, their grandmother stopped by the house to visit. "You should keep an eye on Sandu and Silviu," she said privately to their mother. "People say that they like to spend time by the old dry well on the route to the mountain pass. My neighbor, Floarea, saw them there twice when she was bringing her cows home from the pasture in the evening."

"They like to spend time by themselves, but they have always kept out of trouble," the mother replied.

"They go to a dangerous place," the grandmother warned. "Two people recently died in that area, first the village fool (God knows how he died) and then some stranger who was traveling alone. The man was found dead by the well, his heart was eaten, and there was not a single drop of blood left in him." The grandmother added, "I am telling you, the place is haunted by vampires."

The mother told the boys, but they were not impressed. "We never go there," Silviu assured her with indifference.

One evening, about a week later, the father had to conduct some business with a man whose house was at the margin of the village, close to the old stone bridge that led toward the south plains. The road was narrow and winding. As he drew near the gate, the father saw his two sons walking across the bridge. A strong yellow moon was shining on them. The light made them appear different, in a hard-to-describe way.

"This is strange," the father thought. "I had left them at home. How could they have gotten here before me?" But he, then, continued upon his walk, for there was business to conduct.

The next day, everybody was talking about an unusual incident. The bridge broke, and a poor traveler's cart fell into the river. Both the horse and the man were dead.

More news about the deaths began to spread. It was said that there was no blood spilled at accident. "The vampires are back," an old man asserted. "There have been periods with strange deaths before this. Several people in the region were killed by vampires when I was a little boy. One of them was my uncle. I remember how I hid under the staircase in the house in order to hear the adults talk about the lack of blood and what it meant."

"It will be very hard to find them," he continued. "Sometimes, vampires appear as normal people living among us and mingling daily with regular people. Whether these vampires are living or not, we are all in mortal danger."

But nobody had seen any vampires. Nobody had any idea how to find them. The villagers were naturally suspicious of strangers, but there were few of these, and they had just passed quickly by. It was hard to believe that the threat was coming from someone familiar, someone inside the village.

It was thus normal for skeptics to reply, "What vampires?" one man commented to those drinking and talking at the inn. "We know everybody who lives here. Nobody saw any suspect strangers walking around. These are just old wives' tales. Besides, we all are aware that the old bridge was damaged badly after the floods last year." Although some maintained their fears, the subject was dropped temporarily. Quiet rumors of mysterious deaths continued to circulate.

Two weeks later, the parents of Sandu and Silviu journeyed to a town fair to sell their potatoes and purchase necessities for the winter. They had planed to stay for three days, but they finished their trades faster than anticipated and decided to return sooner.

The return trip was uneventful but long. As they left the forest and started upon the road descending toward their village, the couple decided to stop, water the horses, and let them rest freely in a clearing near the big well at the last crossroads.

"We should feed the horses, too," the man suggested. "Then we will have less to do when we arrive at home. I also could use the rest."

The wife agreed. "Let us sit on this tree-trunk and eat apples. There is still enough light, although evening is racing upon us." So they gave each horse a sack of grain and then sat down near to their cart at the margin of the clearing. They were, unhappily, thus in perfect position to witness a gruesome scene.

The shadows were growing long, and a strange silence descended. A lone man came walking down the road. He reached the well, put down his backpack, and turned the wheel to get water. The pulley chain rattled as he lifted the filled bucket upward. From nowhere, two men suddenly appeared and grabbed him from behind. The lone traveler did not have time to defend himself. The attack was quick and violent. The attackers bit him on the neck, taking turns drinking his blood, and left him dead.

The couple was spellbound in horror. They had just watched their own two sons kill an innocent man, sucking out his blood before disappearing mysteriously. Heartbroken, the two returned home. The realization was crushing. The vampires that everybody dreaded, they now recognized without doubt, were their children.

"Woman, we have to do something to stop them," commented the father sadly. But the mother was not ready to accept that her sons had fully become evil. "Maybe we could save them. Maybe we can ask the priest to help."

"We must hand our boys over to the law. There is no denying the fact that they are vampires, and vampires must be killed. There are particular ways to do it, in order to protect that they will never return."

"We are their parents. We are supposed to help them," pleaded the mother.

"But what if they turn against us?" the father lamented. "What if they try to kill us, too? Who, then, will stop them?"

"They won't kill us. They could have killed us a hundred times already," the mother insisted. "We should talk to them. Maybe there is a cure. We cannot agree to treat them cruelly. They are our sons."

The two parents confronted the boys with their information, their fears, and their hopes for redemption. Things did not go as planned. Sandu and Silviu simply told their parents that they should accept the situation. "There is nothing you can do," Sandu said. "We are who we are. If you love us, you will have to learn how to live with it."

"After all," Silviu continued, "it is your fault we are as we are. You were the ones to conceive us at the wrong time, so that we were brought into this world on doomed nights. Children born on certain nights, everyone knows, often become vampires. I was born on St. Andrew's Eve and Sandu on St. George's Eve."

"We were born different," Sandu boasted. "You have sons who are not like ordinary people. We can do remarkable things together. We are special."

The husband and wife were in shock. They felt so guilty. "Oh, my God," the mother lamented. "What, oh what, are we going to do?"

"We are going to send them away," the father declared. "They will have to go into the wide world, and we will forget that we raised two sons. We will forget they ever cast their shadow on the earth. I have made up my mind."

"Please, just wait another day," the mother pleaded. "They are flesh of our flesh. We cannot just throw them out like dogs. I will go ask the old monk who lives in the hermitage at the foot of the cliffs to say prayers for their souls. I will go to him today. His place is only half of day's journey away. Maybe he can help. I will be back by tomorrow."

The father agreed to wait for one more day, for his wife's sake. "Go and do what you must to appease your conscience. But do not have much hope. If the old monk fails, they will have to leave. I don't want to sleep under the same roof with two monsters."

But the next day, after the woman returned home from her desperate trip, there was more bad news. The schoolteacher of the village died mysteriously in the night. The parents knew that the two boys never liked him.

And they now realized, with reluctance, that simply sending the sons away would not stop them from willfully inflicting great harm upon others. "Woman, there is no hope," admitted the husband. "Our sons are wicked vampires. They killed again last night. I know they were not here at midnight. Their beds were empty. I checked."

"I know," the wife said in a small voice, as if the weight of the world were sitting on her chest. "The old monk did not give me any hope."

"We made them. We brought them into this world. The task falls to us. We must rid the village of them," the men said. "Somehow, I will destroy them with my own hands."

"And I will join you," the woman vowed. "We will kill them together. If we fail in our duty, there will be more many deaths, and they all will be counted against our souls."

The next day, the two parents took Sandu and Silviu into the forest under the pretext that they needed help bringing some firewood home. There, they killed their sons. The parents drove sharp spikes through the hearts of the boys, so they would never return to haunt the living. They then buried the bodies in a small clearing and put wooden crosses at their heads. No names were carved on the crosses. There was only one line to be seen: "God, please have mercy."

Back home, the parents informed the village that their sons had decided to go away to test their fortune in the wider world. The local people listened with sad faces, but asked no questions.

A year later, exactly to the day, a terrible storm descended upon the village. A bolt of lightning struck the two crosses and burned them to cinders. The impact unearthed some bones.

"Did you know," a shepherd announced to those gathered at the inn later that evening, "there are two shallow graves in the small clearing near the forest. It's the place where the lightning struck. Those buried there must have died with great sins on their conscience. They must have so angered God that he did not even let them rest in peace underground."

A long, heavy silence fell on the people who had been drinking and talking merrily a minute before. Then an old peasant remarked, "It is not our business. Let us simply be thankful that the harvest has been good and that the violent deaths in the village have ceased."

Two Widows

It is important to mourn for the dead. It is equally important to let their souls depart. This part ends with two short, parallel stories, in which widows seek to hold onto marital relationships beyond their natural time. As a result, they welcome vampires into their beds. It requires great strength of will to reject a loving husband transformed into a creature of the night.

The first story is inspired by two very similar brief accounts that Pamfile collected from popular storytellers in the Mehedinti and in the Romanați counties and later published in the folklore magazine Şezătoarea (1896–7, No. 8: 19–20 and 1911, No. 13: 156). The second story is based on an account recounted by Niculiță-Voronca, and published in Familia (1898, No. 8: 88–90). All of these narratives describe the predicaments of widows who keep being visited by their dead husbands at night.

There are several lessons in the stories. The first is that members of the village community watch out for one another. It is especially important to look after widows, so that they do not become consumed by their grief, and help them to reintegrate into the normal rhythms of life. Another is that community knowledge is useful and can help solve even the most delicate personal emotional dramas. There are many chants and magic spells when common sense is not enough. Finally, the stories instruct that people should learn to let go of their dead. The two realms, the living and the dead, can only interact through the vampire, a destructive rather than creative relationship.

Valeria was a young widow. Her husband had died three months before in an accident. He was cutting wood for winter, and a tree fell on him. They had been married for two years but did not yet have children, so Valeria was lonely and heartbroken. She cried all the time and lost interest in everything.

"Oh, Traian, why have you left me? Who's going to take care of me now?" she lamented.

In the beginning, her friends tried to console her. "It was God's will to take Traian. You just have to accept it."

But she did not want to accept her fate. She wailed and cried each night.

"You have to stop this," the older women of the village told her after two months. "You have to let him go. He will not find rest if you keep on crying. His soul will not be able to depart. He will stay here, and there is only one way to do that. He will stay as an undead."

But Valeria was inconsolable. She mourned for Traian all the time. Her farm fell apart. Soon, her animals started to die. They just lay dead in the morning, and Valeria did not seem to care.

"You see," a friend told her. "Now you will have to stop your wailing. You have angered God because you do not accept his authority over life and death. Bad things have begun to happen."

"God is not angry, and my wailing has, in fact, born fruit," Valeria announced one day with strange serenity. "Traian has returned. He comes back to me each night."

Her friend was confused by this confession. She decided to keep a closer eye on Valeria. Could it be that the young widow was losing her mind, hallucinating out of grief?

Secrecy is not something that comes naturally to the inhabitants of a small village. Soon, everyone knew about the nocturnal visits that Valeria claimed to receive. The majority did not take the stories as a sign of impending danger. "Poor Valeria," they said sympathetically. "If she is happy believing that her husband visits her at night, maybe we should not interfere and cause her more pain."

Nevertheless, there were some who took a different view, suspecting that something unholy was going on. "Traian is dead. When the undead walk on this earth, terrible things walk with them."

These voices became stronger as the number of mysterious deaths increased, affecting the entire community. Animals that never before had been sick were lying lifeless in the morning, all blood sucked out of them overnight. These did not look like accidents. They looked like vampire attacks. People recognized the signs as they had had similar cases about a decade ago. They remembered, too, that the horror started with animals and then spread to humans. Suspicion started to take shape in people's minds. The vampire attacks had begun with Valeria's farm. Her incessant mourning had attracted disaster.

"Traian died a premature and bloody death," an old and wise man said. "Valeria was so lonely and desperate that, with her wailing, she put a spell on him not to leave. He could not find his peace and so he made a pact with the devil. Now he has returned as a vampire."

"If so," another villager observed, "there will be more deaths."

The conclusion seemed plausible to her friends and neighbors, but

Valeria did not want to hear of it. "Silly people! Traian is no vampire. He does not bother anybody. He returned only to comfort me."

During the following week, two persons from the village were found dead with no blood left in their bodies. The terror had spread to humans, just as predicted. People suggested, in an attempt to be certain, that Valeria open Traian's tomb to examine his body. If he appeared to be the cursed vampire, she had to cut off his head and give him a special burial.

Valeria refused obstinately. "Traian is not a walking dead. He is lying in his grave. But at night he sees my pain. He does not want to leave me all alone."

Some of the villagers became annoyed. "If you refuse to help us," they threatened, "we will act without your permission. We are going to open the tomb and cut Traian's head off tonight."

"No, no, no! Don't do that!" Valeria cried. "It is a terrible sin to mess with the dead. Give me a little more time. I will think of something tonight. I will ask Traian when he comes to visit me."

"We will wait one more day," the villagers conceded. "But we need proof that it is truly Traian who visits your house at night. If he is leaving his grave, then he must be the vampire doing all the killing in our midst."

When night came, Traian appeared in Valeria's room, as usual. They chatted contentedly about small things, again as usual. He inquired whether her Uncle Marcu had finished the house he was repairing. He asked about other members of the community.

Before the cock's crow, the time when Traian would always disappear, Valeria grabbed one of his boots and hid it under the bed. The next day she showed it off proudly. "You can see for yourself," she said. "This is Traian's boot, from the nice pair he bought in Budapest which everybody admired. My husband comes to keep me company, but he is no monster. We even talked about my Uncle Marcu's house."

"You silly woman," was the reply. "Your uncle was found dead this morning, lying near some sacks of grains that he had to take to the mill. There was not a single drop of blood left in his body."

The people of the village did not waste any more time. They found the priest, went to the cemetery, and dug out the coffin. Traian was, as expected, wearing only one boot. He also looked suspiciously unchanged. His cheeks were ruddy, and there was fresh blood on his lips. There could be no doubt. Traian was a vampire.

The priest assisted by some courageous men drove a spike though the vampire's heart. Fresh blood burst forth. The vampire screamed and then turned ashen. The men then cut off the vampire's head and placed it at the other end of the coffin, face downwards. The priest splashed holy water over the body and said his prayers. They nailed the coffin shut and re-buried it in holy ground.

All mysterious deaths stopped. Valeria learned to live with her grief and never spoke of Traian again.

*   *   *

Eugenia had been married only for three years when she became a widow overnight. Her husband, Gheorghe, died unexpectedly in a freak accident at the mill. As happens with such tragedies, Eugenia's life was transformed dramatically.

She and Gheorghe had recently moved into the new house that they had painted together. She had barely begun working on the embroidered curtains intended to ornate the house. Now, her needlework would have to wait. She was a strong woman, and she was confident that she could manage the household successfully. But she was lonely. The nights were very especially long, and she hated spending them all by herself.

During the daytime, the house was cheerful. The rooms were full of light and smelled of the fresh paint. At night, however, the mood changed radically. The same rooms became thick with darkness. The air turned heavy, and strange sounds invaded.

"I have trouble sleeping," Eugenia complained to the other women in the village. "I feel that somebody is in the house with me at night."

"It is not a cause for worry," an older woman advised her. "You may have somebody there. It is your deceased husband watching over you to see that you are well."

"Deceased people sometimes wander on the earth for a while before they leave to the other world for good. They do it especially if they have unfinished business in this world."

As the older woman predicted, a few nights later, the household noises became transformed into a more visible presence, for Eugenia's dead husband appeared to her as she lay sleepless in bed.

"Is it you, Gheorghe?" she asked with surprise.

"Yes, my dear. I am back home," he said casually, as if he merely had been away for a few days on business.

"Why have you come back?" Eugenia asked, a little confused by his matter-of-fact response.

"I will keep you company at night," he answered. "You do not like to be alone. We know that bad things can happen after darkness has fallen."

Gheorghe did not offer any further explanation. His demeanor indicated that questions were not welcome. And so Eugenia simply accepted things as they were. Her husband appeared after dusk and was gone by morning.

For a time, Eugenia was happy leading a double life. She did her housework during the day, and she enjoyed Gheorghe's company at night. The arrangement was so satisfying that she started to decline invitations to go to village get-togethers and offers from her friends to come and visit in the evenings.

Eugenia's conscience, however, eventually reminded her that the situation was most unnatural. Moreover, she had begun to lose weight. She became weaker and felt as if life was trickling out of her little by little.

Eventually, she decided to get some advice from an old woman, Baba Oana.

"My dear," she was told quite bluntly, "your husband is dead. If he came back, he is a *strigoi*—an unholy vampire. Only they can rise from the dead and walk on this earth again. It is a sin to make love to a vampire. You should put an end to it."

"I know I should not live like this anymore," Eugenia confessed, uncomfortably. "But I do not know what to do."

"It is in you power to get rid of him," said Baba Oana. "Tell him that you no longer accept him as your husband. You must indicate that you do not need him anymore."

Eugenia went home and prepared herself as she would for a big event in the village. She took a nice bath. She put on her best clothing. She then sat in front of the fire, brushing her hair, waiting for Gheorghe to appear.

Like always, he arrived after dark. He saw her dressed up so beautifully and was impressed. "Where you are going?" he asked.

Eugenia did not answer him. She just smiled and started to pleat her hair meticulously. When she finished, she turned to him and asked, "How do I look? Do I look good?"

"Yes, my dear. You look very good. But where are you going?" he insisted.

"I am going to a wedding," she said. "Your brother is going to marry your sister."

"But that cannot be!" he answered with disbelief. "Brothers and sisters cannot get married to each other."

Eugenia looked at Gheorghe, straight into his eyes, and said slowly but with clear conviction, "Then the dead and the undead cannot stay married to each other, either. The dead should be with the dead, and the living with the living. Go back where you have come from."

The vampire froze in shock, surprised that she dared to confront him. His face became distorted as realization set in. His body started to shrivel. Soon, all that remained was a pile of white dust on the floor.

Eugenia was frightened, but she knew she had to show strength. "The dead should be with the dead, and the living with the living." She repeated the phrase for her own ears this time.

A gust of wind came from out of nowhere. It blew the white dust pile into the air and out the window. And Gheorghe became only a memory.

PART III

Interlude—How to Recognize a Vampire

This brief interlude, placed approximately at the halfway point of the stories, is intended to make certain inherent themes explicit and to emphasize the difference between the authentic Romanian folklore vampire and those now prevalent in the popular culture.

As is obvious from the stories, the Romanian vampire is the quintessential outsider. Often, he lives at the frontier of the village, haunting the space between the comfortable familiar and the wilds of nature. Other times, he inserts himself within the village, living hidden in plain sight, bringing terror to the familiar.

Vampiredom is not a glamorous occupation. Living in the murky world between life and death, between the civilized and the animalistic, he is haunted as well as haunting. The Romanian vampire not only threatens the peasant village, he comes from the village. He is entirely familiar with the daily rituals of the small, isolated, rural community but cannot enjoy the comradeship. He understands the habits of its members and the motivations that drive them, although he no longer shares those motivations. He cannot escape the lure of the village, even as he works to destroy it. He is a peasant turned into a misfit.

The Romanian vampire is driven by basic needs. He must kill in order to feed and survive. Yet it is a minimalist survival. To the degree that his soul is dead, he can form no attachments, understand no mercy, and exercise no wider reason.

The Romanian vampire is more a coward than a tragic hero. He attacks from the margins, from the shadows of the night, stealthfully luring people away from the paths of safety and security. His attacks are individualistic, targeting the innocent and weak, and secretive, so that he never confronts the strong opponent. He is the enemy that comes from the darkness.

The spiritual life of the Romanian village is infused by the official religion, Greek Orthodox Christianity. At times, therefore, the vampire appears as a henchman of Satan, to be combated with holy water and icons from the Church. Yet traditional vampire folklore is also heavily informed by a far older, pre–Christian mythology. There are resonances of polytheism in which the forest beyond is populated by terrifying deities and demons. The wilderness outside the village borders is the symbolic location for dark superstitions and lurking dangers. The vampire, as a creature who can transform shape into a dog or a wolf, is only one in the panoply of mystical inhabitants of the savage nature useful in peasant cultures to explain the origins of bad fortune or unanticipated death.

The folklore village vampire is certainly not an aristocrat occupying some decaying, remote castle in the mountains (in contrast to the character from Bram Stoker). Equally, he is not physically deformed (in contrast to F.W. Murnau's film *Nosferatu*). He can pass virtually unnoticed through the village and even participate in its ceremonies. He can hide his otherness, although not from the most watchful eyes, strategically in order to feed on village inhabitants.

Most importantly, this vampire has virtually zero resemblance to the teenage heartthrob so prevalent in contemporary popular romance. It is a common adolescent's dream that young love will live forever. The vampire can live forever. It is a common adolescent's fantasy that the outcast boy, with a somewhat mysterious dark side to his personality, is especially exiting on the condition that he is willing to be tamed. The "good vampire" is, thus, easily counterpoised against those beyond redemption in a dichotomous battle of good versus evil. These are simple tales, stripped from tradition and limited in social and cultural significance.

The folkloric vampire is as important for what he signifies as for who he is. The reciprocal of the "misfit Other from the outside" is the "one who truly belongs inside." The two identities help to construct each other. Traditional communities depend heavily on the distinction between us-and-them. Identity and difference play a crucial role for personal validation within the community, establishing rights to legitimate membership, extended kinship, collective protections.

The vampire, a being no longer from this world, serves the role of enforcer for acceptable conduct. The survival of the small community depends on its shared system of beliefs and established patterns of behavior. Strict prohibitions exist against anti-social practice; dire penalties are threatened for those who deviate. In the folklore, the vampire lurks waiting for those tempted to stray. The consequence of his bite is eternal ostracism. In this guise, the village vampire is not just a demonical attacker, but an administrative servant of village norms, working "from the outside" on behalf of socio-cultural integration "on the inside." Historically, some Romanian peasants actively believed in the existence of vampires around them. Yet, even without the belief, the mythology of traditional stories proved deserving of repetition and reinforcement because of its function as a concrete lever through which useful values were infused.

It is therefore useful to ask, within the Romanian folk tradition:

Who might become a vampire?

How can we recognize vampires living among us?

What actually do vampires do?

When are vampires especially active?

How best can we defend ourselves against vampires?

The following sections provide answers to these questions, based primarily on late 19th and early 20th century references to vampire accounts, compiled primarily by amateur Romanian ethnographers and published in edited collections or local journals on folklore and peasant customs. For those who, today, are still worried or watchful, these sections might usefully help to identify vampire traits and tendencies, culled from historical sources. For those with a more intellectual interest, the sections provide insight into the peasant culture that gave rise to the vampire tradition and into characteristics that made the vampire an enduring part of folk legend.

Who Might Become a Vampire?

Not everyone had an equal probability of becoming a vampire. Certain individuals faced far higher risks. These risks could be increased by one's own behavior, breaking established rules of the community. They could also be increased by the behavior of others, especially improper burial or the failure to complete establish burial rituals. Others seem predestined by birth, possibly because they were conceived on the wrong day; their affliction was often indicated in infancy by visible signs or markings. Nevertheless, there were those apparently randomly selected by misfortune in life or accident at death or simply because they were ill-favored by fate.

People Who Break Established Rules

Christianity established strict rules regarding what was considered a mortal and unpardonable sin. The penalty was eternal damnation in hell. In the Romanian village such sins, particularly those that threatened established community norms, gained a second condemnation. The individual might well become a vampire, desperately haunting the world of the living. There was, thus, a double set of punishments—religious and mythological—that insured that the sinner would be cast out forever. It was a sign that violations were treated seriously. In a village based on collective traditions and unwritten norms, there had to be significant prohibitions against those who endangered the core of interpersonal group trust.

At very high risk was *the priest who said mass in a state of mortal sin.* For the Christian church, it was a sacrilegious act. For the laic community, it compromised the institution constituting the main social pillar of the village. Religion and mythological interdictions overlapped. The sinner in local superstition was to be penalized twice, becoming a vampire before his soul was condemned to eternal damnation.

Similarly, *old women who had dealings with demons* and *people who engaged in witchcraft* faced high risk of double condemnation. Those who tempted the power of the dark contradicted the teaching of the Orthodox religion. They also tended to end up as vampires. Black magic put excess power in the hands of one individual, who could use it for selfish gain opposed to the communal interest. This threatened symbolically to upset the balance of man and nature, reinforced by the church, that was essential to harmonious village existence.

People who committed perjury or swore untrue on the Bible were doubly doomed, as were those who *lived and ended unrepentant of their sins.* The village was insistent upon enforcing moral norms. Its mythologies reinforced a worldview in accord with the cycles of life and nature. The enduring strength of this worldview was indicated by the degree to which it became integrated into the official religion. The vampire was not a subordinated version of the Christian devil. Far more powerfully, the vampire became an independent enforcer of Christian teachings, and, in turn, the local church was given an active role in helping to eradicate vampire threats. The religious and the mythological stood as two pillars in defense of social stability.

Suicide also faced a double interdiction. In both Christian religion and Romanian mythology, life was viewed as a sacred gift. *Those who committed suicide* became vampires because they severed the link not just between man and God, but also between man and community. It was a declaration of independence and power in defiance of the natural order. In turn, they were abandoned by that natural order, existing forlorn as members of the walking undead.

It was also declared dangerous *to feast upon animals killed by a vampire*. Sharing food was a communal act. People who "broke bread" with vampires, and by implication endorsed their bloody acts, risked joining their congregation. Beyond this, however, was a plausible dietary prohibition. One should only eat animals slaughtered within family or village boundaries and according to its rules. One should especially avoid eating animals found dead from unknown causes. Mythology, thus, served to emphasize the value of hygiene and to protect people from infectious diseases.

Those who violated community values were threatened with becoming a vampire. It was the penalty for *those who challenged authority* without strong justification and for *those who were mean or did harm to their neighbors*, particularly lying, stealing, fighting, or killing. The village depended on close communal relationships and collective security. It was crucial to unite against common dangers from the outside and avoid behavior that might have corroded internal structures. An evil death became just recompense for an evil life.

Those who violated the family hierarchy were similarly threatened. Young people became vampires when *they disobeyed their parents* or refused to accept their parents' choices when it came to marriage. It was the fate reserved to *young women who eloped with strangers or outsiders*. Romanian peasant villages were strongly patriarchal. Marriage as a social institution determined the transmission of property and secured kinship alliances. A mythology filled with dire threats and ominous consequences was a mechanism of forced obedience.

Children who started sucking again after being weaned might well become vampires. It was a common interdiction in the folklore. It was a sin against biological clock and a threat to family harmony, and it seemed reasonable because, often in peasant households, one child had to stop being breastfeed and voluntarily accept this fact for another child was about to appear. Equally, *children who were cursed by their parents* were doomed to become vampires. In Romanian peasant society, parents were absolute rulers, respected and trusted implicitly to have their children's interest at heart. They were to be honored and obeyed. The hierarchical family unit was an essential aspect of community maintenance. A mother's curse, although rare, was the ultimate act of social rejection. One was immediately condemned, without hope of mitigation or appeal, to existence in the shade.

Control over sexuality was inherent to most Romanian societal, religious, and family warnings against improper behavior. *Individuals who neglected their prayers at night, young maidens who roamed about after dark, widows unwilling to let the souls of their dead husbands depart* were all threatened by the vampire curse. In the conventional tale, animal desire stood opposed to necessary social order and, thus, had to be regulated. Requirements of chastity and limitations on sexual play were articulated and firmly reinforced by an oral tradition of stories detailing the mythological descent of those who strayed.

People Who Failed to Receive a Proper Burial

The cult of the dead was important in Romanian spirituality. It was the sacred duty of the survivors in each family to organize funerals for their departed. Although apparently focused on the deceased, these rituals helped to heal the community, weak and defenseless when faced with the finality of incomprehensible death. They replaced tragedy with a sense of normal rhythm. They occupied the mourners, telling them how and how long they were to mourn. Thus, the mythology of the vampire assisted in the immunization process. People were commanded to occupy themselves with small rituals in order to prevent a greater evil, for the deceased would transform into a vampire unless the survivors tended correctly to their responsibilities.

The deceased might have become a vampire *if a dog walked under the hearse* carrying the body. Burial was about returning to nature through interment. The vampire was an untamed and unnatural being. It might have sought to steal from the body as it was being placed in the ground, preventing the soul from achieving its peaceful resting place.

There were many forms of interdiction against what animals were or were not allowed be in the vicinity of a coffin before burial. Ultimately, these were warnings against leaving the body unsupervised. In many villages, a *deceased person might have become a vampire when cats, mice, or even fowls walked over (or under) the body.* Proper supervision was a sign of respect for the deceased. The body was not supposed to become desecrated by animals. The deceased, moreover, should not have had to face the other world alone. With many local variations, Romanian villages developed elaborate rules and rituals concerning wakes. The vampire was lurking if these were not followed.

The mourning period was also regulated, requiring that the survivors remained actively involved while the deceased took his or her final journey. According to Orthodox Church precepts, a requiem mass had to be performed forty days after burial. *Those who failed to receive the mass after forty days* could have become vampires, their souls remaining on Earth to torment the living.

The highest probability for becoming a vampire at death occurred for *infants who died before being baptized.* Again there was a unity of religious and mythological belief. In Orthodox Christianity, the door toward spending the next life in eternal bliss was opened only for affiliates. In a world of high rates of infant mortality, the family had an obligation to arrange the baptism quickly, to insure that the innocent baby would be automatically elevated to heaven rather than condemned to hell. Folk superstition added additional incentive. The condemned child would not only suffer damnation; it would also, most likely, return to prey upon the village and upon the family that neglected its spiritual care.

Infants Born Under Special Circumstances or with Certain Signs

Predestination was not central to Romanian folk tales. Usually, there was a critical moment when the main character had to choose one route or another. Where manifest, Romanian fatalism was conjoined not to anger or tragedy, but to a sense of resignation and serene acceptance. In vampire mythology, predestination most often referred to the circumstances under which person was conceived or born.

Conception fears emerged as a dimension of village sexual control. For instance, one was not supposed to fornicate on nights of celebration and drinking, of customary visits to neighbors, or of religious ritual. Thus *children conceived on Christmas Eve or New Year's Eve* were destined to become vampires. On Christmas Eve, youths used to go caroling in the village and were said to bring good luck and prosperity. Christian skits were performed about the birth of Jesus, but older traditions still persisted. Among the most widespread was "The Goat," where a costumed group chanted in comical ways best wishes for the coming year.

Similarly, *children conceived on the Easter Eve* were destined to become vampires. On this night, Romanian Orthodox churches held an elaborate midnight mass that ended with the entire congregation carrying burning candles and walking around the church three times. In many villages, people used to bring baskets of good food to the church. The priest blessed the food, and, afterward, there were communal visits and much eating until the wee hours of the morning.

Almost all societies had interdictions against incestuous relationships. *Children conceived by close relatives, especially siblings or first cousins* were doomed to become vampires and would likely return to prey upon their own families.

The prohibition extended to almost all behavior of sexual immorality. Thus, *children born out of wedlock* might become vampires. The risk extended over time. Even if an illegitimate child was accepted socially and lived a life integrated into the community, the *offspring up to the third generation* could still become vampires. In the case *of children born out of wedlock to a woman who had herself been born out of wedlock,* their fate was guaranteed. No witch could intervene; no magic ritual was strong enough to save them from the walking undead.

Many cultures have a fascination with numbers. In Romanian folklore, the seventh in a sequence has special resonance. Great distances are "over seven countries and seven seas," and being very happy is synonymous with being "high in the seventh sky." The *seventh of seven brothers or the seventh of seven sisters* was cursed to become a vampire. On occasion, the pattern was reversed and the seventh brother, as the youngest, saved his family from vampire fate.

Children could be predestined to become vampires from the actions of their mothers during the pregnancy. They came into this world with their fate already sealed. Romanian villages constructed elaborate rituals in the attempt to insure the safe birth of a baby. For instance, one was not supposed to start to make clothes for an infant until it was born, for otherwise fate would punish such conceit. With many local variations, the vampire threat reinforced such prohibitions, intended to teach and protect. Most strictures concerned insuring a safe lifestyle and diet. *Pregnant women who went outside the house without anything worn on their head* were in danger of giving birth to a vampire. Equally, *children born to a woman who, while pregnant, drank unclean water or ate animals killed by a vampire* were doomed to become vampires.

At the sacred moment of birth, it was the duty of the midwife to see that all necessary rituals were observed, to insure that the Goddesses of Fate (*Ursitoarele*), those mythological witches in charge of predicting the infant's future, were all appeased. At times of difficult birth, villagers would resort to disenchantment spells and magical rhymes. Despite the pains of childbirth or the depths of post-partum depression, the mother had to be careful. *Infants cursed by the mother during their birth* were certain to become vampires and afflict their families in the future.

Some babies were born with malformations or unusual appearances. To Romanian villages, these were signs of difference and Otherness, of not being normal and not fully belonging, revealed at birth before they could be masked or hidden away. There is no surprise that superstitions abound when ignorance and fear of the unknown meet. *Children born with teeth,* or *born with a lot of hair on their bodies, or born with a tail* would grow to be vampires. *Children born with a caul or membrane on their heads* were destined to become vampires or else to be extraordinarily successful since they came into this world already marked.

There is something profoundly saddening about a stillborn baby. Where people were ignorant about possible causes, it was normal to assume that malefic forces were already at work. In many regions of Romania, *infants who were stillborn* were doomed to become vampires, seeking from the shadows to live the life that unfortunately had been denied to them.

Random Victims

The Goddesses of Fate were sometimes arbitrary. In villages, people died for unexplained reasons and without any prior signs or warnings. Vampire mythology provided some degree of explanation. The fight against vampires was reassuring, promising power against forces from the unknown.

Those *attacked, bitten, or killed by a vampire could become vampires.* There need not have been special circumstances. Evil could be catching. Some people were simply random victims. In a world where unanticipated death was common, bad things sometimes did happen to good people.

A vampire's curse provided mythological clarification when untimely death claimed a life. It was generally believed that *people who met a sudden or violent death—by drowning, shooting, hanging, or simply collapsing and falling down dead,* were doomed to become vampires. As countermeasures, there were numerous enchantments and magical rhymes to help in cases of violent deaths.

There were times when the risks were higher than others. Vampires were believed to be especially active on the nights of St. George and of St. Andrew. *People bitten by insects during St. George's or St. Andrew's night* were sure to become vampires of the worst kind. Individuals who went out after dark on those nights were considered daredevils and, thus, deserved their fate.

Finally, there was purely haphazard occurrence. Although the signs may not have showed at all during their lifetimes, *some unlucky people* simply became vampires at their death. Not everything in the village world could be or had to be accounted for.

How to Recognize Vampires Among Us

Romanian folk vampires often disguise themselves among the living, strategically easing their quest for fresh blood. Some are not even resurrected corpses escaping from the grave to attack the village. Instead, 'living vampires' hide in plain sight, pursuing apparently normal lives within the village while maintaining a secret identity as bloodsuckers and killers at night. Ironically, they partake of the society that simultaneously they threaten. Thus, in Romanian folklore, fantastic beings can walk the earth and mingle freely with humans. It is a symbol of duplicitous human nature. Good and evil are both present in the ordinary and everyday. The sacred realm and the profane realm become intertwined. The Other is ever watchful and can exist in the guise of a neighbor or even a loved one.

Given the dangers, it was most useful to be able to know the true nature of one's neighbors and to recognize vampires living inconspicuously among the villagers. According to Romanian folk wisdom, there were signs, but sometimes it required an experienced elder or a wise priest or a knowing witch to recognize them.

Living vampires could be identified by the characteristics that made them stand apart. For example, *people with abnormal physical powers* were feared, for they could be vampires by night. Romanian peasants, like individuals living in small, homogeneous communities, were suspicious of outsiders and those who were different. Belonging was granted to those with shared characteristics. Being exceptional was interpreted more as a curse than as a gift.

A widely spread superstition throughout the Balkan region is connected to the infamous Evil Eye. *People who allegedly have the capacity to jinx others* were said to be living vampires, as they were accused of having abnormal power over others.

In the village, the Orthodox Christian Church and much older mythological beliefs formed an odd cohabitation. Christianity was the declared archenemy of the pagan vampire, yet the continuing vampire legend served to help reinforce Christian values. Those who did not recognize the official village church or were offended by its symbols had self-identified as outsiders and were automatically suspect. For example, *people who could not tolerate the smell of incense or who showed fear at the sign of the cross* most probably were vampires.

All those who looked different were also suspect. In general, villagers felt at home with others who looked like them. *People with red hair*, or with *very dark and intense eyes*, or with *touching eyebrows* would be identified as probable living vampires.

Villagers were suspicious of those who avoided the customary folk defenses against vampires. For instance, *people who did not eat garlic* might be vampires. Rejection of the famous antidote gave them away. Reciprocally, villagers were suspicious of those all too willing to risk their fate. According to local lore, vampires roamed freely on specific nights, including St. Andrew's in late November and St. George's in late April. God-fearing people sought to stay at home. By contrast, those who ignored good advice and chose to *sleep outdoors during the nights of St. Andrew and St. George* could well be living vampires.

Finally, village existence was quite transparent, as individuals lived largely in full view of one another. Village celebrations were open affairs in which all were invited. Everyone knew most of the details regarding other individuals, what they possessed, and how their households functioned. In this climate, *people who were too secretive* in their comings and goings, *those who went away on travels, those who disappeared for long periods and then reappeared without explanation,* and *those who could not account for their wanderings at night* were naturally considered to be probable living vampires.

What Do Vampires Do?

Kill People

Vampires are feared because they destroy life. They *suck the blood of their victims*, who then become weaker and often die shortly after. The Romanian vampire is a practical and efficient killer.

The wicked creature spills the blood of unsuspecting, innocent victims. The story is of abnormal death, inexplicable and especially stealthy. Unlike in the stories of popular culture, there is no aestheticism and no ritual attached to the act. Unlike the modern gothic horror, in very few of the Romanian folk tales do we have bloody scenes, gory images of death, or elaborate descriptions of the drinking of the red and warm liquid. Sucking the blood is often but a metaphor, meaning sucking the life out of somebody. It is nothing more than an act of destruction, however brutal, necessary to keep the perpetrator alive.

Paradoxically, the vampire is an inherently relational character. He needs other people to exist. Moreover, he is most often the byproduct of the particular community that created him. In a strange way, he is the refuse generated by that specific group of human beings. Vampires sometimes roam and feast upon strange communities, but most of the time they haunt the place of their origin. If they feed upon animals, it is most often domestic animals living in close proximity to humans, not those in the wild whose death would go unnoticed. Romanian vampires most often come from the community on which they prey, not the wide world "out there," and they usually attack their own kin first. Although they often hide in the forest wilderness, they tend to stick close to the territory surrounding their home village.

In Romanian folklore, the loss of blood can connote *the loss of virginity*. The vampire lures young people, mostly teenage girls, to follow him into the dark world. There is a thinly disguised promise of freedom from social constraint, ecstatic liberation, and sexual fulfillment. Yet, he is merely the messenger of painful death. His only objective is to bite and kill those who do not protect their purity and chastity.

Sometimes, the peasant folktales do not even mention blood. Instead, the vampire attacks the organ that pumps it. He extracts the life out of his victims as he *eats people's hearts*. This is again a metaphor. The vampire is heartless. He forms no relationships of caring and affection with others. He feasts without moral feelings upon humans the way humans feast upon chicken or pork. Ironically, however, he seeks to obtain by violence what he no longer retains by nature. His quest after human hearts brings, at best, temporary relief from inescapable hunger.

Annihilate Fertility

In primitive societies, the gods and goddesses of fertility were major figures, for they insured the fecundity of animals and the productivity of the land. By contrast, those powers that diminished fertility and took away the *mana* were especially evil, for they threatened the foundations for life. This theme, long pre–Christian in origin, maintained its relevance in Romania through the enduring vampire mythology.

Romanian *vampires killed and ate livestock,* often belonging to people with whom they had quarreled. There were tales regarding vampires returning from death to continue their fights with neighbors. In the local village, unresolved conflicts could poison the atmosphere across generations. The moral lesson was that individuals had to solve their own conflicts and repair relationships while still alive.

In most stories, there was nothing elegant to the folk vampire. He was merely a sordid despoiler of life and those things necessary for life. His offenses could range from large to small. He was, thus, sometimes accused of *secretly drinking the milk* from cows, sheep, or goats. He was blamed for *stealing grain from the fields* and even *spreading infectious diseases.*

Transform Into Animals

Zoomorphism is the main magical power of the Romanian village vampire. He is master over the animal world and can understand and control animals. He can *transform himself into nearly any animal,* most often wolves, black dogs, bats, or crows.

In Romanian folk mythology, the connection between vampires and wolves was so close that it did not make a clear distinction, as other cultures do, between the vampire and the werewolf. Peasants tended to use them interchangeably. Vampire folktales could circulate in a variant that has a werewolf instead as the main character. The main exception was that, somewhat frequently, the werewolf had the power to eat the moon. A degree of scholarly confusion stems from the fact that Romanians across regions tended to use different words when referring to the vampire. Transylvanians usually preferred the term *strigoi*, while Wallachians in the south mostly used the term *moroi.* The words should be understood simply as regional synonyms.

The wolf is the most important animal of Romanian mythology and among its most ancient symbols. Many historians claim that the tribal ancestors of modern Romanians, the Dacians, got their name from the fearless wolf. The patron saint of the wolf, Saint Andrew, is also the Romanian national saint. The traditional folk calendar divided the year into two fundamental seasons: winter—ruled by the wolf, the master of darkness and coldness, and summer—ruled by the horse, the master of light and warmth. It follows only naturally that the vampire commonly transforms himself into a wolf, whereas the horse is used to identify the vampire's tomb.

In many parts of the country, children are baptized with the name Wolf because it connotes a powerful and tenacious fighter. In some regions of Transylvania, when a young child is extremely sick, s/he is handed out through the window to a person dressed in wolf skins. The child is then re-baptized with the name Wolf (or sometimes Bear) and then is returned to the house through the main door as a new person, with a different name, whom death will not recognize.

Finally, the wolf can have a sacred dimension, even found in burial customs. As a young woman, I attended the funeral of an uncle at Bratca in Bihor County. A peasant woman with almost no formal education recited a long ballad describing the final journal the departed was to make. The special task of accompanying the deceased and guiding him on his complicated last journal was assigned to the wolf.

Times When Vampires
Are Especially Active

Vampires are creatures of the night. They reign deep in the darkness of the unknown. They are most active when people are asleep, a time of extreme vulnerability. Yet, they are not creatures of the dream world and do not convey subliminal messages. Vampires tend to *appear around midnight and depart with the third crow of the cock*, signaling the arrival of the new day. It is a symbolic statement of the regenerative powers of nature.

Traveling was considered especially dangerous. It was a voyage from the village to the realm of Otherness. Roads were places where people might get robbed or even killed. The passage from one settlement to another often took them through mountains and forest wildness. There is a rich Romanian folk tradition of stories, including vampire stories, about the bad things that happened during travel, especially in *bad weather and during heavy storms*. The relevant slogan was "Stay put in bad weather, as vampires are active during storms."

Vampires are *associated with the full moon*, a time of mystical significance in many cultures. They are also associated with specific days of the religious calendar. They are especially active *on the eve of St. Andrew's feast* (November 29–30). This night, celebrated as "The Commencement of Winter," is equally signified as "The Night of the Vampires." It was believed that, at this time, all vampires come out and roam the world. In the villages, young people congregated for a special ritual, the Protection of Garlic. They would gather at various houses, especially those of young girls, in order to construct a large pile of garlic and protect the pile from vampires who would attempt to steal it. The ceremonies were merry, with dancing and singing, and would last all night. In the morning, everyone went home with some of the garlic, which would be placed on windowsills and the top of doorframes throughout the year.

While St. Andrew's marks the approach of winter, with its coldness and darkness, St. George's feast (April 22) marks the arrival of spring. On *the day and eve of Saint George's feast*, vampires were said, again, to be very active, an indication that they responded to the energizing powers of spring. On this day, in many parts of Transylvania, young men were expected to visit all the houses where there were young females and sprinkle pure water over them as a sign of protection.

Upon death of the living body, the vampire had to make its appearance as a self-declared member of the underworld. There was no consensus across regions regarding how soon after burial *the departed revealed themselves as walking dead*. In some sections of the country, it was said that they became active only *nine days after the funeral*. In others, it allegedly happened *after forty days*. Some accounts reported that initial activity occurred in *six months, three years*, or *even seven years*. The differences were the product of contrasting numerologies. For instance, the Orthodox Church mandates religious rites (*Parastas*) at three years and seven years after death, after which the deceased is permanently installed in Heaven. Various Romanian vampire legends, while not entirely consistent, nevertheless, do show strongly recurring themes and patterns.

Defenses Against Becoming a Vampire

Fending off the vampire threat involved both individual and community obligations. It required a cooperative enterprise that helped to bring the village together. There were preventative measures that individuals took to reduce the risk of becoming infected. There were preventative measures taken to protect the dead. Finally, given the presence of an actual vampire haunting the village, there were procedures to kill the vampire and prevent it from ever returning.

Preventive Measures During One's Life

The message was quite simple: remember to *live by the norms, rules, and moral codes* of the village. One should not be dishonest or violent or insatiable in one's wants. What one did, day by day, was the true measure of human worth. It was necessary to *live in harmony with the other members* of the community, *with the natural environment*, and *with the Church*. For instance, traditionally in Romanian villages, people had a benediction performed each year between St. Basil's Day (January 1) and Epiphany (January 6). During these days, the local priest visited each house and blessed it with a silver cross. He then sprinkled holy water in every room using a basil twig. This was said to promote prosperity and provide protection against disease, death, and vampire attacks.

Prevention also came through the *virtue of cleanliness and good housekeeping*. A household that was clean, with pots washed and put away; and with empty jars and glasses turned upside-down, kept one's objects safe from the vampire's command when he appeared at night. Villagers knew that chaos could invade their private lives at the slightest invitation and, therefore, took steps to avoid it.

There were also steps directed explicitly against the vampire threat. Garlic is a medicinal plant, known for centuries as a natural remedy to help cure infections. In folk wisdom, it equally worked against vampire infection. In some parts of Romania, local lore advised that people should *rub garlic on doorknobs and windowsills*. In others, they were expected *to hang garlic wreaths* in all rooms, or *burn garlic in the fireplace* to prevent vampire access through the chimney. A particularly elaborate recipe comes from the Maramures region in the Northern part of Transylvania: pick garlic flowers from a clove planted in consecrated ground (usually a church graveyard), put these together with the head of a snake especially killed for this purpose, dry them, and keep them in the house for guaranteed protection.

Stronger remedies were required when actual vampire activity was suspected. Villagers were expected to *recite certain magical rhymes in a specific ritualistic manner*. A common variation required that somebody in the suspecting family, often an older woman, recite the rhymes three days in a row, using a bunch of basil made up of three twigs and three white eggs from a black hen. The exact words and gestures varied by village. The inherent meaning, however, was that subtle knowledge rested with the wise ones and was passed on across generations.

Preventive Measures for the Dead

It was the *responsibility of the living to protect the departed*, especially at the vulnerable moment when they moved across the threshold from life into death. The implication was clear, that the bonds that united people in families and as neighbors should not dissolve abruptly at death. Vampire mythology asserted directly: what living people do can affect the dead; what the dead do can affect the living.

There is an extensive cult of the dead in Romanian culture, reinforcing the idea that society is a-temporal, transcending time. The rationale behind certain practices has been lost in history. When I asked, I was merely told, "This is how things are done around here."

A recurring theme, with local variations, is that *bread should be offered as a gift after the interment* and that *wine should be sprinkled on the grave*. Although related symbolically to the body and blood of Christ, the practice also seems to have been inherited from older, pre–Christian religious practices that venerated the cycles of regeneration. In Transylvanian villages, failure to offer the sacrifice of wine would make the deceased return as a vampire, complaining that the ground was too dry. In Maramures, the *family would spread grains and also put coins inside the coffin*. On the way to the cemetery, more grains were sprinkled along the road. It was said, "One grain per year / only after you eat all of them / can you return to meet the rest of your kin."

Often the family was instructed to *place a grain of incense in the nostrils of the deceased* so that it could not breathe, in the ears so it could not hear bad advice, in the eyes so it could not see a vampire or the devil, and in the mouth so it could not reveal the names of its relatives. Little pebbles, garlic, or millet were used in a similar manner. In many regions, clothes and other objects that belonged to the departed had to be given away, to vest the entire community in defending the name of the deceased.

According to other superstitions, it was necessary *to place thorny twigs at the feet of the body*, so it would trip if it ever attempted to get out of the coffin. In many parts of the country, especially in cases of violent death, *the body had to be buried face down* to prevent it from escaping the grave.

Finally, when there was reason to suspect that the deceased was a strong candidate to become a vampire, the recommendation was *to cut the head off and place it at the other end of the coffin*, so that the eyes do not recognize the route and could no longer command the legs to travel homeward. Sometimes a stake or *a long needle or pin was stuck into the heart*.

How to Kill a Vampire

When confronted with an actual vampire attack, the first objective was to identify the grave or resting place of the creature. Often, it was someone who had recently died in the village. With determination and a bit of stealth, it never proved too difficult to follow the vampire back to its lair. In cases of uncertainly, one solution was to bring a horse to the suspected tomb (in some regions it had to be a white horse). If the horse acted nervous or rejected water or refused to walk over the grave, it was most likely home to a vampire.

Under ordinary circumstances, it was a sacrilege to disturb the sleep of the dead. Sometimes, however, necessity required that one dig out the coffin. Technically, this was not exactly legal, and, therefore, it was best to have consent, even assistance, from the local priest. Nor surprisingly, in the folk stories, suspicions (although they may have been slow in forming) always turned out correct. The vampire's body would lie in an unusual position, for example facedown or turned around in the coffin, or else it appeared surprising fresh colored and lacking in decay.

There are remarkably few stories in Romanian folklore involving direct, open combat between the slayer and the monster. Instead, the vampire was most often killed while resting, through the use of a formal, but not especially complicated ritual. Usually the ritual required more than one living participant, including at least one who had been close to the undead person when he or she had been alive. Although there are many variants, most involved combinations of decapitating, stabbing, burning, holy water, and sunlight.

In one common version, the ritual required that, simultaneously, the vampire's head be cut off and an iron or wooden spike be thrust into its heart. The body would then be burned in the light of day and the ashes re-buried, accompanied by a religious mass at the graveside and a liberal dousing with holy water.

In some versions, a relative of the undead had to exhume the body and thrust an iron rod or silver dagger into the heart. In some, long iron nails (including one through the heart) had to affix the body strongly to the coffin, which was then re-buried. In some, the heart was cut out and burnt. In some, the extracted heart was boiled in wine, the remainder of which was sprinkled on the tomb or even drunk. In some, the decapitated head must be buried separately from the body. In some, the strong rays of the sun were sufficient to turn the body into ashes. In some, burnt ashes were scattered over the ground, often in the nearly fields or forest, or tossed in a flowing stream.

Regardless of the variant, none of the stories required a vampire hunter with extraordinary abilities. Some courage was needed to confront the undead. But the slayer was always an ordinary person who lived comfortably within the village. He was not a superhero. He almost never was a village leader, and he possessed no special powers. The act of killing the vampire did not elevate his life. Instead, it merely allowed him to return to the now-peaceful community. Similarly, in none of the variants could there be compromise or negotiation with the vampire. It could not be redeemed or reformed, whether by reason or by love. It could not turn back from its terrifying path. Unlike in contemporary popular fiction, in Romanian folk culture, the only good vampire was a dead vampire.

Conclusion

Did Romanian peasants living within traditional villages actually believe the folk stories about vampires in their midst? It is impossible to tell. There is no enduring written record. Accounts compiled by Romanian ethnographers (Şăineanu, Pamfile, Dumitraşcu) date only from the late 19th and early 20th centuries, and their reports were limited. Some more recent writers (Cremene, Senn) asserted that residuals from the tradition could still be found in the villages during the post-war communist period, although it was not much discussed with strangers because it contradicted official party ideology. At the end of the 20th century, Hedeşan discovered that peasants still enjoyed talking about vampires. Today, however, especially to young urban Romanians, vampires are more creatures imported from Hollywood than home grown from native roots.

Ultimately, it does not matter whether vampire legends were consciously believed or not. They provided stories to be told on long nights. They carried moral lessons about proper behavior. They taught community integration. They linked the natural and the mystical in intricate ways. They represented the rhythms of birth, life, and death. They produced explanation for dark and unknown terrors through the existence of unworldly creatures that attacked viciously and without warning, but they also gave to humans defenses against and responses to those creatures. They gave physical form to the horrifying "Other," and through it, they reinforced normalcy.

Embedded in these folk vampire tales is a revelation regarding the Romanian soul—it is at peace with the world as it is. The vampire is not the embodiment of ultimate evil. Fears are manageable, and the vampire is not invincible. Humans have some degree of power over the mystical world and can, eventually, restore natural balance. It is my hope that some of the rich complexity is visible in the stories found in this volume.

PART IV

Identifying and Eliminating Vampires

The Soldiers and the Old Woman

In a world populated by the living and the non-living, it is important to be able to identify those of the latter category and to protect oneself from their bloody intentions. The Romanian village might be populated by family, friends, and close acquaintances. But one must be wary of the dangers that come from the strangers encountered along the road.

The first story in this section recalls the adventures of four soldiers traveling together. Fortunately, good faith and good luck kept them safe.

The story was inspired by an old uncle of mine who lived in Valea Neagră, Bihor. He smoked a pipe and was recognized as the most worldly and well-traveled person in his small mountain village. As a young man, he had been drafted into the Emperor's army, when Transylvania was a part of the Austro-Hungarian Empire, and had traveled as far as Italy.

A group of four soldiers were traveling through Transylvania on their way to Vienna. For more than twenty years, they had served the Emperor. They had fought courageously and had seen the world. Now, they were going to meet the Emperor in person. They were journeying to his magnificent palace to take part in a ceremony organized every three years in celebration of retiring soldiers. Some were to be awarded medals; the lucky few would receive a few golden kreitzars, the fabulous Austrian coin.

A sergeant, the leader of the group, was one of the fortunate ones. He rode across the countryside full of hope, anticipating that the sum he had saved and the amount he was expecting would be enough to buy a house with some land.

"Who knows," thought the sergeant, "perhaps I will choose to live somewhere around here. I have always liked this region. I was born and raised on the other side of those mountains, not very far away. I would like to own a little farm when I retire from the army, maybe even start a family."

The men were riding slowly, admiring the scenery—lovely green hills and the winding Crişul Repede river—when their road bent sharply to the right and led them near to a house sitting by itself on top of a small hill overlooking the river.

"Look men," said the sergeant. "That house over there is quite nice. I would like to own a property like that. It has a parcel of good land next to it and a great orchard behind it."

"I see what you are saying, sir," one of the soldiers commented. "Besides, the forest is not far, so it will not be hard to gather firewood."

As they drew closer, they noticed that the garden in front of the house was full of weeds. Next to the house, however, there was a large stack of dry hay.

Înmormântare la ţară (Burial in the Countryside), Camil Ressu (1880–1962). This painting of a Transylvanian village funeral shows the assembled community humbled in the face of death. Burial rituals are shown as essential to the community, and they help to prevent the departed from joining those unfortunate souls stranded between Heaven and Earth (courtesy Cluj-Napoca Art Museum).

Interior țărănesc (Peasant Interior), Camil Ressu (1880–1962). This painting, of a woman sitting by the hearth, shows the interior of a Romanian peasant dwelling. It is usually two-room, simply furnished with ornaments more functional than decorative. In the typical story, women who do not take good care of this inner domain can be vulnerable to vampire attacks (courtesy Craiova Art Museum).

"I had hoped," sergeant said, getting off his horse in front of the gate, "that we would find some food for us here, but it's fine if there is hay for our horses. The sun is beginning to set, and we must soon make arrangements for the night."

There were no fowls in the yard, no dog either, but an old woman dressed in black appeared somewhat suddenly on the porch.

"Good evening, Auntie," said the sergeant. "We are not from around here and are wondering whether you would sell us some hay for our horses. We are in the service of the Emperor and can pay with good money."

The old woman did not answer right away. She examined them with a cold expression. She was not in the least friendly, nor was she frightened of them. She merely pointed to the haystacks and nodded.

The sergeant, thus, ventured another question. "I say, Auntie. Maybe you will let us spend the night here. The next village seems to be a little further away than we would like to ride tonight."

The old woman did not seem surprised. Finally she spoke, as if it cost her some effort. "The house does have empty rooms. You will have to make your own beds."

"Don't think twice about it, Auntie," said the sergeant, quite relieved. "We are weathered soldiers. We sleep wherever we can lay our heads."

"Say, Auntie," asked one of the soldiers, joining in the discussion, "now that you've allowed us to feed our horses and promised us a place to sleep, maybe you also have some food for us. I am so tired of the lard and onion that we are carrying with us."

"We have money to pay. You are not going to be at a loss, don't you worry!" another soldier added.

"No," the old woman said, almost mumbling to herself. "I will not be at a loss."

Then she disappeared as silently as she had appeared. After a while, she returned, carrying a plate with cheese and bread and a small pitcher of wine. Without a word, she signaled them to follow.

The room she gave them looked as if it had not been occupied in a long time. Things were covered by a thick layer of dust. The soldiers did not mind. All they noticed was that it had four beds, nicely arrayed with soft furs.

The old woman brought them an oil lamp and showed them an adjacent room where they could find pillows for their heads.

The adjacent room looked much like the first. There was dust over everything, and the air was stale. A long-dried bunch of lavender rested in a hand-painted clay vase in the middle of the center table. The towels hanging on the wall showed their age, as the brightly colored stitches had faded to pale.

Somebody had once put a lot of effort into the house. It must have been, at some time in the past, quite beautiful. The hand-carved chairs and bed-frames, hand-woven linen, and the embroidered pillowcases could still be seen. But clearly, it had been years since the house and its furnishings had experienced care. There was something strange about this house, but the soldiers had been through many experiences in their travels. They did not think twice about it. They were tired and hungry.

While three of the soldiers went to feed the horses, the sergeant stayed behind to pay the bill. He took out a purse with some coins in it and asked, "Auntie, how much do we owe you for all this?"

"You will pay me, never fear. You will pay me in the morning," the old woman responded with strange sparkle in her otherwise inexpressive eyes.

"Suit yourself," he said, a little surprised. "But we will be leaving very early, at the first light of the morning. Are you not concerned we might leave without paying?"

"Never fear," she answered. "We will settle your payment by the time the cocks crow."

"Good night, then," the soldier said and put the purse back into his pocket. "But wait," he added. "Let me give you this as a way of saying thanks." The sergeant took his hand out of his pocket and with a fast, almost playful move dropped something into the hand of the old women before she even had time to react.

"It is a little cross I brought from the holy Mountain Athos, which I visited on a pilgrimage this past winter," he explained.

The old woman looked at her palm in disbelief and fled.

"That was a fast one. Good night to you too!" he shouted after her.

The four soldiers slept through the night and woke up the next morning quite early, as they had planned.

"I feel that I have been sleeping the sleep of the dead," one of them exclaimed. "It must have been the drink. That old wine was much stronger than it appeared."

"I guess so," another answered. "I cannot remember the last time I slept so deeply."

"We have to be going," said the sergeant. "We have a long journey ahead of us. I will find the old woman, or one of her servants, to take our money."

Soon he returned with an odd expression on his face. "There is nobody in this house, not a single living soul. This house is uninhabited," he announced.

The men could not believe their ears, but they knew better than to doubt their leader. They went off to search the house. They opened all the doors, one by one, slowly and carefully. The rooms were all furnished, the house looked spacious and well endowed, but the signs indicated that it had not been occupied for a very long time.

"What is this, a ghost house?" one of them asked. "Let us make sure we have looked everywhere. Maybe there is somebody in the stable."

So they looked some more. There was nobody in the stable, just very dry hay and cobwebs. Similarly, cobwebs covered the barrels and chests stored in the attic. The cellar, however, told a different story. Under the house, in a large basement, there were seven coffins.

The four soldiers, although experienced in the world, decided that they had seen enough of this strange house. They rode away in a hurry and did not rest until the next village. There, they stopped at the local pub.

"Welcome, soldiers," the innkeeper told them. "Come join in the joy. The men over there have just shaken hands regarding the purchase of a house. Now they are 'wetting the deal' as they say around here. Everybody present is offered a free drink."

The four soldiers accepted gladly and began talking with those present. The sergeant wanted to learn more about the mysterious house in which they had spent the night.

"Speaking about houses to sell," he started, "we saw an interesting farm further upriver, one with a nice garden all covered in weeds. Does anybody live there? Is it for sale?"

"You are talking about Trifu family house. That is a cursed house, man. It would be a nice property, but nobody has lived in it for more than twenty years. There used to be seven people in the family, but they are dead, have been for ages."

An old man sitting quietly by the fire continued the story. "They all were turned into vampires. We stay clear of that property. It is unsafe to enter the house or grounds. It is said that the vampires kill anybody who spends the night there. The evil undead take pleasure in feeding on innocent travelers who happen by."

The locals told them more strange stories about the house and the mysterious disappearances of travelers who stopped there. As is customary among men sitting in the pub, discussion soon moved to other issues, those of more direct interest to the local villagers, like the forthcoming harvest or the quality of the plum brandy this year.

Yet, the four soldiers were most intrigued by the stories of the cursed house. Having fought in real wars and faced vicious enemies, they were not easily scared. However, they realized, something strange had happened during the previous night.

"But we slept in the vampire's house last night, and we are all alive," the youngest of the soldiers blurted out.

"May God help you!" said the innkeeper, crossing himself.

"Make certain to cleanse yourselves from all spells and from the evil eye," another man suggested, looking at them with suspicion.

The more they thought about it, the more confused the soldiers became. Had the vampires in the house attempted to suck their blood? Had they been spared? Why would that happen?

The soldiers realized that they could not just leave and move on. They were responsible servants of the Emperor. They felt an obligation to return to the cursed house and destroy the vampires, if they still were there. Only then would the road be safe for other travelers.

"Talk to our new, young priest," the old man by the fire suggested. "He has performed disenchantment prayers in a nearby village. He might know what to do."

The priest was well educated and did know exactly what to do. The next morning, he accompanied the four soldiers to the infamous house, intending to lift the curse forever. They went directly to the cellar. There, they found the seven coffins, just as the soldiers had explained.

Six of the coffins were closed, but the lids were not nailed shut. The seventh was open, and the corpse it was supposed to contain was lying on the ground next to it.

First, the men carefully opened the six closed coffins. The priest made the sign of the cross over each body. He splashed holy water on each body with a bunch of dry basil. Then the soldiers took out their swords and cut off each vampire's head. They knew they had to act very quickly—cutting the head off does not kill a vampire; it only weakens them temporarily. Finally, the men thrust their bayonets through the hearts saying, "Disappear forever, you vampires! Let your souls go to Hell and your bodies turn to ashes."

There was no blood when they cut the heads off, but the hearts told a different story. The hearts were full of blood, fresh blood that spilled on the ground making six small, dark pools. A horrible hissing sound came out of the mouths of the creatures as the men performed their holy ritual.

The priest splashed holy water on the bloodstains and chanted a prayer in an old language that the soldiers did not understand. The stains began to boil. Soon they dissipated leaving no traces behind.

The seventh vampire remained, the one on the ground next to the open coffin. The men recognized her. It was the old woman dressed in black who had greeted them the day before. Unlike the others, her body was dry and still. It did not appear to have any blood in it.

Indeed, before the men could cut off her head, she completely turned to ashes. There was no need for them to drive a bayonet through her heart. All that was left on the ground was a broken Athos Mountain cross and a pile of white ashes.

"God forgive her!" said the priest.

"Is it possible that my cross killed her?" wondered the sergeant.

"Yes. The holy cross is death to a vampire," the priest replied. "It saved you, and it saved her soul at the same time."

The men burned all the coffins that had held the vampires and washed away the remains. Before leaving, the priest burned incense in every room and sprinkled holy water on the doorsteps. He then placed a small wax cross on top of each door to prevent evil spirits from again entering the house.

Having performed their duty, the soldiers went on their way to meet the Emperor. They followed the narrow, winding road uphill in silence. When they arrived at the top, they turned around to look at the house one more time.

"Who knows," thought the sergeant. "Perhaps I will return to this region some day. It has a strange attraction for me. My heart is heavy as I take my leave."

He looked at his hand and noticed a small cut that was bleeding. "I hope you will be healed by the time I reach Vienna," he thought and then forgot all about it.

The Cursed Family

Risks exist even inside the village. It is often dangerous for a family to have a vampire living within the household. The danger only grows once the vampire departs this life for the other side, for it quickly forgets the protective affection it once felt. Family members, then, become available prey, and their familiarity singles them out as especially choice victims. The vampire is, thus, especially hateful, for it violates the sanctity of the family, essential to village life.

This story was inspired by an account mentioned by Pamfile in his Mitologie Românească *(1916/2000, 123). It is a summary of a story previously printed in the folklore magazine* Şezătoarea *(1900–1, No. 12: 155).*

Pamfile's version ended in death for everyone in the family. My story instead incorporates learning. It is more reasonable to posit that peasants gather information and respond to the events in their world, rather than simply accept their fate. In addition, my story emphasizes an important characteristic in Romanian folklore, that the youngest boy in a family has special qualities and frequently saves the day. It reflects the optimistic faith that Romanian villagers have in younger generations, as capable agents of transmission from present to future.

Once upon a time, there was a husband and a wife who had seven fine sons. Their house was on a hill at the crossroads between two villages. They were a little isolated, but they were content. Their house was solid, and their land and stock were fertile. Nobody knew, however, that the woman was a vampire.

Such creatures can live apparently normal lives, mingling with ordinary human beings. At some point, nevertheless, they have to join the realm of the dead to which they truly belong. Then, there is no rest for such creatures. They have to wander Earth, sucking people's blood or eating their hearts. The only way to stop them is to kill them with special tools and give them a special, vampire's burial.

When the woman's days as a living vampire came to an end, her death was quite sudden. Her husband and sons were surprised but did not suspect anything unusual. She was given a conventional funeral. She was buried in the family cemetery on the family property. The husband and sons, although saddened, soon returned to their conventional existence.

Upon her death, as happens with vampires, the woman forgot all the love she felt as a wife and mother. Her earthly feelings simply disappeared. In search of fresh blood, she returned to this world to drag the members of her family after her.

First, she returned as a fly. For three evenings in a row, she entered her former house as a big, black fly. Each time, she sat on her husband's face and bit him.

"What is wrong with these insects?" he said to his youngest son who was helping him tie some sacks of flour. "This damn fly just bit me. Even the flies have turned aggressive these days."

"Daddy, I know you told us that one should not kill any of God's creatures unnecessarily," the youngest son asked, "but what if an animal bites us?"

The father answered, "Sometimes we have no choice but to defend ourselves. In that case, killing is necessary and justified. Otherwise, we must be kind to animals, taking only what we need for food."

Three days later, the father began feeling sick and took to his bed. Soon, he was dead.

The seven sons were sad having become orphans so unexpectedly, but they had no reason to suspect anything unusual. They gave their father a proper funeral and buried him in the ground, next to their mother. Unfortunately, conventional religious rites—the ones performed under normal circumstances—have no power over vampires.

A terrible cycle started. The husband became a vampire. Now he, too, was doomed to wander the earth and suck people's blood. Such a cycle does not stop until the last member of the family is killed.

A few days after the father's death, the oldest of the sons was sitting on the porch, eating a slice of bred, when a stray dog entered the yard. It was a small grey mutt. It looked tired and hungry, and the lad took pity on it. The dog seemed quiet and tame, so he decided to adopt it.

"I will name you 'Vagabond,'" the young man announced. "You will live here and be my pet."

The lad started sharing his food with the dog. In the evenings, he would walk through the orchard to relax after work, and the dog would accompany him.

"Little brothers, let us play a little! Come and meet my dog!" he shouted. But the others had not yet finished their chores and could not join him.

In a few days, a strange weakness overcame the oldest brother, and soon he died, just like his parents.

The six remaining brothers hid their grief, buried their brother according to custom, and moved on, not knowing what else to do. They barely noticed that the dog also had disappeared.

One morning, not long after, the oldest of the remaining boys noticed a stray cat in their yard. The lad had been sitting alone on the porch, finishing his meal and watching the sun set behind the horizon.

"Hey, kitty! Would you like some milk?" he asked it. He poured some of his milk into a small plate and placed it on the floor for the cat to drink. The lad took to feeding the cat every day before he started his chores and every evening as the sun went down.

One evening, as he was leaving of the kitchen with a mug full of milk, the youngest brother shouted after him, "Hey, bro, don't take that mug outside. Finish your drink in here and leave the mug on the table. I am in charge of the dishes today."

"No, I need to feed my cat," he answered as he went out.

"We do not have a cat, silly," the little brother exclaimed.

The lad fed the cat for about a week. As happened before, he then took to his bed. And, as happened before, the brothers had yet another funeral to arrange.

"This family is cursed," they said. "So many deaths in a row."

The five remaining brothers were heartbroken, yet they did not know what to do. They had a large household to manage, and now there were fewer of them to work the land and take care of the animals. "We all will have to work harder now," they decided, "and make sure we take good care of our health."

Life followed its normal course. The brothers reorganized their work so that each of them was in charge of something.

The oldest of the five remaining brothers was the strongest, so he was put in charge of the firewood. Every day, he made sure that they had enough wood for the kitchen and the fireplaces. Whenever the pile of wood—kept in the shed at the back of the yard—was insufficiently large, he would sharpen the axe and chop some more. He would always whistle while chopping. His brothers knew where he was because he whistled all the time.

One day, while he was in the shed working and whistling, the youth heard a different kind of music. A bird was crowing nearby.

"Aha! I have competition! You like singing, too," he exclaimed, and he started to whistle at the bird.

The black crow answered back as if playing a game. After that, the bird was always there, waiting for him. One morning, the lad invited his little brother to come and hear the duet he was making with a bird. "You want to hear this. There is a bird that I have trained, and we sing together."

"What are you talking about? You cannot train a bird. That's silly," answered the youngest one, ignoring his invitation.

Soon the third brother began to feel sick and weak. He fainted by the woodshed. Later, he could no longer walk. He took to his bed, and died.

Now, there were four brothers left. They were dismayed. The household seemed to be cursed. But they saw nothing that they could do other than yell at the fates. After a proper period of mourning, they returned to their household labors, and life moved on.

One of the brothers was particularly good at hunting. He used to accompany their father when he went shooting. Now, it became his job to bring home game, possibly a pheasant or a hare. The lad went out to hunt early in the morning. "I won't be long! We will eat game for the next days, and, if I am really lucky, somebody will have a new fur hat," he shouted as he left.

He returned that afternoon smiling, for the hunt had been success-ful, and the brothers would eat meat for the next few days. As for the fur hat, that did not quite work out. He had indeed shot a fox, but he only wounded the animal in the leg and then brought it home to care for. "I just could not kill it," he announced. "I am going to watch over it until the leg is healed, and I can let it loose in the forest."

The brothers were a little surprised, but did not really care. Let him do whatever he wanted, they thought, and they minded their own busi-ness. But a few days later, the hunting brother complained of weakness. He, too, took to his bed and died.

Another funeral followed, accompanied by further mourning and total confusion. "A terrible curse is ravaging our family," they concluded, but they could not figure out why it had descended on them. Nobody noticed that the fox disappeared. Had they noticed, they would probably have thought with relief that it simply ran away.

Of the original family, the mother and the father were dead, and four of the seven brothers were dead. None of them had been sick. They had simply withered, almost overnight, as if something or somebody had sucked all the life out of them.

After further days of mourning, the three remaining brothers had no choice but to resume their lives. They reorganized their tasks and moved on. All three together worked the land. In addition, one took care of the animals, one chopped the wood and managed the supplies, and the youngest brother ran the kitchen.

The new arrangement did not seem to be succeeding. There was too much work and too few hands. "We have to do something," they admitted. "We might have to sell this place and move out." Before taking drastic action, however, they agreed to seek advice from those who were wiser and more experienced.

The plan was interrupted by further tragedy. The next morning, the brother charge of the animals had bad news. Their horse was acting strangely. "You would think something is possessing it," he complained. "Ever since the poor animal was bit by something in the back leg, it has been unrecognizable. It is agitated, restless, and aggressive. I don't know how I am going to clean the wound, as it does not let me near. You would think that it does not recognize me anymore."

The youth decided to spend the night in the stable with the horse, to try and ease its suffering. In the morning, both the youth and the animal were dead.

The two remaining brothers were now extremely frightened. If there was a curse on their family, then they, too, were in imminent danger. But what were they to do? They had no idea what they were fighting against. Five brothers seemed to have been killed quite suddenly by a mysterious disease that wore them out without warning.

"It is possible," the older of these two suggested hopefully, "that the deaths are not connected, and that we are not really at risk. I am certain that, at least, two of the deaths resulted from bites. Our brothers were bit by something."

"Bit by something?" the youngest brother of the family asked in wonder. Then, his mind began to work. He remembered the old stories and realized: "It is a vampire. A vampire's bite can kill. It has been a vampire all along."

"You are really scaring me," his sibling stated. "You mean, there might be a vampire hiding here on our farm. It is possible, I guess. Now that you put the idea into my mind, I am afraid to go outside to feed the owl."

"What owl?" the youngest brother asked, very alert.

"There's an owl that appeared in our nut tree two days ago. I noticed it after the last funeral," he answered. "You know that I love all animals. Our parents taught us always to take care of animals, even stray ones that appear at our house."

"Animals can bite," the little brother exclaimed. "I remember father telling me that sometimes we have to defend ourselves from such animals."

"I understand everything!" he continued, surprised by his newly found insight. "The animals that have appeared in our yard lately, they are not just animals. They are vampires. They are the curse on our family. There is no natural disease. We are in a battle against the unnatural undead."

His brother grasped the point immediately. "I remember the tune that our grandmother taught us:

> *When you are out late at the night,*
> *Beware the small vampire bite.*
> *From this bite there is no healing,*
> *For the vampire lacks human feeling.*
> *You will wither and wane,*
> *All medicine is in vane....*

The remaining two brothers came to a sad conclusion. There was no way they could bring their two dead parents and five dead siblings back to life. But they could try to save them from the fate of walking the earth at night, hated by all. They could give them peace, and in the process save themselves from a terrible death.

The two boys prepared their tools carefully. They cleaned a small hatchet so there was no trace of rust on it and they used it to make seven pointed wood spikes. Then, they hung garlic on every door and window of the house so that no vampire could enter while they were away. They also burned feathers in the fireplace so that the chimney also could not be penetrated.

While the sun was high in the sky, they went to the family cemetery. They dug up the seven coffins of their family members, those who had died recently of suspicious deaths.

Just as the lads suspected, the seven bodies showed no sign of decay. There were indications, however, that they had moved about. All seven were lying with their faces downwards, a sure sign that they were vampires. There were bloodstains in the coffins.

The boys knew exactly what to do. They did not hesitate. With sure hands, they thrust the seven wooden stakes into the hearts of the vampires and nailed them down deeply using the small hatchet. Then, they cut their heads off. After that they burned the bodies and spread the ashes over the fields.

Knowing that they had done the right thing, the two boys went home. There were no further mysterious deaths in the family.

Dangerous Promises

Mothers want the world for their babies. However, it is dangerous to promise too much, for some children die young and might return as vampires to seize their unrealized reward. In this story, a young boy and an old priest together solve the problem and implement the solution.

My story was inspired by an account collected by Dumitrașcu (1929, 16). His source was an old man from his village in the Dolj region, who claimed that the events actually happened half a century before to Dincă Mărinaș, the relative of a friend.

At the core of the story is people's incapacity to explain why some babies are stillborn or die in infancy. It is easy to blame unnatural forces that come to capture the baby especially those who have not been baptized. My version also incorporates a moral theme. Mothers in the vil-

lages have clear responsibilities to their babies and to the community. The mother in the story fails in her duties, and it falls to her older son to make amends.

Sabina became a widow overnight. Her husband had never been sick. One day he simply died, leaving her with a 12-year-old son, Sorin, and another baby on the way.

The young widow was heartbroken. Little did she know that her troubles were only beginning. The unborn baby soon started crying in her womb, sobbing incessantly in distress. Nothing that Sabrina did seemed to help.

"Come on, dear, stop it. I will sing you a lullaby," she offered, attempting to soothe it. "I will tell you a nice story." The baby would not listen. "I will give you these carved wooden spoons to play with, later when you are born. They will be your toys," she tried again. Nothing appeased the baby. It kept crying.

The following day, while the baby again was crying in distress, the old cat came and sat next to Sabina, purring. "Oh, do not cry again," the mother said in desperation. "I will give you anything. I'll give you this cat if you stop." And guess what! To the poor mother's relief, the baby stopped its wailing. "Do you hear, old tomcat? You belong to my baby, now." The cat just purred. What does a cat know? The older boy, Sorin, heard his mother and laughed. "Imagine if your promise came true. The baby would have a pillow with sharp claws."

Next time the baby began to cry in her womb, the mother remembered the cure she had found. The dog, the good guardian that it was, was barking at some passer-by and drew Sabina's attention. "Hush little baby. Stop this crying," she said. "I will give you the dog. Hector is going to be yours." The older boy teased, "That's a better promise, mother. The baby might need a friendly guardian. But there is a problem as Hector is my dog. You cannot give him to the baby." Sabrina paid him no mind, happy that the crying inside her womb miraculously stopped.

From then on, Sabina used this strategy as a way to calm the baby. She started offering it gifts, naively, as if it was all a game.

One time, she was looking out through the window into the neighbor's yard, smiling at the family's small daughter who was running after a flock of noisy geese. Again, the unborn baby started crying in her womb. "Hush, hush, dear. Don't cry. I will give you this pretty girl. She will be your play-pal soon." The baby stopped its crying.

Another day, an older relative, Uncle Cornel, happened to pass by the gate. He had been away to the Negreşti Fair and had bought three young sheep to add to his herd. As Sabina hurried to the gate in order to see them, the baby began to cry. She patted her belly and cajoled, "Hush, hush, now. Stop crying. Look at the sheep. I will give them to you. They will be yours."

The boy heard his mother and frowned. Later, he told her, "Mother, you have to stop promising the baby things that are not yours to give. You are not thinking about what you are saying. Nothing good is going to come out of such promises."

"Don't worry," she said dismissively. "Do not take my comments seriously. Besides, Uncle Cornel does not have heirs, so it might anyway become true that you and the baby would inherit the animals from him."

But Sabrina did not forget her son's comment. The next time her unborn baby began to cry, Sabina carefully did not offer it something she did not own. She promised it something that was hers to give, her heart.

Months passed. When the due date came, Sabina's baby was born, and it was born with a caul, or a veil as some call it, on its head. "That is sign of good fortune," the midwife predicted. "The baby will be rich one day."

But the prediction did not come true. On the third day, before people had the time to baptize it, the baby died. "I just hope that it will now find peace," Sabrina commented sadly. The baby was buried at the margin of the cemetery, in a special section outside of the holy ground especially assigned for children who did not get to be baptized.

Sabina mourned the baby, and then slowly started to heal. "Death is a normal part of life," she said with resignation. "It is something we must accept."

As if to prove her right, more death soon visited the house. One morning, she and her son woke up to find their old tomcat dead near the fireplace. "Its time had come," Sabrina explained to Sorin. The cat was old, and they accepted its death with serenity.

Then, one week afterward, they had to say goodbye to another pet. They found the dog lying dead on the threshold. This time, Sorin could not be easily consoled. "Why did he have to die? He was young and healthy," the boy whined. Moreover, he felt, without the faithful dog, the house became defenseless. Dogs keep away bad people during the day and evil spirits during the night.

Less than a month passed when there was more talk of death. Uncle Cornel's sheep suddenly died. He complained about his bad luck to everyone willing to listen. "I bought these three sheep only last fall. I carefully selected each of them. They were all healthy. Now they are all dead. I'm telling you, these were not normal deaths," he announced. "My sheep were killed by a vampire. There was no blood left in any of them."

Uncle Cornel was the first to mention the possibility of a vampire attack. The other villagers did not take him seriously or, if they did, they did not show it. Sorin, however, became frightened. He had never before heard tales of vampires so close to home. A bad premonition lingered heavily upon his soul. He was the man in the house now. It was his job to protect his mother and their household the best he could.

Yet again, ugly death soon showed its face. This time, it was their neighbor's little daughter, who died with no apparent explanation. The unhappy parents told a sad story. "The poor child complained of chest pains on Wednesday morning. She kept repeating that she felt as if somebody was eating her heart. Three days later, she was dead."

Mother and son were both moved by their neighbor's tragedy. "How sad to hear of a child's death," Sabina said. "There was a time, not so long ago, when I had hopes that my baby and this girl would be playing together."

The boy listened in silence. Then he remembered the strange gifts that his mother had promised the baby as she tried to soothe it. Slowly, he reviewed the gifts that his mother had promised—the tomcat, the dog, Uncle Cornel's sheep....

After a long pause Sorin asked, "Mother, did you promise the Suciu family's little daughter to the baby?" A heavy chill settled between them like a dark cloud. Mother and son just looked at each other. Sabrina did not utter a word, but Sorin knew. Still on the list, moreover, was his own mother's heart.

Realizing that he would get no explanation from his mother, Sorin decided to consult the village priest. The old man had been kind to him and on several occasions had given him chores to do for the church. The priest listened to the boy's story with sympathy. One of the details especially disturbed him. The dead baby had been born with a caul and was buried without having been baptized. Putting the facts together, he suspected the baby had been returning from the grave, feeding upon the living and claiming the lives that its mother unwittingly had promised to it.

The priest explained to the boy that vampires could emerge from various causes and were not only evil murders or those who had dealings with the devil. He discussed the dangers that they pose to the living. He told Sorin of his fears regarding the baby brother, yet he also assured the boy that such creatures were not invincible. They could be destroyed once their identity and resting place are discovered.

Sorin wept with sadness and anger. If his baby brother was a vampire, he cried out, then there was no time to waste. They had to act immediately. The old priest understood the need for urgency, but he counseled against premature judgment. "We are not absolutely certain that the deaths resulted from your baby brother. We must make sure that our suspicions are confirmed. It is a terrible sin to disturb a body for no good reason."

It was already a little after noon, and, although the summer day was long, they had several things to do before sunset. The priest and the boy first went to the river, stopping at the ford where the water was shallow. They selected three large round stones that had been washed by the water and dried by the sun. They, then, went to the thicket where the wild dog rose bushes grew, and they cut off a few prickly branches to take with them. Finally, they borrowed from one of the villagers a white stallion. Such horses are not common. Fortunately, the owner consented to let the priest take him for a while without asking any questions.

Thus equipped, the boy and the priest went to the cemetery, to the section reserved for those who died without baptism. The priest inspected the baby's grave carefully, noticing a small hole in the ground right next to where the coffin was buried. "Look here," he said. "It is an important sign. This might well be a hole used by the vampire to get in and out."

The priest, next, tried to lead the horse across the tomb. As it drew near, the horse stopped abruptly. It raised its forelegs several times and neighed in distress, refusing to step any closer. "As I feared, we now have our proof," the priest announced. "White stallions will never cross a vampire's grave. Your baby brother has indeed become a vampire. We will return tonight and put him to rest."

A little after midnight, the two vampire hunters, one old and one young, returned to the grave and began to dig. It was hard work for them, but they soon uncovered the tiny casket. As they had expected, it was empty. The vampire was out, hunting for new victims.

They turned the tiny coffin around, in order to confuse and disorient its occupant. They placed the three round stones into it—one where the head would go, one at the chest near to the heart, one at the feet. They closed and covered the coffin, and they placed the prickly dog rose branches into the hole next to the grave.

Sorin and the priest waited and watched in silence. In the thick night air, minutes slowly drifted past. Just before the first signs of dawn, the vampire returned. Trying to get into the grave, it had first to fight through the branches. It was obvious that time was running out. Light was slowing glowing on the horizon, and the cocks were ready to announce the day. Then, the creature discovered that the coffin was full. Rocks had taken its place. There was no room place for it to hide. The cocks' crows announced the arrival of mighty the sun. As the first rays shone down, the creature caught fire and burned with a hiss.

The boy and the priest realized with satisfaction that their work was done. The new day cast a serene light over the peaceful little grave.

The Vampire's Revenge

Thwarted love can be painful, but suicide should not be seen as welcome relief. The act of suicide both defies Christian teachings and severs the link between the person and the community. One, then, joins the unholy dead, returning to inflict harm and seek vengeance. This is a story of a fickle young man and a jilted girl, who seeks revenge against a former friend. In the end, it shows how help, sometimes, can come from unexpected sources.

My story was inspired, in part, by a story that was published by Furtună in the literary magazine Ion Creangă *(1912, No.1: 11–12). In it, an innocent girl becomes suspicious that the person leading her into the forest is actually a vampire. She breaks a string of beads and bends to pick them up, in order to gain time. She then attempts to hide inside a small cabin. At the last moment, a hen (and not the lazy cock) comes to her rescue, in a comical reversal of gender roles.*

There are many versions of this story. Mine utilizes a female vampire (strigoaica). Women from the mystical world, including witches and fairies, are frequent in Romanian lore and are more often associated with revenge than their male counterparts.

There had been gossip regarding the circumstances of Viorica's birth. An epidemic of vampire attacks had been ravaging the village. Her mother became sick but did not die. People whispered that Viorica's real father was the killer vampire. The mother, it was said, must have made a pact with the unholy creature. She gave him a child in exchange for her life. Some predicted that the child would have bad luck, or that the vampire would come back and reclaim it later.

By and by, the gossip was almost forgotten. Viorica's parents died relatively young, but that was not especially unusual. As life followed its uneventful course, the girl grew to be a beautiful young woman. Eventually she fell in love with Mitru, a young man from the village.

However, Mitru's parents did not want Viorica as their daughter-in-law. They could not ignore the stories that surrounded her birth. "Don't waste your time with Viorica!" his mother told Mitru. "You should look to the other eligible young women in our village. There are plenty of good ones that we would approve of."

The father had expressed his disagreement even more clearly. "I would never accept this Viorica as a daughter-in-law. You must look for somebody else."

Nevertheless, for a while the two young people continued to see each other, often talking long walks together through the old orchard. Some of the girls even giggled in secret that the two had gotten so very close that they might be forced to marry soon.

But nothing happened. Quite the contrary, for men can be fickle in their attentions. Mitru abruptly settled upon another, a pleasant young woman named Ileana. The family was pleased with his new love, who was popular in the village. The wedding date was soon announced.

Viorica was devastated. She stopped taking part in the village social gatherings and neglecting her friends. She was seen less and less walking through the local pathways and lanes, and then she was not seen at all.

"Of course she disappeared," some people said. "Why should she have lingered here? She must have gone to live with relatives beyond Piatra Craiului mountain, where her mother came from."

"I do not remember her ever mentioning relatives," a former friend commented, somewhat puzzled.

"It matters not where she went," was the reply. "Her goal was to get away. This village was no longer home to her, so heartbroken was she because Mitru dumped her."

"I am afraid that she might have taken her own life," the friend continued. "The last time I visited her, all she did was sit and cry, as if she had nothing left to live for.

"Now that you mentioned it," one villager confessed, "I have an unusual story to tell. Last week, I went to visit my brother in Cold

Springs, and I took the shortcut using the old wooden bridge over the gorge. Near the Round Cliff, I decided to rest my feet a little. I sat down to eat an apple in the shade of the roadside trees. Shortly after, Viorica came walking quickly past me. She did not notice me sitting there. She appeared lost in thought. I know she did not take the turn toward the old bridge. Instead, she went up the narrow path uphill towards the Dead Man's Jump."

"That is a cursed place," one woman commented and crossed herself.

"I didn't know what was on her mind, did I? I thought she might be after wild berries or mushrooms. A few minutes later, as I was crossing the bridge, I looked up toward the cliff, and, there she was, or so I thought. Somebody who looked like her stood there, gazing down into the precipice. When I looked again, there was no one standing there at all"

"Oh my! Poor lost soul! And what did you do?"

"What was I to do? I crossed myself and said a quick prayer. But then I looked carefully into the gorge. I did not see a body, and so I could not be sure anyone really had jumped. When I returned home after two days, there was no talk of someone dead or a body found in the river. Naturally, I put the whole thing out of my mind."

"If that was her," people said, "if she really took her life, she is now damned forever. What a unholy thing to do."

"God helps us all," an old woman predicted. "If Viorica took her own life, she has turned into a vampire, and we are all in danger. She will come back. We have not heard the end of the story."

Viorica's disappearance remained a mystery. People searched, but no remains were found. It was easier to believe that she had just gone away. Some of the more wicked-minded started making jokes. "She will return, just you wait. She will reappear immediately before Mitru and Ileana's wedding with a child in her arms."

And the young woman did, indeed, reappear.

One mild evening, only a few days before the wedding, the bride-to-be was returning home from a cousin's house with some golden summer apples when she saw Viorica watching from across the road.

Ileana was surprised and a bit afraid to see her rival, for she was aware of the village gossip. Yet Viorica appeared serene, smiling warmly as she called out a greeting. "Good evening Ileana," she said in a strange but mellifluous voice. "Nice apples that you are carrying there."

The wind stopped, and the air turned chilly. The shadows became darker and deeper. Ileana didn't know what to say, still frozen in surprise.

"I hear that the wedding preparations are going well," Viorica continued. "I bear you no ill feelings. In fact, I want to give you a gift as proof," revealing a string of beautiful beads. The beads shone in the dark, and Ileana could not take her eyes off them.

"I have," she said with a strange gleam in her eyes, "many more beads like these for your embroidered costumes and also a beautiful golden scarf, perfect for a bride. You have never seen anything like this, trust me."

With fascination, Ileana reached for the beads and grasped them tightly. "Thank you," she heard herself answer in a small voice.

"Come with me," said Viorica with determination, talking Ileana by the hand. "Let us go to my place!"

Ileana felt that she barely touched the ground. It was more like flying than walking. She knew she should be going home with her apples, but she was under a spell and had to follow obediently. A greater force was controlling her.

They soon arrived at Viorica's house, but they did not enter. Instead, they walked past it toward an old, overgrown orchard. It was where the graves of Viorica's parents were found, along with a few old tombs guarded by a thick oak tree.

"Here we are," Viorica announced when they reached the tree. Absolute silence engulfed them. "Go in!" she commanded firmly, pointing to a large hole in the crooked trunk.

Ileana had felt powerless, a rag doll in Viorica's hands. But the black hole in the tree—appearing like a toothless, hungry mouth—made her heart jump with fear. Frightened for her life, Ileana's feet stuck to the ground as if anchored.

"Please go in," the vampire lured, shifting to the softest of tones. The poison of the strange voice was most tempting, yet Ileana still managed to say, "You go first. You have to show me the way."

Viorica stepped inside and disappeared, swallowed by the dark hole. She called out, "Come, follow me!"

But Ileana still hesitated. She lingered for a moment, adjusting the basket of apples on her shoulders. As she did, the string of beads that she had been holding tightly in her hand all this time caught on the basket and broke. The beads spilled out, all over the ground. They sparkled at first, but then their inner light died and dissolved away. The controlling spell lost its power, sucked into the bowels of the earth.

"What am I doing here? What is this place?" Ileana thought frantically, and then she understood. "It is not the real Viorica who returned to be my friend, but a wicked vampire that brought me here to eat my heart."

"Come inside, now!" Viorica ordered from within the tree.

"Oh my," Ileana replied carefully, in the sweetest voice she could manage. "I have dropped my beads on the ground. Give me a minute to pick them up. I will be with you shortly."

Ileana moved quickly. She stuck the golden apples into the hole of the old tree. The power of the sun within them, would delay Viorica's pursuit temporarily. Then she ran for her life. In confusion, however, she ran away from the village and toward the hills of the outskirts. There was no time to reverse direction, for the vampire soon would be following her.

Ileana saw a small light ahead, coming from a farmhouse at the margin of the forest. There was nobody home, but the door was unlocked. She entered, locked the door behind her, and hid under a table in the corner of the kitchen.

As her breathing eased, Ileana looked about the room. She realized that she was not completely alone. A hen and a rooster were perched on top of the stove. The noise of her entry had awoken the hen, and it was watching the situation with curiosity.

It did not take long for Viorica to arrive at the farmhouse. Angrily, she pulled at the door but it did not open. This did not deter her, for the jealous vampire was determined to get her revenge. Vampires have ways of gaining entry into locked houses.

Fortunately, the hen was wise. It fully realized what was going on. "Hey, rooster," it said. "Wake up and see what is happening here. There is a vampire trying to get into our house and eat a young woman. "

But the rooster was not impressed. "Let me sleep," he answered.

"Come on, " the hen persisted. "There is a young woman trembling with fear in our house. We cannot let the vampire get her."

"What is it to me?" replied the rooster with indifference. "I do not care. Let me sleep."

"Don't be like that," the hen clucked. "This girl is just like our young mistress, and you know that she always feeds us well."

By now the vampire was opening the door.

"Please, rooster!" squawked the hen. "You have to do something. The vampire is getting in."

"Let me be," said the rooster. "There is nothing I can do."

"Of course there is," the hen insisted. "All you have to do is crow. Crow that it is morning, and the vampire will disappear."

"It is not my time to crow. It is not yet dawn. Let me be!" the obstinate fowl responded.

The vampire entered and began searching for Ileana.

"Crow and save the girl! You have to save the girl!" the alarmed hen howled.

"You are always telling me what to do," the lazy rooster mocked. "You save the girl if you care." And it closed its eyes and returned to sleep.

So, the hen did crow. She crowed like a rooster three times, and her crow made the vampire disappear.

Sometimes some apples and a hen can save an innocent girl from a wicked vampire set upon revenge.

The White Flower

Vampires do not like to be disturbed while on the hunt, and they do not like to be recognized. Their revenge can be terrible. There is somewhat of a magical element to the following story, in which the girl from the fairy tale meets the monster from the undead. The prince finds his true love in a young woman who had been entrapped as a flower. The complication is that she is also stalked by a vampire who wishes to keep his identity hidden.

This is a story of accident more than intention. We find it in the initial encounter between the girl and the vampire, in the meeting of the girl and the prince, and in the final resolution. Unlike in many Romanian folk tales, agency and choice are less important than fate.

My text is based on a short story collected by Şăineanu, "The Vampire and the Girl" (1895/1978, 560). Pamfile recounts a similar story (1916/2008, 127) that he learned in the small town, Râmnicu Sărat. His version was translated into English by Agnes Murgoci (1926, 333–4) as part of her famous article that first introduced the Romanian vampire to wider audiences.

According to Şăineanu (570), a story of this sort also circulated in Russian folklore under the title "Nechistoj" (The Unclean/Devil). The equivalent term in Romanian is "Necuratul." In my opinion, this is the origin of the name, "Nosferatu," a word that has come to represent vampires in popular culture but does not exist in Romanian, nor can be found anywhere in the regional folklore.

Maria wiped away her tears as she walked home slowly. She had just visited her parents' graves. It was her only comfort these days. They had both died unexpectedly, only a few days apart. Now she was living by herself, scared and haunted by what she had seen.

She did not mind being alone during the day, as her farm required much work. The chickens would wake up early and signal for the day to begin. She had to milk the two cows and send them out with the village herd. The farm animals then needed attention. Even the household animals had to be fed before breakfast (her faithful dog, a lazy cat, and a noisy family of peacocks that roamed the yard simply to ornament it). Later, there was work to be done in the vegetable garden—planting, weeding, and harvesting for her meals.

When night came, however, her world became scary. The animals seemed to feel that way, too. Her dog would often act strangely. All of a sudden, it would whine and shiver, the hair on its back became stiff, and it would show its teeth at the slightest noise. Out of the blue, the cat would start to meow and jump into her lap for protection, its pupils dilated. The other animals would sometimes make strange noises when they were supposed to be asleep and quiet. Some of the animals lately had begun to show signs of weakness. A few had died.

Maria thought to herself, "I know when this started. It was that terrible night when I walked by the old, dry well. It is my fault. Everybody knows that the place by the old well is cursed. I should have listened and avoided it. But I was there, and I saw him, and now he has started to come after me. What am I going to do?"

One evening a few months before, Maria was walking back home. She had been at a friend's house, helping her to install a new loom. They had practiced their weaving and some wool dyeing tricks, and the two girls forgot about the time.

As it was late, Maria decided to take a shortcut home. She followed a grassy path past the old cemetery. The burial ground had not been used for years, and the stone well next to the gate was dry. People no longer had much reason to come there. "Even the water became frightened and ran away," they would say, "leaving the well quite dry. Vampires have taken over. It is their kingdom now."

The sun had set, but the night was not especially dark. A full moon was shining, covering things with a silver light. The shadows were short. Nothing was moving. The wind had died away. Silence reigned.

Maria was not especially afraid. An old aunt had taught her how to protect herself against vampires and evil spirits. She washed her face only with rainwater and carried dry basil leaves underneath her clothing, against her breast, for protection. "Keep in mind that one should never speak to a vampire," the aunt had instructed. "Never address him and never answer any question that he might ask."

Now, Maria knew that things were not quite so simple.

On that terrible evening, a few months ago, she felt a sudden chilliness overcome her as she approached the dry fountain, on the grassy path by the cemetery. She saw a man lying on the ground and a black dog next to him. The dog appeared to be eating the man's heart. She was horrified but did not lose her composure. She was confident with dogs, no matter how big and ferocious they were. She picked up a good sized stone to arm herself—a piece of an ancient, crumbling cross from the tombstone on her right—and ran toward the dog, intending to chase it away.

The dog turned around and looked at her with a snarl. Its fangs were red with blood, and its eyes glowed red as well. Maria was about to shout at the dog, but as she opened her mouth, the ferocious beast transformed itself into a tall, pale, dark-haired man with dark eyes and an ugly face. It happened right before her eyes. Maria's heart skipped a beat. She understood immediately that she had encountered a vampire feasting on its prey. She looked into his eyes and, through them, into the other world. A curse descended upon her. She knew, instinctively, that her life would be changed forever.

The creature had glared at her with fierce, intense eyes. "What did you see?" he demanded.

Maria remembered to stay silent. Under no circumstance was she to speak to him. It might be the only thing to save her life. Horrible things happen to those who talk to the undead. Without thinking, she threw at him the stone she had just picked up. She threw it with all her might, doubled by the intensity of her horror. The vampire with a confident sneer caught the flying stone in the air, with no effort at all.

But then he did react. He looked at the stone with surprise and annoyance, and dropped it as if it were burning hot. The stone left a mark on his palm. The stone that wounded the vampire had a golden spot on it. The gold was a portion of a cross that had been painted on the old tombstone from which it had fallen.

Maria turned and fled, running as fast as she could toward home. Fortunately, the vampire chose not to follow her. For now, she had won her safety, but it was not enough.

One day, the vampire appeared to her, materializing as she was picking vegetables from the garden. "Tell me what you saw," he demanded.

Maria knew that she could not answer. She knew the prohibition against uttering a single word to a vampire. She just turned and walked into her house. Within a week, her father suddenly fell ill. He did not appear to suffer from any recognizable disease. He did not have any aches or pains, but he was exhausted and grew weaker by the day. Then he died, his body shrunken and dried out.

The vampire returned a second time, appearing in her path after the father's funeral. "What did you see?" he insisted. "Tell me or your mother will die." Again, Maria refused to answer. She turned and ran, although it was no escape. Within a week, her mother died, in exactly the same fashion as her father.

After that, the vampire would appear often to Maria. She was tempted to ask him, "Why do you torment me? You know I saw you eating a person's heart." But she always remembered the interdiction, "Never speak to those from the other world. You would start down a road of no return, for you would end up a vampire, yourself!"

Maria felt some possibility of hope. The vampire might continue to frighten her, and it might afflict her animals, but it might not be able to kill her because she had never spoken to it. Apparently, however, such hope turned out to be false. One dark night, the vampire came after her, and she fell deathly ill.

The people of the village chose a spot for her grave on a pleasant hill next to the road. Curiously, on the very next day after she was buried, a beautiful white flower appeared on her gravesite. The flower was sparkling white and fragrant. Everyone who walked by noticed and admired it.

Yet, this is not the end to the story. A few months later, a prince of the realm was passing through the village on his way to a hunting ground. He stopped his horse and gazed at the beautiful flower growing from a gravesite. He was tempted to pick it and wear it from his hatbend, but some mysterious force deterred him. For a day, all he did was sit and gaze at the flower. He was captivated. Then, he ordered his servants to extract the flower, taking care not to disturb any of its roots. It was transported to his palace and replanted in a pot on the windowsill of the prince's bedroom.

Every night, after the prince fell asleep, the flower turned into a beautiful young girl. (Had anyone noticed, there was a strong resemblance to dead Maria.) The girl would look down at the prince, not with evil in her heart, but with love. She would tidy his room, and then lie down to sleep next to the young prince, remaining until almost daybreak.

After a while, the young man started to feel despondent. He lost his interest in worldly activities. He cared nothing about the hunt or the dance. He took no interest in managing the family estates. He moved about without energy, as if nothing pleased him. He preferred to be in bed, where he slept away the hours.

"I do not want to awaken anymore. I feel that I have another life in my dreams," he would comment.

The parents of the prince were bothered and confused. Their son had never acted this way before. They feared for his health and even for his life. In desperation, his mother, the queen, consulted an old witch with a reputation for concocting potions and casting spells. She came and watched the young lad sleep. She asked him questions that he minimally answered. She examined her cards and read his palm. She went away without comment but returned one day later with a potion for the prince to drink and a spell for the mother to recite after prayers.

That night, when the flower turned into a girl, the prince was not asleep. He looked at her with affection and begged her to stay with him in human form. The charms worked. The girl was a joy to behold. Everyone admitted her beauty and her intelligence. The prince rapidly regained his energy. The couple was soon married, and their life proceeded pleasantly.

There was only one complication. The bride did not wish ever to leave the house. It was as if some great fear haunted her. She only felt safe within its walls. She asked that the windows be covered with heavy curtains, and that they be drawn at all times.

One day, however, the inevitable that was destined to happen, did happen. The young bride had to leave the house. She needed to attend church to pray for the good health of the child she was expecting. She had long anticipated this day. She knew full well what was waiting outside, but her obligations as a mother-to-be were preeminent and sacred.

As expected, the vampire was there, watching her as she stepped outside. He stood in her path, halfway between her home and the main church door. The young woman was calm, as if she was prepared to accept her fate. She looked directly at the unholy creature and walked deliberately toward him.

"What did you see?" he demanded.

The woman had been walking slowly down the path, but at the last intersection, she turned suddenly to her right and ran as fast as she could toward a small, old, wooden door at the side of the church. Somehow, she knew it would be unlocked.

The vampire raced after her, but she managed to reach the small door first. She entered the church and threw herself down at the feet of a large silver icon of the Madonna and Child. The vampire reached the church right afterward. As he began to grab her, his hot breath on her neck, there was a noise like thunder. The icon came free from the wall and fell upon him, smashing the vampire to the floor. The surrounding votive lights and candles all went out and then, a few second later, magically relit. They twinkled peacefully. A dark cloud hovered in the church air for a while, then lifted, and disappeared.

The vampire was destroyed, and the young woman saved. As the saying goes, she and her husband and the family that they raised lived happily ever after.

The Red Flame

It is the goal of most village men to meet and marry a worthy woman. Although it is said that a good husband should not pry too deeply into his wife's past and private affairs, the situation changes if the wife might well be a vampire. Blind love, in such a case, can result in fatality.

The theme of finding out surprising things, not always positive, about a loved one appears occasionally in Romanian folk tales. My story is inspired by a brief summary by Pamfile in his Mitologie Românească *(1916/2000, 105), based on a story published initially in the folklore magazine* Şezătoarea *(1893, No. 247).*

The most interesting thing about this story is that village gossip turns out to be correct. Quite often in stories, gossip is a source of misrepresentation and confusion, expressing petty jealousies and uninformed suspicions. In this case, by contrast, eyes from afar are more seeing than those from the bedroom.

Once upon a time, there was a man named Martin. He was a nice looking fellow, honest and hard working, but not very lucky with the girls. All the other village men his age already were married with children. His parents naturally hoped to see him with a family of his own. He was their only living son, and they wanted heirs for the little wealth they had acquired.

"It is time for you to settle down, my lad," his father said. "We are not so young anymore, and we would love to see kids again in this house. Life is short, and one cannot wait forever."

But Martin was not attracted by any of the girls in his village. One day, however, he attended a fair in the city, a long ride away along the river valley. There he met a young woman. She was a weaver, selling the fabrics, towels, and carpets that she made. She had red hair and pale skin. She did not talk much, but her eyes captivated Martin. Soon he was under her spell. They traveled back to Martin's village together, as husband and wife.

Martin's parents were so pleased to see him wed that they did not complain. "If she is the one he chose, what can we say? We were afraid we would die and never see a daughter-in-law. Now we can rest assured that he will not be alone in his old age."

Other people, though, loved to gossip. "What a strange woman, not friendly at all. She just sits in her house and weaves. I guess she does not like the hard farm work and housework that we do. Lucky her, to find a husband who does not make her do anything else around the house."

"It's too bad that our own girls showed no interest in Martin. He turned out to be a better husband than many others around. Now this strange woman from the city gets all the benefit."

"She is not from the city. They just met there. Martin told me she was from somewhere else, farther away. She's from the village of Black Lake, in the Bihor county."

"No, it cannot be. You have it wrong. Black Lake used to be a village a very long time ago. Nobody lives there any more. It is now a ghost village comprised of ruins."

"What are you talking about?"

"I know the place. I have been there, by accident. When I was about twelve, I went with my grandfather to fetch lumber for the house. At some point, we took a wrong turn. I do not remember most of the details from the journey, but I do remember Black Lake as if I had been there yesterday. I will never forget the thick fog and my feeling of overwhelming fright. Martin's wife cannot be from Black Lake. You must have misunderstood."

"Fortunately," one of the women concluded, "we all live in a happy village."

But happiness can be fleeting. Good times are often followed by bad. Slowly, things began to change. Most disturbing, there were as number of sudden deaths and mysterious lethargies, in both animal and people.

Among the first persons to die—only a few weeks apart—were Martin's parents. They apparently withered away. They turned pale, lost their strength, and succumbed in their sleep. "At least they died in peace, satisfied that Martin was not left alone," villagers commented.

Yet, village gossip soon sounded a different note. Some individuals (not the most reliable, as they were the ones who drank heavily at the pub) insisted that his parents had no reason to be satisfied as they had seen Martin's wife entering (or was it leaving?) the houses of two certain single men. In fact, one of the men died soon after, and the other was now quite sickly.

Meanwhile, Martin's wife spent her work time inside the house, weaving at her loom. Her only companion during day was an unusually large black cat, always asleep in a dark corner.

Finally, the gossip reached Martin's ears. He did not believe a word of it, and he did not tell his wife about it. Instead, he laughed and made a joke. "One of these nights," he said to her with a teasing wink, "I am going to stay awake and follow that cat of yours. It seems to me that it wanders through the neighborhood having great adventures." His wife said nothing in reply.

From that day onward, Martin's health began to alter. He grew weaker and started to lose weight. The rosy coloring disappeared from his cheeks. At night he slept very deeply. He would arise, not rested, but instead totally exhausted.

News of Martin's illness spread through the village. As could be expected, it launched a new wave of gossip. Many became convinced that something unnatural was going on and that the red-haired wife was the cause of it.

People turned to the old midwife, Baba Rada, who was famous for her knowledge of remedies against evil spirits and spells. She made her living by selling potions and lotions, a lucrative business since many people trusted her with their diseases and ailments. She also had cures for the evil eye and remedies against all sorts of hexes that she had learned from her mother, also a skilled sorceress. Baba Rada was familiar with the stories that were circulating in the village.

"There seems to be a vampire in our midst," the midwife declared. "Although I rarely leave my house, I have seen the bad omens, more clearly than those who travel. I am positive that some of the latest deaths can be blamed on the living dead. Sudden loss of strength, paleness, a deep and unhealthy sleep—these are signs of a vampire's touch."

Somebody suggested Martin's wife, the recluse.

"I cannot yet tell," said Baba Rada. "I need to see Martin, talk with him, and cast a divination spell in order to discover the truth."

By the end of the month, Martin was very weak. However, he had to go to the Autumn Fest to sell his produce and buy food for the winter. He gathered his strength and went to the market.

Baba Rada knew he would be there and went in search of him. She had known him since his birth. She had been close to his mother and felt an obligation to help if she could. The old midwife located him without difficulty. One quick glace confirmed her suspicions. Martin had indeed been infected by a vampire. He was in mortal danger.

"My boy, something is very wrong with you. You seem to be dying."

"It is my fate," Martin answered with sad resolve. "I guess my time has come."

"No," the old midwife insisted. "I looked into your future. Your time is not supposed to come yet. My cards never lie."

Baba Rada gave Martin a special concoction. "Drink this. It will help you get some strength back. You will feel a little better."

Martin trusted Baba Rada and drank what was offered. The beverage did make him stronger. It was as if part of the heaviness on his chest was lifted. He felt more alive than he had been in a long time.

"You see; I've told you," she said. "You are jinxed. You brought the wrong woman into your home. You married a vampire. She is sucking your blood at night and draining you of all power." Yet, he was still far from convinced about his wife.

"What are you talking about, Baba Rada," he said. "You must have lost your touch at telling people's fortune. Nothing happens at night in my house. My wife does not drink my blood. She does not drink anything at night. She doesn't move. She stretches out silently at night, not even visibly breathing. The only creature alive at night in my house—very much alive—is her faithful black cat."

What he told Baba Rada was absolutely true. His wife would lie down on her back and fall asleep almost instantaneously. A few minutes after that, her breath would die away, and a red flame would come out of her mouth. The lazy cat immediately would awaken, and it would leave the house on the prowl.

"She sleeps perfectly still until morning. It is the cat who wakes her up when it returns from its nightly roaming, just before the cock's first crow."

"Aren't we lucky!" Baba Rada exclaimed. "Things are better than I had thought. Had I known this, we could have prevented other deaths. But let us act quickly and be certain, at least, to save your life, dear boy."

"What are you talking about?"

"You have given me convincing proof that your wife is a vampire. She does not really sleep—she merely takes leave of her human body, getting in and out of your house as the black cat. Once outside, at night, she can take any form that she wants. That's how vampires are. But she has to be back home and make the transition to her original body by the time of the cock's third crow in the morning."

Martin found this hard to believe. Yet Baba Rada was wise, and he was afraid of returning to feeling listless and helpless.

"You must follow my advice," Baba Rada insisted. "You have nothing to lose. If your wife is a vampire, then getting rid of her will save your life. If she is not, there will be no harm done."

Martin eventually agreed and went home, waiting for the evening to come. He drank more of the concoction obtained from Baba Rada and felt renewed strength. Yet, as instructed, he complained of weakness and went to bed early. Soon the wife followed him to bed. He pretended to be asleep, but he was aware of every move. The wife lay down and closed her eyes, completely still. Then he saw a red flame come out of her mouth. Right after that, the cat came to life and disappeared into the dark night.

Martin tried to awaken his wife. He shook her firmly and shouted her name. As Baba Rada had predicted, the wife did not respond. Her body was cold, as if dead. Martin carried the body into an adjacent room and hid it under some extra covers. He made sure to close all doors behind him.

He then waited for the cat to return. As the night wore on, he felt increasingly weaker and weaker, as the effect of the special concoction faded away. On the other hand, his determination grew firmer, for he was now finally convinced that his wife was not human. This gave him the power to stay alert.

The cat returned right before dawn. It entered the room quietly, just as it had departed. But it showed panic when it found the bed empty. The cock crowed for the first time. The cat howled in despair. The cock crowed again and the cat frantically began to search about. It was scratching hysterically at the door to the adjacent room when the cock's crow sounded for the third time. The initial rays of sun appeared. With a hiss and a tormented cry, the cat simply disappeared. Reddish smoke lingered briefly in the air and then blew away.

Martin opened the door and rushed into the adjacent room to look at his wife's body. He found nothing under the covers. The body was gone. Soon, Martin was back in perfect health.

Whenever people inquired about his wife, he answered, "She just left me. She felt lonely and returned forever to her people in Black Lake."

PART V

Vampires as Friends and Lovers

The Vampire's Friendship

The stories in this final part differ considerably from those that went before. They contain more wit and irony. The vampire is not longer as threatening and dangerous. These stories indicate the variety of historic Romanian folk tales about the living undead, revealing how the central theme was twisted into intricate forms by innovative village storytellers.

The first narrative in the section was inspired by an account in Pamfile (1916/2000, 112) that summarized a version collected and published by Rădulescu-Codin (1913, 261–2). In this story, the vampire gives a valuable gift to a peasant who had done him a kindness. The creature, generally believed to be the embodiment of evil, nevertheless lives by the rule "One good deed deserves another." My version also incorporates a number of other slogans common in the villages, including "a dog is the man's loyal friend," and "in the proper family, it is the cock who sings and not the hen." It also reflects the close relationship between humans and animals inherent to the peasant household.

Ionel Piperu was a man whom everyone liked. He had many friends because he was clever and funny. He offered a good word to all and never thought twice about helping his neighbors.

"What can I say," he would explain. "The sun is always shining on my side of the sky. Why not share it with others."

In the evening, once a week, during the warm season, the people of the village would gather in the central square for the dance—*the hora*. This was everybody's favorite event. For the young ones, the dance was an opportunity to meet and get to know one another. For the older men, it was a good time to talk about their work and crops. For the women, it was an occasion to gossip about housekeeping and sewing. For the young children, it was just another playground to chase one another merrily and, of course, noisily.

Ionel loved to dance. He was among the best dancers because he

127

Peisaj de toamnă/Car cu boi (Autumn Landscape/ Ox Cart), Nicolae Grigorescu (1838–1907). This painting by Grigorescu, the most famous Romanian painter of the 19th century, depicts a family traveling by ox-cart along a dusty road. Travel away from the confines of the village was infrequent and believed fraught with danger. The vampire could lurk in the forest and attack unsuspecting voyagers on their slow march homeward (courtesy Cluj-Napoca Museum).

was slim and agile. In fact, his dancing qualities gave him his nickname—Piperu (the pepper).

One evening, he had been dancing for almost an hour when he decided to take a break. Anxious to see a girl that he liked arrive for the evening, he sat on a bench by the dancing area.

While he was catching his breath and watching the hora, Ionel shouted funny verses to the dancers:

> *Green leaf, green leaf,*
> *One, two, three,*
> *I know all girls want to dance with me.*

The young girls in turn answered:

> *Green leaf one, green leaf two,*
> *We'd rather chop wood*
> *Than dance with you.*

It was amusing to follow the verbal duels, and everybody contributed to the fun. Despite the general laughter, Ionel noticed, there was one man, a stranger, standing near him, who was not smiling at all. There was something unusual about him, and so, Ionel quietly but carefully took a better look. The man had a vampire's tail, almost hidden but still showing from under his coat.

Very discretely, Ionel drew the man's attention to it. "Hey, I am sure you don't want to show that to others. I don't think you want to start a commotion here." And teasingly, he sang out a verse:

> *Vampire, vampire,*
> *Stay away from fire.*

Ionel did not sense that the vampire was a danger to others at the dance. Or maybe, who knows, he did not think about such things at all; maybe it was simply his good nature prompting him to help another creature. He was of the belief that we are all God's creatures, and that everyone had their crosses to bear.

The vampire was surprised. The man did him a favor! No such thing had ever happened to him before. "Thank you. I seek no trouble," the vampire said. "One good deed deserves another. I do not want to be a debtor."

Ciobănaş (Shepherd), Nicolae Grigorescu (1838–1907), Private Collection. This painting, also by Grigorescu, shows a typical friendship—the young shepherd and his dog—as they lead the sheep towards pasture. Animals are essential to the Romanian peasant village, and, thus, they figure often in local vampire stories, either as victims or as embodiments of the bloody villain (courtesy Mrs. Dana Ciorapciu, photograph by Lucian Groza).

On this particular night, the vampire indeed was more interested in watching the fun than disturbing the happiness. He was fascinated by the gaiety shared by the village people, and he was studying them with awe and envy.

"I will make you a great gift," the vampire promised. "I will give you something no other human being has." But, he told Ionel, the gift would have to be given away from the crowded village. "You have to come to the old Silver Forest. I will meet you on the top of the hill in the clearing that the locals call 'The Two Worlds Crossing.' Do not come alone. Make sure to bring your best friend with you. Come anytime you choose."

"Sure, I will," Ionel laughed and turned his attention back to the dance. He did not take the vampire seriously. Soon, he forgot entirely about him.

A number of months later, Ionel was married, to that same girl he was awaiting at the dance. He had his own house now. He had a nice wife, and he had a nice farm with good land to toil and animals to manage.

One evening, he was on the porch cleaning the dog's house when the same vampire appeared. "You have not come for your gift," he said. "There is no reason to be afraid. Remember to come with your best friend." Then he disappeared.

"OK, I will," Ionel thought to himself. "Why not! One should never disregard presents. This vampire seems to believe that he owes me something. If he wants to give me a gift, I should not hurt his feelings."

Ionel was happy as a newlywed and wanted to be with his wife all of the time. There was no doubt, he decided, that the wife qualified as his best friend. She was, therefore, the one who should accompany him on the trip to the clearing known as "The Big Crossing."

The young woman prepared a big basket with food for the journey. Ionel spread some extra blankets onto the carriage seat to make it more comfortable. They, then, left on their first long trip together.

As they were leaving the yard, they noticed that the dog had curled up and was sleeping in the carriage, among the extra blankets by the picnic basket. They stopped and ordered it to the ground. "Out! Get down from the carriage! Go watch the house for us! We can watch the food baskets ourselves," Ionel said laughing.

The Silver Forest was a full day's journey away, but traveling together made the trip enjoyable. When they arrived at the designated clearing on top of the hill, the vampire was waiting for them. He seemed to be angry.

"What were you thinking? Didn't I tell you to come here accompanied by your best friend?" There was no time for an answer, for the vampire quickly blew fog over Ionel, and he suddenly felt tired and fell into a deep sleep. You see, vampires are known to make people fall asleep, just like that.

But Ionel's wife saw something completely different. For her, the vampire was a handsome young man, and she fell for him immediately. The bewitched young woman looked over at her sleeping husband with disgust and decided to be rid of him. She grabbed a hatchet and intended to kill him. As she was raising her hand to strike, the vampire made Ionel wake up. He made the wife stop her actions, fall asleep, and forget everything.

Ionel understood. The vampire didn't want to harm him, but teach him a lesson. "You silly young man. Your wife is your wife, not your friend! Go home, and, next time, come accompanied by your best friend!" The vampire, then, disappeared from sight.

One week later, Ionel set out to reclaim his gift, selecting his brother as traveling companion. They chose not to take the carriage but to ride their horses for the exercise. As they were leaving, the dog began to follow. Ionel, again, sent it back. "We do not need you to defend us," he shouted. "We are two grown men on horseback. We certainly can take care of ourselves. Go back and watch over my wife and the house for me!"

They rode all day and arrived at the established meeting place toward the evening. As they were unsaddling their horses, the vampire appeared, still annoyed. "What were you thinking? Did I not tell you to come accompanied by your best friend?" Just like the first time, the vampire blew fog over Ionel, who suddenly felt tired and fell into a deep sleep.

But the brother saw something completely different. For him, the vampire was a beautiful young woman, and immediately he was in love. He looked over at the sleeping Ionel and saw a potential rival who had to be killed. He grabbed the hatchet, yet, just as before, the vampire shook Ionel awake and made his brother stop, fall asleep, and forget.

Again, there was a lesson. "You silly young man. Your brother is your brother, not your friend. Go home and next time come accompanied by your best friend!"

Ionel felt obliged to claim his gift, but he had no idea whom to take along on the third trip to the designated crossing. Reluctantly, he decided to go alone, even though the vampire would remain angry. As he rode from his home, Ionel noticed his faithful dog following from a distance. "Oh, well," he said. "I guess you can follow me if you want. You might get tired, but it will be nice companionship."

By and by, Ionel arrived at the meeting place. The vampire was waiting for him, smiling warmly at the dog. "Oh, I see. This time you finally brought along a true and faithful friend," he said.

"I will give you the gift that I promised, but it comes with a warning. You can never tell any human being of the power I am going to bestow on you, or you will die. If you ever tell about my gift, I will come and drink your blood myself, to strip you of the power and retrieve it back."

The vampire for the third time blew fog at Ionel. As he was falling asleep, his eyes as heavy as lead, he heard the vampire say:

> *From this day on, whatever you do,*
> *You will speak the language of the animals, too.*
> *You'll be healthy and wealthy, all your life through*
> *As long as your tongue doesn't get the better of you.*

Then, as if in a dream, he heard his dog tell him, "Sleep with no worry, Master. I will be watching over you!"

From that day on, whatever Ionel touched was a success. It was certainly not difficult to manage the farm. All Ionel had to do was walk among his animals, and he would learn of their needs. His cattle were contented and multiplying, knowing that he was considerate of their pains. The birds and bees would tell him when the crops needed water, when it was time to pull the weeds, and when the plum trees were ripe for harvest.

When his friends in the village asked for the cause of his good fortune, Ionel would answer with a twinkle in his eye that he had a great secret, given to him by a vampire. It became a matter of teasing when the men were out drinking after a long day of work. "Ionel," they would say, "come share your great secret with us." And Ionel would reply, "Tell the secret, and I would die." The friends would laugh as if it was a joke, and they all would enter the pub together in excellent spirits.

Ionel's wife, however, was more inquisitive. With womanly curiosity, she just would not let the topic drop. She kept insisting that Ionel reveal his secret. She never grew tired of the refrain. She would nag him, almost every evening, "If you love me, you must tell me your secret. I am your wife. You have shared your food and bed with me. You have to share your secret with me, too. I want to know what the vampire gave you."

Over the years, Ionel grew tired of her insistence. He worried about the matter for months, and it was affecting his health. He had been growing weaker and weaker. Finally, he decided to tell the wife everything. He would do it on the coming New Year's Eve. Of course he knew the price he would have to pay, but he was a good husband who did not like to refuse anything to his wife.

"Oh well," Ionel thought to himself, "everyone has to die some day. Besides, the gift that the vampire gave me, the gift of languages, is not a normal power for a human being to have. I have enjoyed it, but I should not think of it as a legitimate possession."

One morning he was walking across the yard when he heard his dog talk to the horses. "I am so worried. My master is troubled by some terrible thoughts. He looks sick. I'm afraid he is going to die soon."

"That would be sad," said his favorite horse. "He is a good master. I do not want him to die."

"Oh, he's a fool," said the cock that was perched on the fence. "He is nothing but a fool because he is letting a woman rule over him. Look at me. I have 30 wives, but I easily keep them all under control. He cannot control just one!"

Ionel quickly turned around and went into the house with determination. "Woman," he said, "I love you very much and happily share my life and my bed with you. But there are some matters that must remain private. Some things I know that you do not need to know. Please stop pestering me about the secret. I am asking this once and for all times. Trust me. It is far better this way."

The wife heard Ionel clearly, and she respected him. She never again asked about the secret. Ionel lived to be a hundred and many years beyond. He may still be alive, for all I know.

The Drunkard

There is a popular Romanian saying, that God protects the happy drunkard. This is true, it seems, even when the drunkard encounters a group of mischievous vampires out for some evil fun. In the end, however, it is the drunkard who saves his fellow villagers.

My version develops from a very brief story found in Pamfile's Mitologie Românească *(1916/2000, 123). It emphasizes the belief, com-*

mon in Romanian folklore, that vampires, devils, and evil spirits cannot successfully enter any house where the inhabitants said their evening prayers. There are many of variations about how much prayer is enough to constitute defense and guarantee security. The combination of foolish humor and serious danger makes this story both unusual and profound.

Once upon a time, there lived a man whose name was Cosmin, but everybody called him Thirsty (*Setosu*). He continually complained, whenever you met him, that a terrible drought was tormenting him, and that he needed a drink to allay it. In fact, he did drink all the time, and his favorite beverage was wine. Thirsty was inebriated many hours of the day, almost every day, but people did not mind. He never bothered anybody. He was never belligerent. He never got into fights. When he was drunk, everything became a joke. He made people laugh.

"Thirsty has a faithful guardian angel," the villagers would say. "Somehow, he always manages to find his way home."

One night, Thirsty was returning home late. As usual, he was more than a little drunk. He was talking to himself, not to feel lonely. "Hey, path," he said, "don't move! Why are you always straight during the day but winding at night? What's wrong with you?"

He walked a little, then stopped and tried to light his pipe. But he did not succeed for he got the hiccups. Thirsty gave up and walked a little further with uncertain steps. He tried again to light his pipe, and he failed again. "Hey old lady," he addressed his pipe. "Stay still, will you! Have you, too, turned against me?" he whined, hiccupped, and giggled.

Paying more attention to his pipe than to the route he was taking, Thirsty ended up near the old cemetery at the back of the churchyard. For stability, he learned against the wooden fence, and he saw in the cemetery a small fire and some darkened silhouettes gathered around it. He was too drunk to realize it, but these were not regular humans. They were vampires, gathering to organize the night's activities.

"Hi there, good guys!" Thirsty shouted merrily. "That's just what I need. Hold that fire still a little! Let me come and light my pipe," and he stumbled over the fence. "The world does shake, doesn't it," he mumbled to himself.

The vampires were so surprised at the apparition that they did not know how to react. Thirsty drew close to their fire and tried to light his pipe. As he leaned forward, he hiccupped loudly and had to stop. He began to lean forward again, with the same result. The vampires started to laugh.

"I have the hiccups because I'm thirsty," he explained innocently, fighting all the while with his pipe.

The vampires were now confident that he was not a danger to them. So they decided to amuse themselves for a while. "You say you're thirsty. And what would you fancy to drink?"

"Oh, man! Anything!" he replied.

"Anything?" one of them teased him. "I am more particular. I drink only blood."

"You are spoiled," Thirsty answered with a smile. "I'm not particular. I drink anything,"

"Let's suck his blood and be done with this idiot human," one of the vampires suggested, impatiently. But the others were having too much fun. The youngest among them commented that drunk people are not full human beings. They do not see well, hear well, or know what they are doing. "Let us treat our thirsty guest to a warming beverage. He deserves it, since nobody has entertained us so well."

It was time for the vampires to feed. To play a joke on him, they gave Thirsty a mug and told him to accompany them into the village. They were certain that, in his drunken haze, he would not object and would not remember.

They arrived at the first house but were met at the door by a little dog. It began barking and did not let them in, so they went away to try their luck elsewhere.

They went to a second house. This time, they stopped at the outside gate. The house and its yard were guarded by a much bigger and more aggressive hound. They ran off fast.

At the third house, they were able to open the front door, but inside they found only half a man. Disappointed, they went away without touching him.

Eventually, during their search, the vampires found houses that they were able to enter easily. In them, they fed on the inhabitants' blood until they felt satiated. From the last houses raided, they filled their mugs with extra blood, saving it for later.

"Thirsty, now it is your turn," commanded a female vampire whom he had followed inside one of the houses. "Come here with your mug and fill it up with drink. It is almost time to leave."

When the vampires had completed their bloody task and had satisfied themselves for the evening, they all returned to the cemetery.

At first, Thirsty didn't understand what had happened because his head was full of the wine. During the long walk back, however, he began to sober up. Now, he felt very confused. "Hey friends, what had just happened? Will somebody explain to me please! Where have we been?"

"We went into the village for food, you idiot!" they laughed at him.

"We went to drink some blood, silly man" one vampire clarified, "and you came with us."

"That's what we, vampires, do," added another. "We feed on blood from humans like you!"

"You boasted that you would drink anything," reminded the woman vampire. "Just look at your mug! What do you think that is? Drink up the blood."

But Thirsty was still in a fog of confusion about the events of the evening. "What happened at those houses? Why couldn't we get inside some of the places?" he asked.

The vampires gave him an elementary lesson. "At the first house we visited, we were met by a small dog, the night guardian of the house. The dog was there because the master had said his nightly prayer – 'The Holy Father'—before going to bed. It defended him. Vampires cannot get into houses where this prayer had been said."

"The second house we visited was guarded by the large and angry hound because the master had said not only 'The Holy Father' but the entire 'Creed' before going to bed. The guardian dog was prepared for us. We vampires cannot even get into the yard of such houses."

"Didn't we see half-a-man in one of the houses?" the drunkard asked.

"Yes, that is how he appeared. These aren't really half-men. They merely look to us that way because they said only half-a-prayer before going to bed. We can get into their houses, but in general we do not touch them."

"There are always plenty of houses where the people have not said their prayers before going to bed. We enter those houses with ease. These are places we like to visit and revisit—as long as the person lasts, of course. They die pretty quickly on us."

Thirsty finally realized what was going on. "Those people are going to die!"

"That's what happens to people who lose their blood," the vampires answered with sarcasm and indifference. "But who cares!"

"Is there nothing that can save the people we visited tonight," Thirsty asked, "to reestablish their strength or bring those who died back to life?"

"You really do know nothing about our world," was the bored reply. "They can be restored by returning to them some of the blood that was taken."

"I certainly will not give them back my share of the treat," the woman vampire said with cruelty, and she drank what was left in her mug.

At that moment, the cock crowed the first signal of the new day. By the time it shouted for the third time, all the vampires had disappeared.

For a moment, Thirsty thought he had awoken from a bad dream. "What a terrible nightmare I had," and he reached for a drink. Then he froze, realizing that he was holding in his hand a mug full of blood.

Quickly, Thirsty ran back to the houses the vampires had raided and put a few drops of blood into the people's mouths. Soon they woke up, a little tired and weak. Nevertheless, they all arose to another day.

It is hard to say whether or not the villagers actually believed Thirsty's incredible story. Since that night, though, they have been especially careful to say their prayers correctly before they went to bed.

The Journey Together

There is no reason why a vampire, living comfortably in the village, cannot make a loving and caring husband. The wife must be careful, but it is not necessarily grounds for divorce.

A common theme in the Transylvanian folk tales is that a husband (or sometimes a wife) suddenly can turn into a vampire and attack his spouse. In most of the cases, the woman is able to defend herself while she slowly learns the identity of her attacker. Senn (1982) collected more than twenty-five accounts of such stories from his interviews with local peasants. In some versions, the spouse becomes frightened and dissolves the marriage, but in others, the spouse accepts and accommodates the situation.

My version, inspired by the many strong women cherished in the Romanian folklore, focuses on the wife as heroine. Her acceptance thus emerges as a conscious decision and not an act of resignation.

The newlyweds were very happy. They were young, healthy, and had just moved into a new home. Some days later, the husband had to travel to the market fair, a journey of two days, to buy things for the farm. The wife, not willing to be separated, volunteered to accompany him.

They traveled all day but were still more than an hour from their destination. The wife mentioned that she was hungry, expressing a desire to eat something warm. The young man, the good husband that he was, offered to build a small fire to heat up their meal.

The couple stopped their carriage in a small clearing on top of a hill, and the man went into the forest to collect the necessary kindling wood. No sooner had the man walked into the forest, than an unusual chill came over the wife.

"My dear, come back! The sun is about to set," she shouted after him. "I am afraid to be left alone here, even for a short time. Let's keep going. We will eat at the inn. I certainly won't starve." The faithful husband quickly returned to her, and they continued on their journey.

When time approached for another trip to the market town, the husband suggested that his wife stay at home. "Why not just take care of the household and relax. Traveling can be dangerous. There are many bad people in this world."

"Oh my dear," she answered merrily. "I have never feared other people. My father taught me to treat strangers well, and that they will treat me well in return."

"There are wild beasts in the forest along the way," the man persisted. "I would rather you were safe at home."

"I am more afraid to be home alone," the woman replied. "Lately, a vampire has been killing in our region. They say that many animals and even some people have died, their blood all sucked out."

"The roads are full of perils, especially at night," the man said.

"I'm a married woman now, my dear husband," she answered cheerfully. "I have you to protect me."

"But what if I am not there?" he insisted, but without much success.

As she was so determined to accompany him, the man decided to give his wife a weapon to defend herself. The husband gave her a light but sharp silver hatchet with a short handle. "You have to hit until you draw blood," he instructed. "You should not stop hitting your attacker until you draw blood."

The day for the journey arrived, clear and warm. The couple piled their things into the carriage, and the wife placed her hatchet under her seat within easy reach. Evening caught up with them as they were entering a forest. It was as if, in an instant, they had moved into a different realm, engulfed by shadows. A chilling silence descended. The shade of the trees no longer defended them pleasantly from the scorching sun, but sucked them in an unknown mystery. The wind stopped blowing as if overcome by a greater power.

The husband stopped the carriage at a crossroads. "I need to check that we should be taking the right fork. I will be back soon. Do not be afraid, and do not hesitate to defend yourself, if need be, with your silver hatchet. Hit until you draw blood," he said.

No sooner had the husband disappeared than a snarling black dog raced from the forest and attacked the young wife. She was frightened but grabbed the hatchet and did as she had been advised. She hit the beast, and it ran away, wounded.

Immediately after, the husband returned. He looked disheveled. The wife, still shaking, told him what had happened. "Oh, my husband, you will never believe what has just occurred. A ferocious black dog jumped at me, out of nowhere, and tried to bite me. How lucky I had the hatchet at hand to defend myself. I aimed at its head. I think there are a few drops of its blood on the blade."

"You are so courageous, my woman," the husband complimented. "I am sorry I that was not here to defend you."

She noticed a small wound behind his ear. "But what happened to you? You have a cut behind your ear. It's bleeding."

"It is nothing, a superficial scratch," he said dismissively. "Don't think twice about it. I was caught in a dry branch. Let us continue our journey, as it is getting late."

That night, they stopped at an inn just on the outskirts of the market town. They both were tired and went to bed almost immediately. In the morning, people were talking about a vampire attack. Someone at the inn had been killed sometime after midnight.

"You see, my dear," said the husband. "You should stay home in the future, for bad things can happen on the road." But the remainder of the trip was uneventful, and they returned home safe and sound.

A harvesting season passed quietly, and eventually there was cause to visit the market town again. As before, the young wife insisted on accompanying her husband. "I will be afraid to stay home alone. I know that nothing bad has affected our home, but the vampire is still haunting the village. Besides, I want to go to the market fair for I need new ribbons and some dyes for the wool I am spinning."

Again, they journeyed together, and evening, again, caught them on the road. They had but a short distance left to go. In fact, they could discern the lights of the town at the bottom of the valley ahead. As they crossed a small clearing, they saw a stone well and decided to stop for a drink and a quick rest. "It is just what I need," the woman said merrily as she hurried to the well and began to lower the water bucket.

Suddenly, the wind stopped. A chilly silence descended upon her. The wheel of the well screeched strangely. A nearby black bird screamed in panic. The bucket hit the water surface. The wife stopped the wheel and grabbed the chain to steady it. The cold metal sent a shiver down her spine, and a deep fear overcame her.

She turned around in search of her husband, but she could see nobody. She was alone. With clear purpose in mind, using quick and firm steps, she approached the carriage and grabbed her hatchet. At that instant, a wild boar jumped to attack her. She aimed the hatchet at its front legs and with a steady hand hit it firmly, drawing blood. The beast yelped and ran away, wounded.

No sooner had the boar disappeared into the forest than the husband returned.

"My husband, please do not leave me alone in such places. Again, I was attacked when I was all by myself. How wise you were to give me the hatchet. Otherwise, I might have been killed."

As they rode away, the young woman noticed that her man was hurt. "What happened to your hand?" she asked. "It's nothing, just a scratch," he answered. "It caught on a thorny bush as I took a shortcut back to the clearing."

They arrived at an inn and slept there. The next morning, they awoke to hear more rumors of vampires. Apparently, there had been violence during night. Some unlucky person from the inn was dead.

"You see, my dear," the man commented. "This world is a dangerous place. You would have been safer at home. Let us purchase all the ribbons and wool dyes that you want. But, please, make sure you have enough to last you all winter."

"I am so lucky to have you," she answered merrily. "Nothing can happen to me while you watch over me." He was such a good husband, she thought. She was proud to have married him. He was handsome and generous, and he filled her heart with joy. He was hardworking, too. They did not want for anything, and all the bad things happening in the village stayed away from their house.

Spring came, and the man needed to leave for a short journey. It was merely to another village, across the valley on the other side of the river, in order to complete a friendly exchange of goods.

However much he insisted, the wife had no desire to stay behind.

"I do want to go with you. My heart is always happy when you are near. I am never bored with you. Days without you have less sun for me," she told him, and he could not refuse her.

This trip went well. They did not have to travel far, and they were not on the road as evening fell. "Bad thing happen," the wife thought to herself, contentedly. "That's just how the world is. It is our good fortune that they always happen to other people, in other places."

On their way back, however, only a few miles from home, a wheel from their carriage shook loose. As it had to be repaired, they stopped by the river. Hours flew away. The sun was now slowly setting, and the shadows were growing longer.

"I am done. It is all fixed," the man finally announced, proudly. "I need only to wash my hands in the river."

The moment he went away, the wife felt chilled. She felt again as if she had entered different universe, hostile and terrifyingly dangerous. She understood the need to arm herself. She took a firm hold of the silver hatchet.

There was little surprise this time. A dark bear appeared and came menacingly toward her. She waited for it with calm and hit it with the hatchet in the hind leg. One strike only, but it drew blood. The beast immediately ran away.

Soon the husband reappeared from the river. He looked tired and walked with a limp. "I slipped on a wet rock and fell. It's just a scratch, nothing serious," he said.

The wife did not reply. She gave him a piece of cloth for his wound. In silence, she watched him struggle to get into the carriage, his handsome face serious.

"Let's go home," he said.

"Yes, we should do that," she answered softly.

Night was falling quietly. The round moon brightly lit the road, and they arrived home in a very short while. As the man opened the gate to their yard, the young woman remarked with deep affection, "My love, I have changed my mind. I would prefer to stay at home from now on. You will have to go alone on all future journeys."

For Now and Forever

Love is a very strong bond, holding people together across distances and differences. Even the expression "Till death do us part" does not necessarily apply when one of the partners is a vampire. This story gives new meaning to the romantic lovers' vows, that they will remain eternally faithful, and that their love will last forever.

I first heard this story on a school trip to Ciucea, in Bihor county. We were visiting the Octavian Goga house and mausoleum, where the great Romanian poet lived and was buried. After the visit, the guide told us this story. My version expands on the original, consistent with how folktales in the oral tradition get transmitted, yet the spirit of the tale remains the same.

Mihai and Elena lived in a small mountain village near Ciucea. The young couple were very much in love. Mihai had been courting Elena ever since they were teenagers. They always danced together at the *hora* (round dance) on Sunday evenings. Everyone in the village attended. The young ones were there to dance, the others to listen to the music and to gossip about this and that.

The two lovers, as so often occurs, were thinking about marriage, but Mihai had not yet formally proposed. He had just turned eighteen, the age for getting drafted. In his country, it was an inescapable law. He had to go into the army, like all the other young men from the village.

Soon his draft order came, and Mihai started preparing for his departure. He was excited about becoming a soldier. In those times, many believed that the army provided valuable experience, a necessary stage in the process of becoming a real man. Nevertheless, part of Mihai was sad because he knew he had to leave Elena behind. He expected to be away for three years, and he was aware that many things could happen during this period.

Elena was a good-looking girl. She was merry and hardworking. Besides, she was the only daughter of a prosperous family. Mihai did not care at all about her dowry, but he knew that others might be after such things. Of course, he worried. God knows what other men might attempt in the effort to win hear heart and hand.

It was true that the girl had given him indications of real affection. She had not only promised to wait for him, but had made this promise known to everybody, announcing that she considered herself "given away." The two young people even asked to become formally engaged, but her parents would not agree.

"Do not tie yourself with too many ropes," her father said. "One never knows how time turns things around. He will be away for three years. Maybe he will forget about you. Maybe he will find somebody else. Maybe he will never return. We certainly like the young man, but we also want to insure what's best for you."

Of course, Elena did not want to hear such things. She would have been happy to marry Mihai before his departure.

"Don't jinx your luck," her mother warned. "Be reasonable. If he is meant to be yours by destiny, he will return to you in due course. Trust your fate."

On the day before the scheduled departure, the two lovers took a long walk together and renewed their reciprocal commitment.

"Promise to wait for me," the young man pleaded, "and, in turn, I promise that I will return to marry you and be with you, as the saying goes, 'til death do us part.'"

"What a lame promise," Elena teased him. "If you want me to wait for three long years, promise me that not even death will separate us. Promise that. No matter what, you will come back and marry me."

He answered firmly, "By everything I hold dear, I promise to come back to you. I swear that not even death will have the power to separate us."

And so, three years passed. Nothing unusual happened. Village life went on and on, in its customary fashion.

Elena waited patiently for her man to return. At first, she received a few letters from him, very simple ones, the type that are sent from the army—usually written by a sergeant more familiar with writing than the regular soldiers. During the third year, however, the letters stopped. The men had been sent away to fight a war. The Emperor in Vienna preferred to send his Transylvanian troops to defend his Western borders. As a result, the soldiers were required to travel quite far from their native lands. Sometimes things ended well, as they got to see the world. Sometimes, they never returned.

The girl did not lose hope when the letters stopped. She kept waiting for Mihai, meticulously marking in her log every day that passed.

Mihai, in fact, returned to the village exactly as scheduled, precisely three years from the date he had left. There was no mention of the long silence.

Soon after his return, to no one's surprise, the couple was married. And so their life together began—but the life of the village started to change. A strange disease afflicted the region. Some people got weaker overnight and died within a few days, without any clear signs of a previous illness. Many were strangers, people who happened to be traveling through, but others were individuals well known to them all.

It is a natural temptation to dismiss the possibility of evil among us. The local innkeeper ventured, "Maybe dangerous robbers have been visiting our area lately. Maybe they are to blame for some of these deaths." The schoolteacher offered a different possible cause. "Maybe the unfortunate travelers were exposed to an epidemic during their journeys. Who knows where they had been, or what they may have done."

People die all the time, of course, even young and apparently healthy ones. But strange stories soon circulated, frightening the villagers. Some claimed that the dead returned to haunt the area. Those who died during the night, without having been sick a single day, it was said, returned to haunt their families.

Elena and Mihai ignored the rumors circulating within the village, even after a tragedy struck next door. Their neighbor's brother died suddenly and, allegedly, he returned to prowl around the house several nights in a row. Several family members said that they saw and recognized him, and that he left only after they grabbed their crosses and repeated the prayers over the dead.

The neighbors went around advising everyone on the street to hang garlic wreaths above all doors and windows and to paint the sign of the cross on each house using the soot from a church candle. Also, they insisted, people should place a votive light in every room after the sun set.

Elena asked Mihai what he thought of the situation, to which he responded laughingly, "My dear, you know I am not afraid of death. Let other people do what they have to do."

Elena ignored the village stories. No one in her family had died yet. Her parents were well, and she had no siblings. Moreover, she had her own important worries—but these were of a different nature.

The young woman was becoming increasingly jealous. She had the feeling that curious things were happening inside her very household. Mihai sometimes would disappear for more than a day, and he did little to explain these absences upon his return. He merely said, with a disturbing lack of detail, that he had things to buy or matters to manage in some other village. Elena worried about what might happen to him on the road. God only knew what beast or evil creature, human or not, might attack him on these journeys. Even more troubling, she was tormented by doubts about what he was doing.

This was not the worst of it. Elena also had the impression that her husband, even when he was at home, did not sleep in his bed all night. She tried to stay awake and observe, but she did not seem to be able to resist deep sleep. Once in bed, she did not stir at all until morning. She began to suspect that there was even something mysterious about her sleep.

Determined to learn the truth, the young woman decided to ask for help. She went to the old gypsy (many said that she was a witch) who lived at the margin of their village. The woman listened to Elena's worries without comment. She examined Elena's palm but still did not say anything. She cast some white beans and read Elena's present and future in them.

The old gypsy looked at the young bride with sadness. Softly, she finally spoke. "You live with somebody whom you love and who loves you, but this man has a very great secret. You both swore an oath, but one of you has not kept the promise. I see a dark wall separating the two of you. Because of this darkness, you cannot see his real face. Only when you see your husband as he truly is, will you know what you are dealing with."

Elena did not understand the meaning of these words. She cried and begged the gypsy to help her. "If you truly want to see your husband's real face," the gypsy instructed reluctantly, "go home, and make yourself a special potion. Fetch fresh water from the well, water that has never seen the light. Do it in the evening after the sunset. Pour a little of the water into a small tumbler, and add some dry wild blackberry flowers or leaves. Then light a match and drop it into the water. It will go out with a sizzle. You must repeat this seven times. Each time you light the match, make sure to say: 'Keep me awake; make me see! Keep me awake; make me hear! Keep me awake; make me understand! So be it!' Make sure you have recited these words seven times.

"It is absolutely essential that nobody else is around when you brew this potion. No one may see you doing it. If it looks like somebody might interrupt you, stop, hide everything from sight, and continue later when you are alone."

"Wait for night, some particular night when you feel especially troubled, and drink all the water. Go to bed and pretend to fall asleep right away, but wait to see what happens."

Elena paid one golden coin to the old gypsy woman and left. She was now far more frightened than when she came. So she delayed taking any action for a few days, until her fears and jealousies became almost unbearable. Elena then did just as she was told. She made the potion after sunset, reciting the assigned phrases seven times, and then drank it. She hurried to complete the task in private, while Mihai was finishing some work around the house. When he returned, she announced that she was sleepy and went to bed.

Mihai blew the candles out and quietly lay down next to her, until he thought she was fast asleep. He then got up and left the house without making any sound.

Elena right away jumped out of bed. She dressed quickly and went to follow his moves. With surprise, she noticed that she was not sleepy one bit. Once outside, she was a little scared by the darkness. She remembered how worried people in the village were about vampires that haunted the village. She knew that death sometimes waited for one in the dark. She was determined, however, not to let anything stop her.

Elena had one thought in mind. Mihai had promised that nothing, not even death would separate them. She had to find out what or who was creating a barrier between them.

She followed her husband carefully. To her surprise, he did not head towards the village. He was not going to tavern, or to house of any neighbor. Instead, he took the path that led in the opposite direction. It was easy to follow him this way, for there were few lights and many shadows from overhanging trees. Mihai soon arrived at a place where three major roadways crossed, near the old well. The major intersection, with the availability of good water, meant that often some late traveler might be stopping there.

Mihai stood quietly in the shadow of the well. Elena stopped too, and waited. The moon cast a strange, cold, grayish light that made the shadows seem impenetrable. The wind had died entirely, as if sucked in by the darkness. The silence was so deep that Elena felt like holding her breath.

For a long while, nothing happened. Then, a moving speck appeared in the distance, along one of the roads. It kept drifting toward them and soon became a small carriage that eventually stopped by the well.

The coachman lazily climbed down from his seat. Mihai raced out, grabbed him from behind, and bit him on the neck. After drinking, he dropped the lifeless man to the ground near the carriage, turned around, and began walking back toward the village. Everything lasted one short minute.

Elena had seen enough. She understood everything. Mihai was a vampire. He was a member of the walking dead, a *strigoi*. Strange as it may seem, she was happy. In fact, she felt relieved. He was not cheating on her. He loved her, and he came back to her in spite of his death, just as he had sworn to do. He had kept his promise!

The girl now knew what she had to do. She took the shortcut home. She felt light as if she were flying. The darkness did not scare her anymore. She was no longer afraid of death.

Elena arrived home quickly. She went to the kitchen for a cup and a knife. She cut sharply into one of her wrists and let the wound bleed into the cup. Almost immediately, Mihai arrived at home.

"You should have told me. You should have known that you could trust me," she reproached her husband mildly. Then she handed him the cup with her blood. "This is for you," she said. "This way I too can keep my promise. Nothing ever will be able to separate us."

Then, Elena lay down to sleep.

Over the years, many people claimed to have seen an odd couple waiting by the old well, at the three-roads intersection near the village of Ciucea. And, sometimes, unlucky travelers never reached their destination.

The Vampire and the Thief

The last story in this collection of Romanian folk vampire tales leaves us on an optimistic note. Two kindred souls meet in the night, and it appears that they are following the same road. One of them, however, is not beyond redemption. It is a cautionary tale that is more deep and profound than apparent at first glance. The story teaches that the road to perdition may well start with an innocent-looking prank. Yet, there are important transition points along that road. Surprising turns provide opportunity to rediscover one's moral conscience.

My version is inspired by a highly compressed account published in Pamfile's Mitologie Românească (1916/2000, 115). The story is based on the alleged parallel between the thief, albeit a small time offender, and the vampire as the embodiment of extreme evil, and it ends with a miraculous sneeze. Interestingly, the sneeze has an occasional role in Romanian folklore, first commented upon by Niculiță-Voronca, in Ion Creangă (1914, No. 2: 51).

This story, like so many in the collection, combines entertaining narrative with moral instruction. It reinforces traditional norms of good behavior, warns of the dangers from violation, and demonstrates the patterns of human relations fundamental to stable village existence.

It was a windy winter night, at the hour when wolves begin prowling in the hills above the village. But bad weather has never deterred a wrong doer. In fact, the thief found it a perfect night to go about his wicked deeds. This time, he had set his eyes on a strong young stallion owned by the local priest.

He took a back alley to get to the man's house, a narrow shadowy lane that passed by the old cemetery. He was in a good mood and kept singing a little tune to himself,

> "I don't care, rain or shine,
> I just take what I want to be mine."

As he made the last turn towards the priest's house, the thief was startled by a dark figure hiding behind the fence. It was vampire—a very short, thin vampire with a gaunt face, small mean eyes, and sharp teeth.

"Oh, you startled me. Get out of my way! Ugly man, what are you, anyway?"

The creature gave him a crooked smile, and greeted him warmly. "Good evening, my friend."

"My friend? What friend? Get lost! Beat it, you ugly monster! I've never seen a more hideous creature in my life. Get out of my way, or I'll kick your ass," the thief threatened.

"Ha, ha!" the vampire laughed, not worried by the thief's cocky attitude. "Not so fast, my dear. This is not how you should treat a brother who has done you no harm!"

"Brother? What are you talking about?" asked the thief in confusion.

"We are brothers of a somewhat similar trade," the vampire replied, "for we both steal from people. You might say that we are blood brothers, whether you like it or not. I am a vampire who steals people's lives. You are a thief who steals their livelihoods. Don't play some righteous tune with me."

The thief had to admit that he had been outwitted. "Well," he said with hesitation, "I don't really take anybody's livelihood. I just partake of what they have in abundance."

"Oh yes, I have heard that before," the vampire mocked. "That is what all thieves say."

"I am telling you the truth," the thief defended himself. "I mostly steal money from careless people, clothes and things that people leave unattended. I sometimes take sacks of grain that I can sell for money. I certainly do not kill people. I just remove things from them—you know—the usual stuff."

"That's how everything begins, with small things," the vampire asserted. "But it does not stop there. Tell me—what are you planning to steal tonight?"

The thief confessed, "I am on my way to steal a stallion that I've been coveting."

"You see," the vampire said with satisfaction. "You have already started walking down my path. That is how I started. Just you wait. You will move on to bigger things soon," he predicted.

"What are you talking about?" the thief said hesitatingly.

"I will tell you my story," the vampire offered. "I was born in a village not far from yours. Even as a child, I would get into trouble. At first, it was only small stuff. I stole fruit from the neighbor's fruit trees or took fresh eggs from the henhouse merely to break them. Later, I started stealing sacks of produce from people's barns, selling them to corrupt merchants at certain markets in the area."

"I have done the same," the thief conceded. "I have had dealings with such people, myself."

"Then you must know what follows. Bored in my village, I stole a horse and ran away. I started wandering through the whole county of Salaj, cheating and grabbing people's property at fairs, robbing travelers in forests and on the main roads."

"I always had money in my pocket, and I would spend it foolishly. I drank in all the taverns around the region and started countless fights. Some of the fights got serious. One thing lead to another, and, at some point, I was a wanted man, sought for murder. Since I escaped without being caught, I considered myself invincible. After that, I thought nothing of killing, either in a drunken argument or over some property I desired."

"But my story continues. I was still young, barely twenty-eight, when I was killed in a fight. It was in a small tavern. I started the fight, with a soldier over some plum brandy. We were both drunk, but he was less so, and thus much faster to pull out his pocketknife. Nobody knew my name, so they buried me in an unmarked grave. And now, because of my sinful life and violent death, I am doomed to haunt this Earth at night and feed on people's blood."

The thief was silent. The story sounded plausible, even familiar.

"Where as you going tonight? Whose blood are you planning to suck?" the thief asked, eager to break the ensuing silence.

"I am on my way to the priest's house," the vampire announced indifferently. "I am going to drink the blood from his youngest son. He will be easy pray as the boy never listens to his father, and he never says his prayers before going to bed. I will start tonight, and, most likely, I will be done with him in two or three days."

"Wait a minute," said the thief. "That's exactly where I am heading. I intend to steal the priest's young stallion this night. Tomorrow I will ride far away from this village. Why don't you go and suck somebody else's blood? To be robbed and to lose his youngest son at the same time—that will be too much for the poor priest to bear."

"Ha! What do I care," the vampire replied. "You steal someone else's stallion!"

By this time, the two men had reached the priest's house. Although it was late, one of the windows was lit. Well hidden by the shadows, the two saw the priest reading by candlelight in the room next to his son's.

The darkness was thick, and the silence lay heavy around them. The vampire had crept away from the thief, drawing closer and closer to the window of the young boy's room, when they heard the child suddenly sneeze.

"God bless you! Good luck and good health!" the thief said automatically, before ever realizing that he might give himself away.

Like magic, his words echoed in the quiet of the night like thunder. The vampire cried out, a haunting desperate cry. His ugly face became the image of unspeakable suffering while his body contorted and then shrank with a terrible hiss.

"Don't ... utter ... such ... words," he struggled to say in a harsh but weak voice, for he was turning into smoke and disappearing into the darkness.

In total shock, the thief crossed himself three times quickly. "God have mercy on me!"

"Who's there? What's happening?" shouted the priest, startled.

This tale has a happy ending, to show that not everybody who meets a vampire is worse off afterwards.

The thief confessed everything to the priest, telling the entire story. "You have saved my son's life," declared the priest, "and, in turn, I want to help save your life." To the thief's surprise, the priest gave him the young stallion as a gift but first made him swear that he would not sin ever again.

PART VI

Seventeen Folk Stories About Vlad Ţepeş

(Compiled by Ion Stăvărus, Translated by Adriana Groza)

Just as there exists a small but identifiable Romanian oral folk tradition of village stories about vampires, there is a small Romanian oral folk tradition of stories about Vlad Ţepeş (Vlad the Impaler), also known as Dracula. Importantly, there is no absolutely connection between these two traditions.

The association of Transylvania, vampires, and Dracula is fixed in contemporary popular consciousness. Yet, it is not an association made in Romanian culture. None of the Romanian folk stories about vampires involve the person named Vlad who ruled Wallachia briefly during the 15th century. Reciprocally, none of these Romanian folk stories about Vlad have him returning from the grave or drinking blood as a member of the undead.

The vision of Vlad that exists in Romanian popular culture is well represented by the painting by Theodor Aman, Vlad the Impaler and the Turkish Envoys. *In contrast to the familiar German woodcuts of bloody, impaled victims, we here see a wise Prince dispensing justice in an elegant room, surrounded by supportive nobles. An Orthodox Church is visible through the window. The ambassadors come from Sultan Mehmet II, the most powerful ruler of the era and the conqueror of Constantinople. Vlad, in the painting, appears to have the advantage over them, suggesting his stature in world politics.*

This section consists of a translation into English of the collection of Romanian stories about Prince Vlad compiled by Ion Stăvăruş (Povestiri medievale despre Vlad Ţepeş—Draculea; Bucureşti: Univers, 1993) and derived from oral tradition. They are not historical accounts of Vlad (as found in the few existing German, Turkish, and Russian medieval manuscripts), although the stories are broadly consistent with historical understanding. Rather, they are typical of the tales told and retold in the villages concerning a visible figure from Romanian history.

In these stories, Vlad is portrayed as a cruel but moralistic ruler

Vlad Țepeș și solii turci (Vlad the Impaler and the Turkish Envoys), Theodor Aman (1831–1891). Romanian folklore presents Dracula as a proud Voivode intent upon ridding his land of corruption and resisting incursions from the Turkish army. This highly nationalist painting reflects a famous story in which Vlad dominates over Turkish envoys sent by the Sultan. Claiming to be offended when the envoys refuse to remove their turbans in his presence, he orders the turbans nailed onto the messengers' heads (courtesy National Art Museum, Bucharest).

and a resolute enemy of the Turkish invaders. He emerges as a proud national hero far more than as the embodiment of everlasting evil.

I

Once upon a time, a few great boyars of Targoviste, fed up with the ruler's harshness, decided to get together and devise a plan to get rid of him. Their intention was to catch Vlad Dracula in a trap and send him as a gift to the Turkish Sultan, his sworn enemy.

Dracula, however, was not a man to fall so easily into the hands of traitors. He discovered their cunning and betrayal, and he turned the tables on them.

Out of the blue, on Easter Sunday, when these boyars and their families were participating in the mass, Dracula's men stormed the church and took everybody hostage—great and insignificant, young and old, men and women. His servants made them all march to Curtea de Argeș—Vlad the Impaler's court—and then even further up into the mountains where peaks stand shoulder to shoulder. There, they stopped at a small pass, at the end of a canyon known as the Argeș Gorge.

After they had rested and filled their eyes with the majestic beauty of the mountains, the sovereign himself appeared on a splendid red stallion. He frowned, raised his deadly mace, pointed to the ruins of a old fortress on top of the highest cliff, and shouted:

"Boyars and young gentlemen, ladies and misses, you who have plotted against me, look up at that cliff over there! On that very peak, I command you to build me a new fortress, one that would greet the first rays of sun in the mornings. Make sure you complete the work by Doubting Thomas's Day. Do you all hear me well?" He, then, turned around abruptly and vanished.

The boyars worked hard, day and night. Some broke big stones with their axes. Others carried building materials uphill on their backs, climbing almost vertical slopes, in the effort to finish the fortress by the designated date. They knew only too well that the sovereign was not joking. They were ready to work as hard as they could. They would rather be alive than end up on top of a spear.

Many of the people slipped and fell into the

Vlad Țepeș (Vlad the Impaler), Portraitgalerie, Schloss Ambras, Innsbruck. **This is the only existing portrait of Vlad Dracula. It is a copy made by an anonymous German painter more than a century after Vlad's death, and it shows a man of nobility, wealth, and power, with sharp eyes and a dedicated purpose (Erich Lessing/Art Resource, New York).**

precipice, their corpses eaten by vultures and wild beasts. Nevertheless, on the assigned date, the new fortress stood high on top of the mountain, shining in the morning sun like a fairy tale miracle.

This is how Prince Vlad the Impaler would punish the slyness and sneakiness of his treacherous enemies. Eventually, he forgave those who survived, considering that they repented. But that remained to be seen.

II

A long, long time ago, after the reign of Mircea-the-Old, Wallachia was ruled by Prince Vlad. The Prince was brave and courageous like nobody else, but also mercilessly intolerant with the lazy and wicked, as well as with the enemies of his country. His solution for such people was to impale them, and that is why he was nicknamed, The Impaler.

Vlad was the grandson of Mircea-the-Old. He was adamant that his small country should be free, and not a subordinate vassal to the Turkish Empire. Because of this, he was very much loved by his soldiers, but also feared. Stories of his courageous deeds reached far and wide.

Once, the Turkish Sultan, who was always trying to conquer Wallachia, invaded it with his great army. In the fight, the Turks took one of Vlad's valiant soldiers prisoner and brought him to their Sultan.

The sovereign wanted to know the Impaler's plans and the exact size of his forces, so that he could catch him faster. The Sultan asked the prisoner all sorts of questions, trying to squeeze information out of him in different ways. The Sultan even tried to buy him, offering riches and promising to make him a boyar or even a prince, to replace Vlad at the country's helm. The soldier never talked.

Realizing that bribery was not working, the Sultan changed technique and ordered his men to scare the prisoner. They threatened to break his bones on the wheel, to skin him, even to bury him alive. Nevertheless, the soldier kept silent. Realizing that his life now depended entirely on the Sultan's whim, he finally decided to speak his mind.

"Oh, great Sultan, I know that my life is in your hands. I know you may order me killed, but you will never find out anything from me about Prince Vlad. I would rather die for my country than betray it and my ruler.

On hearing this, the Sultan frowned seriously and replied, "I am impressed. If your Prince has more men like you, he will soon conquer the world and push me out of these lands too."

He, then, commanded his army to retreat. He freed the prisoner and gave him a nice sum of money. The Sultan, thus, left both Wallachia and its ruler, Vlad the Impaler, in peace.

When Vlad found out about his man's behavior, he thanked him and bestowed titles and riches upon him. This is how our former rulers would reward faithful soldiers.

III

There was a time when the Turkish Sultan felt animosity against the Prince of Wallachia and organized a large army to capture him. He put his most formidable general—Hamza Pasha—at the helm of this army and commanded that he catch and deliver Prince Vlad Țepeș.

The Turkish army did attack our country. They expected an easy victory because they had support from some treacherous boyars. Very few of the Turks, however, returned home. Almost all of them left their blood, heads, and red fezes on a forest of spikes.

Learning the news of this humiliating defeat, the Sultan became angry and decided to punish the Wallachian Prince. This time, he gathered an even larger army and led it himself.

The Prince got word of the impending attack, but he was not at all scared. He took his small army of brave soldiers and began to harass the Turkish army, luring them toward a mountainous region.

One night, around midnight, Vlad dressed like a Turkish officer entered the enemy camp. There, he managed to enter the Sultan's tent. He took out his dagger and thrust it into his enemy's chest. Then he ran away shouting, "Catch the murderer, if you can!" His cry created havoc in the camp, and many were killed or wounded in the confusion.

Unfortunately, Vlad Țepeș did not kill the Sultan, but instead one of the Turkish generals.

IV

Once upon a time, Prince Țepeș and seven of his most faithful officers retreated to the Poienari fortress. There, in utmost secrecy, they consulted together to devise a plan to defeat the Turkish Sultan who had set his eyes on Vlad and his small country.

There they were, all seated in a circle talking passionately when, all of a sudden, an arrow zipped in, hitting and breaking the windowpane, severing the candle and putting it out, leaving them in complete darkness. Vlad and his men froze. They had no idea why the light had gone out. "What could this mean? Was it an omen, bad or good? Was it some kind of a miracle?"

One of the men pulled out his tinderbox and relit the candle. To their surprise, they saw the arrow stuck in the middle of the table. The arrow had a roll of paper attached to it. The Prince grabbed it eagerly and unfolded it. "It is a message," he exclaimed. It was from one of Vlad's relatives, a nephew held hostage in the Turkish camp.

"You highness, the Turkish army is drawing near. They have arrived in Pietraria and are now setting up their cannons to destroy your fortress. Run and save yourselves!"

Pietraria was the mountain that stood across from Vlad Țepeș's Poienari fortress. It offered a perfect view of Vlad's meeting place, which now appeared to be at the mercy of the Turkish army.

The attackers did not waste any precious time. Sure enough, they started shooting cannon blasts at the fortified walls. For a while, it looked as if the fortress would keep its hold. But, eventually, the stonewalls gave in and crumbled under the intense fire.

On the third day of the attack, the Turkish soldiers managed to surround the fortress, and they started the final assault, climbing the steep cliff with difficulty. When, finally, they reached the fortress on the summit, they could not believe their eyes—it was absolutely deserted. Not a single person could be found, dead or alive. They searched high and low, but they did not find a soul.

By and by, they located traces of horses, but it was too late to catch them. Vlad and his men had escaped the trap and found haven in Transylvania.

V

Oh, my, our little country did really hurt. The Turkish invaders gave us a bad time during the reign of the local Prince Vlad.

The Turks would often come and kidnap people, just grabbing them to become soldiers in their Sultan's army. Oftentimes, the Turks would take cattle from people as a form of taxation; one out of every ten they would seize. And that was not all. They also took sheep. In those times sheep were among the most important household possessions, and people had them in abundance. As the saying goes, "The sheep feed you in summer, and they keep you warm in winter." And people had so much milk that they used it instead of water to make their daily polenta. It was cheaper that way.

As could be expected, Prince Vlad was angry with the greedy Turk oppressors. He constantly went hunting for them, and he would impale them on every occasion he caught them stealing and plundering our little country.

There were times, however, when Prince Vlad punished in a similar way those treacherous boyers who formed partnerships with the oppressors and those who would cheat their own people.

Once, it is said, he organized a grand party to which he invited all of the men he had grievances against. He gathered them together and impaled them on the spot. This is how Vlad treated his enemies.

VI

They say that Vlad the Impaler was a terribly cruel ruler. Whomever he caught lying or mistreating the old or oppressing the poor, he would right away punish by impalement.

He would also punish in a similar manner the Turks who came periodically to loot his country.

Stories report that, in every town and big settlement, the Prince had a special house built where he would judge evil people. He had a hanging gallows with the noose and high wooden stakes ready to impale the guilty ones. The place near to this spot where he would make his judgments was in Albutele, close to Beleți.

Whenever he found a guilty victim, he would judge him and hang him. After the person was truly silenced, he would order him impaled on one of those stakes, for all to see.

VII

During the time when Prince Vlad Dracula ruled in Wallachia, the Turkish sultan, Mehmet II, considered him a vassal and would often send messengers to his court. Vlad resented his vassal position and often found ways to assert his independence, provoking the leader of the expanding Turkish empire.

One day, messengers from the Sultan arrived at Vlad's palace. According to court protocol, messengers from important people would be received in the main hall. Vlad sat on the throne and ordered his men to bring in the Turkish messengers.

The messengers were wearing clothes of silver and mauve brocade with a golden sash. Over this, they wore caftans of golden and green broadcloth lined with purple. Their sleeves were trimmed with expensive furs. The Turks carried curved scimitars, and their heads were covered in turbans.

On entering the throne hall, the messengers were asked to leave their curved swords, daggers, and sheaths outside because these were not to be worn in the presence of the Prince.

They surrendered their weapons to the guards, entered the big hall, bowed deeply, and greeted the Prince full of deference. But they did not take the turbans off their heads. The Prince announced that he felt offended, saying, "You have come to my court without any invitation. I, nevertheless, received you. Why then are you treating me with such profound disrespect?"

"How are we treating you with disrespect, your highness?" the men asked in astonishment. "We are behaving as we would in front of our master, the Exalted Sultan, who sent us to you."

"In our court," they were told, "people who come before the Prince have to uncover their heads. People cannot bow and kneel in front of our Prince yet keep their heads covered."

"It is something we cannot do," the messengers answered. "We are wearing the clothes that our master, the Sultan, gave to us, and we never take our head covers off," they responded in unison.

"Oh, now I understand," replied the Prince. "If this is your custom, I certainly wish to encourage you to follow it."

So he ordered his soldiers to bring hammers and nails, and used them to firmly affix the turbans to the heads of the Turkish messengers. "This way, your head covers will stay put no matter what."

He then let the messenger leave. They were to return to their Sultan with a message from Prince Vlad.

"Go and tell your master," he ordered, "that he might be used to such displays of disrespect, but we are not. Advise him that he should not send his messengers to other rulers in other countries and expect them to follow his customs alone. We will not accept or tolerate them.

VIII

There was a time, in the period when Prince Vlad Dracula ruled the country, when people were put to death for all kinds of offenses, with or without due process. We should be grateful that we no longer live in such times. We should be grateful that those times are gone. May such times never return! Fortunately, today we have, as the saying goes, judgment not just internment.

Once, during those times, Prince Vlad ordered his men to arrest and ready for impalement some boyars who had conspired against him. His order was dutifully obeyed. After a while, the ruler remembered the men and fancied to see the stakes, to make sure personally that everything would be carried out according to his wishes.

He ordered his courtiers to accompany him to the execution place. His people followed him, some more reluctantly than others. One of the boyars in his retinue felt pity for the condemned men and dared to make a comment. Who knows why! He may have been secretly involved with the conspiring group, or he may have been related to one of them. Anyway, his heart gave way.

"Your highness," the courtier inquired, "why have you deserted your castle? The air there was clean, while here it is foul. You should return to your quarters lest this heavy smell be harmful to your health."

"You mean to say that it stinks here," the Prince answered, looking directly and intensely into the eyes of the boyar.

"Exactly, You Highness. You would better stay away from a place that can be harmful to the heath of a ruler who has his subjects' best interest at heart."

Maybe the Prince had stared straight into this boyar's soul, or, maybe he just wanted to give the others a lesson. Anyway, he shouted, "My servants! Make haste and produce a spike three times longer than the others for this boyar. Impale him there. We must make sure that he is placed much higher than the rest, so he will not smell the foul stink of this place."

IX

There was a time when the small country of Wallachia was ruled by a Prince named Vlad Dracula, who was nicknamed the Impaler. He was famous for being a very harsh ruler, but he was also recognized for being just. He would not tolerate the liars, the lazy, and the thieves. Thus, he did everything he could to rid the country of such people. Had he ruled for long, he would have cleansed the land of all the bad apples and bad eggs. But, alas, we did not have such luck!

Once during his time, a rich merchant from Florence, Italy, loaded with expensive merchandise and gold happened to be traveling through the land. The Florentine was going to Transylvania, and he had to pass through Târgoviște, the capital city of Wallachia. He had heard many terrifying stories, especially about what happened to Turkish soldiers at Vlad's court, and so he proceeded with the belief that the Romanians were terrible monsters or, at least, thieves.

As soon as he arrived in Târgoviște, the Florentine went directly to the castle, carrying a valuable gift for the infamous ruler. He entered the throne hall with no problem and was received by the Prince.

"Your Highness, fate wanted me to pass through your country carrying with me everything that I own. I have worked hard for many years in the non–Christian Far East to acquire this wealth. You rule over a faithful, Christian land. I humbly ask you to assign some of your servants to guard me tonight. I do not want anybody to say that a God-fearing Christian merchant was robbed by other Christians in your land, especially after having survived the yataghan knives and swords of the infidel in their land."

Prince Vlad was a clever fellow. Upon hearing such a request, he frowned and answered, "Keep you gift, Christian man. I order you to take your possessions to any of the tiny back streets or out-of-the-way lanes that you can find here in the city. Leave the goods there unguarded until morning. If you will suffer any loss, I will take responsibility, myself."

The Florentine had no choice but do as he was told. There was no disobeying Vlad the Impaler, and so he, reluctantly, deposited his possessions in the street, and, as ordered, left them there overnight. Needless to say, he hardly closed his eye during that night, which seemed to him to be the longest ever.

To his surprise, in the morning everything was as he had left it. The merchant kept staring at his pile of goods, hardly believing his eyes. Nothing had been touched. Immediately, he decided to go to the castle to express his thanks. He had never seen anything like it, he told the Prince, in any of the countries where he had traveled, although he had been traveling since his youth.

"You wanted to give me a gift," the Prince reminded him. "What is its value? How much is it supposed to be worth?"

At first, the Florentine did not want to tell, but eventually he named a price. To the merchant's surprise, the Prince accepted the gift but, in turn, paid him in gold the full amount it was worth. "Now, continue with your journey," Vlad said, "and tell everybody what you experienced in my country."

X

At the time when Vlad the Impaler was ruling over Wallachia, a prominent merchant from Florence happened to pass through his country on his way home from Transylvania. He was carrying nice merchandise and a hefty sum of money.

As soon as the traveler arrived in Târgovişte, the capital of the country at that time, he went to the Prince's palace to ask for protection. He asked Vlad to assign guards to protect himself as well as his goods and money.

The ruler instead ordered that the merchant sleep in his castle overnight but leave his possessions outside in the main plaza.

The Florence was not happy with the way things had turned out. However, he had no choice but do what the Prince told him. He worried about his possession and barely slept during that night.

In the morning when he checked his carriage, he discovered that, just as he had feared, somebody had robbed him. He counted his money and found that 160 golden coins were missing.

The merchant went to the Prince to report his loss. Vlad told him not to worry and promised personally to replace in his carriage the money that was stolen. In secret, however, he ordered his men to add one extra coin to the sum. He, then, commanded his people to find the thief right away, and he threatened to punish the entire town if the culprit was not found.

The merchant returned to his carriage and took inventory of his possessions. He counted his money twice, and he found, each time, with surprise, that there was an extra coin. He then returned to Price Vlad and told him, "Your highness, I thank you for your protection. I found everything in good order. As for the money, because of you, I am not now at a loss. In fact, when I counted it, I seem to have one extra golden coin."

Just as he was saying this, the guards brought in the thief. He had been captured and was waiting to receive his punishment from Vlad the Impaler.

The Prince looked at the Florentine, smiled, and said, "Go in peace, good merchant. Had you not confessed to receiving one extra coin, you would have ended up just like this thief, whom I am going to impale right away."

This is how Vlad Dracula would treat his subjects.

XI

A very long time ago, when Vlad Dracula ruled Wallachia, a foreign merchant traveled through the country.

As ill luck would have it, the man's purse disappeared. He most likely had dropped it. He announced that there were one thousand coins in the purse, and that he was willing to reward the person who helped him recover it. He stood at the crossroads, shouting that he would pay one hundred of the coins to whomsoever would bring it back to him.

Soon, a good Christian soul, like all Wallachians used to be during Prince Vlad's time, came up to him and said, "Honorable merchant, as I was walking down the road behind the fish nursery, I found this purse lying in the dirt. I assume that it belongs to you since you have been shouting so loudly. It can be heard all over town that you lost a purse full of coins."

"That is correct," the merchant said. "I have lost a purse, and this one is mine. Thank you for bringing it to me." He, then, proceeded to count his coins to assess his damage. As he was calculating, greediness took the best of him, and he started to search for ways to take back his promise of a finder's fee.

The good man watched the merchant handling the coins, not exactly understanding what was happening.

After secretively counting the coins, the merchant placed them back into his purse and put the purse firmly away in his pocket. "Well, my good man," he said, "I have examined all the coins, and I noticed that you have already taken your share. There were one thousand coins in my purse before, and now I find only nine hundred in it. That is not a problem. Indeed, I had promised one hundred to the person who found my purse and brought it back to me, which you did. You deserve the money. Now, I thank you and bid you farewell."

The good man was very surprised to hear this. "My most honorable merchant," he answered, "I am confused by your claim that you are missing money. I found your purse and returned it to you just as I found it. I never even opened it to look inside."

"I am telling you," the merchant insisted in a curt tone, "that I lost a purse with one thousand coins, and you brought me back the purse with nine hundred. That is all there is to it. I will not give you any more money. If you want more, sue me, and take the case before a judge."

The good man was so offended that his face turned red. He had done a good deed and ended up being mistreated, suspected of stealing and cheating. So he chose to go to the Prince to seek justice.

The next day, he appeared in front of Vlad Dracula and told him the full story. "This is not about the money, your highness. I am not here because he promised one hundred coins to the person who found his purse and returned it to him. I am suing this merchant because he accused me of trying to cheat him. I want my name cleared because I am an honest, God-fearing man."

Vlad was wise and began to suspect how things truly had evolved. He was determined to find the truth and rule justly. He ordered the merchant to be brought before him also, for him to tell his own version of what happened.

The ruler listened very carefully to both parties. He weighed their testimonies and saw that his scales were leaning in one direction. He looked both men in the eye, as if to read their souls, and then turned to the merchant and said,

"Master Merchant, lying is not acceptable at my court. We punish liars drastically, here. You said that you lost a purse containing one thousand coins. You made a public announcement of it. You announced it loud and clear all over town. The purse that this good man brought you contained nine hundred coins, you say, yet he swears before God that it had not been opened. It is, therefore, absolutely clear that the purse returned to you is not yours. How dare you accept it? You have no right over it."

People started to murmur, but Vlad went on. "My judgment is this: give the good man back the purse he found, and then wait for yours to appear."

"As for you," the ruler said to the plaintiff, "keep this purse until its owner shows up to reclaim it."

And this is how things were settled. There was no way out of it.

Vlad Dracula's word was very strong, and his judgment was final. The merchant regretted his actions for the rest of his life. He had tried to trick somebody, but ended up only tricking himself.

XII

During the times of Prince Vlad, an Orthodox Greek monk was wandering through Wallachia, spreading the teachings of his creed. He was critical of everything he saw. According to him, the Romanian people had lost their good ways and were sinning far too often. The monk argued that the Romanian priests were not properly doing their job in guiding the flock and serving the church. He felt that his calling was to scold people, to make them repent and follow his teachings.

Word about this foreign monk reached Prince Vlad. He did not like foreigners coming to his country in order to proselytize. He was especially suspicious of people who thought that they were better than others. Thus, he decided to meet this monk and make his own assessment.

Soon after, the Prince encountered the monk at church. Vlad was attending a new church near the town of Târgoviște for Sunday morning mass. The wandering Greek monk was preaching in front of the church, proclaiming that everybody had to reform his behavior.

The monk, realizing that the Prince himself was among the listeners, gave a very animated speech. Quoting from the Scriptures, he asserted that Romanians had become too greedy. He decried their gluttony and their tendency toward envy. "One should never covet another's possessions," the monk shouted. "People should follow my example and never take something that does not belong to them." He very much wanted to make an impression on the Prince.

The Prince, however, did not appreciate the monk's lack of modesty. He thought it hubris to preach in front of a sacred church, telling everybody—including simple people, local priests, and hereditary boyars—how to behave. However, Vlad decided to know the monk a little better before he made up his mind about what to do with him.

Later that day, the Greek monk received a surprise invitation. He was asked to join the Prince for dinner. The invitation made the monk very happy. Convinced that he was now a chosen authority, he started behaving with even greater superiority.

At the dinner reception, the monk, seated next to Prince Vlad, challenged the others at the table with questions from the Bible, for he was knowledgeable about the Scriptures. While they were all eating and talking, the Prince merely broke small pieces off his loaf of bread and placed them in front of his plate, close at hand.

The monk, so self-satisfied with his own show of wisdom, paid no attention to what the Prince was doing, to the elaborate manner in which Vlad was arranging his food. Without thinking, he began eating the pieces of bread that Vlad had prepared for himself.

Vlad watched this carefully. After the monk had helped himself to even more of the bread pieces, he said, "Thief! I have caught you. In front of our churches, you proclaim respect for other people's property. Never should one touch something that does not belong to him. God forbid, it is what you preach. But you preach one thing, yet live by another."

The Prince was disgusted with them monk's disrespectful behavior. "Here you are, at my very table, eating my very food. And still, you reveal yourself as a dishonest glutton. You have just grabbed my food from before my plate, from under my own eyes."

Vlad, then, turned to his servants and ordered, "Take this dishonest, false prophet away. We must teach him a permanent lesson. He must learn what happens to hypocrites in our country."

Prince Vlad had the monk impaled. Nobody's pleas could make him change his mind.

XIII

Once upon a time, there was a poor priest. He had spent many years preaching at a church located very close to Vlad's castle, and the Prince had listened to several of his sermons. The priest was a simple and honest soul, and people often came to him for advice. He was generous, and the door of his church was open to anybody. He always had travelers and pilgrims eating at his modest table.

A Greek monk had been roaming through Vlad's country. For some reason, he chose to settle for a while near to the poor priest's church. But his presence was not a positive addition to the community. The monk loved to gossip, and he was a mean-spirited person who looked with nasty eyes upon everything. The Greek would bicker and complain constantly—about the people, customs, and rules of our country.

The monk was especially critical of the local priest. He would call the priest stupid and uneducated, a shepherd of stupid and uneducated people. With superiority, he would forecast damnation for the whole nation.

"If you find us all so terribly stupid and uneducated, then why have you settled here?" the humble priest would ask in response. "Why do you choose to live among such an offending flock? You might prefer to go back to your people, whom you obviously enjoy more."

The squabbling between the two religious men persisted. One day, Prince Vlad learned of it, as he was very well informed about the things happening in his kingdom. He liked to know everything that was going on, especially so close to his castle.

He decided to discover for himself how things stood with the feuding holy men. Vlad was a God-fearing person. In Wallachia, the prince was the official head of the church, and he expected modesty and wisdom from the servants of his church. Prince Vlad, therefore, decided to invite both men to his castle. Neither, however, was to know that the other had been invited as well.

The much-expected day soon arrived. Both the poor priest and the Greek monk presented themselves at the castle. They did not see each other because they were told to show up at different gates, for the Prince was planning to meet them separately.

The Greek monk was very full of himself. He was proud that the Prince had invited him for a meeting at the castle and was anxious to demonstrate his wisdom. The local priest was meek and unassuming. He wondered how the Prince had ever taken notice of him. He was thinking of ways that his congregation might benefit from this special interview with the ruler.

The intention of the Prince was to tempt the hearts of these two religious men, so that he could read into their souls. Vlad Dracula was that type of person who judged by seeing into the souls of other people.

When the Greek monk entered, Vlad said to him, "My good monk! I have been told that you travel through my kingdom assisting in matters of the church. I assume that, in your wanderings, you have met people of all types, good and bad, rich and poor. Tell me, please, what are my subjects saying about me?"

The sly Greek monk warmed with joy. Here was a question, he thought, from which he could profit. So he smiled and assumed a deferent pose, answering, "Your highness, from one end of the country to the other, every subject praises your name. Everybody is delighted with your leadership and says that Wallachia has never had such wise and generous ruler. I, personally, would only dare to add one piece of advice to this. Your highness, please be merciful and generous toward those foreigners who come from the Sacred Land to assist your local holy men, priests, and monks. Then, your name will be blessed eternally by cohorts of heavenly angels."

"You are a double-faced, sly liar." the Prince shouted angrily and frowned. Quite obviously, he knew that the speech was not truthful. As the saying goes, not even the mighty sun can keep everybody happy and satisfied. Vlad summoned his guards and ordered, "Take this hypocrite away. This scheming fool deserves to die!" The order was dutifully obeyed. The monk was impaled right away.

The Prince, then, called for the local priest, who had no idea about the fate of his foe, and asked him the same question.

"Please, your highness, forgive me for saying this," the humble priest answered. "I cannot but speak the truth. The people are not overly happy. There has not been much rebellious talk in the country, but lately many have started to complain. A few have even cursed your name, saying that you show no intention to reduce the high taxes that were imposed by your predecessors."

"Yes, you are speaking the truth," Prince Vlad said in a mild voice. "I will think about it. From now on, you will be one of my counselors. Go home to your congregation in peace."

XIV

I have learned from our old wise men that, during Prince Vlad's reign, honesty and justice ruled in this country as never before. One could not encounter lies or oppression or drunkenness or any other thing that spoils an individual.

Vlad's most impressive improvement was to get rid of thieves and robbers. They say that he caught them all. None escaped his spike. There were no rocks for them to hide under, oh, my God! Hardly had they found a thief, than, they impaled him on the spot.Soon another followed him. The prince's people would raise their stakes at crossroads and leave the poor devils there for everyone to see, with crows hovering above.

This is how Prince Vlad rid the country of thieves. Nevertheless, to make sure that no thief escaped his hunt, he decided to test his subjects. He thought to himself, "Let me set a trap for the dishonest ones. I will have my servants put a golden cup at an often used well near the main road. Let us see whether any of the many travelers who pass by the spot will dare to steal it."

So, he ordered that a beautiful, big, shining golden cup be placed at the well on the busy main road. He gave instructions that the cup should not be chained down or tied to anything. It was to be left there, lying loose.

Very many people passed by. Some used the golden cup to drink from, tasting fresh water that was available. But none were tempted by the devil to steal it, not as long as Vlad was Prince of Wallachia.

XV

Prince Vlad Dracula was a clever man. He liked order and neatness, very much so. God forbid that he might see a scruffy soldier dressed in shabby clothes. He would raise hell for that. He liked people to be tidy and well dressed. He liked them clean and, you know, spruced-up. Those who were not properly dressed would not get to spend much time in his company. He always reacted badly to messy individuals and to those responsible for their mess.

One day, the Prince encountered a peasant. The man looked unkempt. His shirt was too short, and his pants were torn and tight. The Prince did not like what he saw and ordered his servants to bring the man before him. "Are you married, my man?" he wanted to know.

"Yes, I am married, your highness."

"Your wife, she must be one of the very lazy ones. How come she did not make you a shirt fit to cover your body? Such a woman is not worthy to live in my kingdom. We have to get rid of her."

"But I am pleased with her, your highness. Have pity," the man replied. "I can always count on her being at home, and she is honest."

"You would be even happier with another one," Vlad announced. "You seem to be a good, hardworking man. You deserve better."

Without much ado, two of his guards fetched the poor woman and brought her to the Prince. He had her impaled immediately. He, then, ordered that another wife be found for the widower. Vlad insisted that she be told what had happened to the first wife, what she did to bring about her punishment.

Oh my, this new wife did work! She would put a piece of bread on one shoulder and the salt on the other and kept working. She tried her best to keep her husband satisfied so as not to bring the Prince's wrath down upon her.

Did she succeed, I wonder?

Fortunately, there is no Prince Vlad ruling us these days. What a great number of stakes would have to be used to rid the land of lazy, good-for-nothing wives.

XVI

Prince Vlad had a lover. Her house was at the end of a small, dark street in Târgoviște. Nobody knew. Not even the slowly flowing river near the house could hear him coming to her house. The woman adored the Prince. He had taken a fancy to her, as luck would have it, but his interest was more simple necessity than love.

The woman tried her best to keep him happy and merry, despite his worries and cares. He would take for granted all signs of true affection from her. Once in while, however, he would lighten up in her company.

One day, when Vlad was especially downcast, she try to cheer him up and told him a lie. "Your highness! You will be delighted when I tell you the good news."

"What news is that?"

"The little mouse got into the milk pail."

"What does that mean?" he asked with a grin.

"It means I feel heavy."

"You should stop telling such lies," he said angrily.

The woman knew how Vlad punished those who deceived him, so she tried to convince him that she was telling the truth. "I am not lying," she persisted in desperation. "It is the truth."

"No, nothing is happening," he told her with a frown.

"But if it is going to happen, "she dared to add, "I hope that your highness will be glad."

"I have told you that nothing, really, is happening," the Prince shouted, stamping his feet. "I will show you that nothing is happening."

As he uttered these words, he took out his sword and cut open her belly, to prove that she had not told the truth.

As she was lying in terrible pain, he told her, "You see. I told you that nothing was happening!"

Then, he left her there to die, her only sin being that she had tried to cheer up her lover with a lie.

XVII

The story goes that, at one time during Prince Vlad's reign, the number of lazy people increased enormously. Nevertheless, to survive they had to eat. Their merciless bellies asked constantly for food. Rather than work, they walked around and begged. By constant panhandling, they sought to live without having to work.

Sometimes, people would ask the beggars why they did not work. The answer was, "Am I not walking around all day? How is it my fault that I cannot find work?"

The rejoinder from responsible people was often a tease. "I am going search of work. Please God, do not let me find any!"

The lazy one would always find excuses. They would say that the furrier sews all day only to lose his sight, that the tailor works his entire life, but what he makes can be put on the head of a pin, that the shoe-maker gets a hunch from all his toil but goes to his grave without nothing. They had complaints about all the useful crafts.

After a while, Prince Vlad learned of such comments. He saw with his own eyes the multitude of beggars, the majority of them strong men, fit for work. So he began to ponder. "A man should earn his daily bread by the sweat of his brow. That is what the Good Book teaches us. Yet, these beggars have made themselves useless, living at the expense of somebody else's sweat. It is a form of theft. The mugger attacks you and tries to rob you, that is true. But if you are stronger or faster, you can defend yourself and prevent the theft. These beggars are far worse. They take your money or possessions by appealing to your mercy."

After serious consideration, Prince Vlad decided to rid his kingdom of such people. He commanded that all beggars should be summoned to his castle, on the pretext that he was going to give them food and new clothes.

On the appointed day, the town of Târgoviște was swarming with vagrants from all parts of the kingdom. The Prince's servants gave all of them new clothes. Then, they were taken to a big house on the outskirts of the town where tables full of food were waiting. The beggars were delighted with the feast.

"This really is kingly generosity," some said. Yet, others replied, "He is giving us a great meal, but it is paid from the people's taxes. The funds do not come from his own pocket."

The conversation continued. Some argued that the Prince, who once was so critical of beggars, appeared to have had a change of heart. The response from the skeptics was the old saying, "that a wolf can change its coat, but not its ways."

The banquet consisted of lots of good food from Prince Vlad's own kitchen and strong wines from his own cellars. The tramps were seated at long tables, eating and drinking gluttonously. Many were falling off drunk, unable to speak anymore.

After a while, the Prince gave an order to his servants. The doors of the banquet house were closed and bolted. Then the walls were set on fire. Smoke started to appear from all sides, and, soon, the fire reached inside. The poor vagabonds tried to save themselves. They banged on the doors and begged for their lives. They cried and wailed. But all was in vain. In the end, all that was left was a large pile of black ash.

What do you think? Do you believe that Prince Vlad Dracula truly succeeded in eradicating every vagrant from his land? C'mon! Do not believe all that you hear! Grow up! These days, the world is no different than during his times. There will be lazy beggars until the end of time.

On Historical Sources

There exists a vast literature on Romanian myths and folklore. Within this literature, vampire themes are present, but not especially prominent. There are remarkably few sources for authentic vampire folk stories, even within the archives of the *Biblioteca Academiei Române*. Romanians use the terms *strigoi, moroi, vircolaci, priculici, bosorcoi*. The word *vampire* is sometimes used today, often with sarcasm, but it is a late addition to the language.

There is no authoritative collection of Romanian vampire stories in any language. Stories about *strigoi* or *moroi* circulated for centuries among the villages in oral tradition, but it was only during the late 19th century that some of them were written down.

For the most part, the stories were preserved in greatly abridged versions. Elaborate folk narratives were compressed into a summary form that briefly sketched the central plot and indicated the underlying moral theme. The detailed imagery and poetic beauty of the stories were largely neglected. One could no longer hear the cultural memory of a nation recounted by gifted storytellers captivating the village audience sitting by the fire. My goal has been to retrieve this narrative thread and bring these scattered story fragments back to life, retelling them as they might have sounded in their original version.

Our knowledge of Romanian vampire stories comes primarily from enthusiastic, but amateur folklorist and anthropologists writing in the late 19th and early 20th centuries. They wrote during the period of nationalist awakening, believing that the *arta și creația populară* helped to reveal the essential Romanian mentality. These writers were not especially focused upon vampire stories, but vampires do sometimes appear in the stories collected and published, most often in small, regional periodicals. Among the most important are *Familia* (1865–1940), *Șezătoarea* (1892–1949), and *Ion Creangă* (1908–1921).

The first significant Romanian work based on the vampire legend was the poem *Strigoii* (1884) by the most famous Romanian romantic poet of the 19th century, Mihai Eminescu. It concerns the conquering Norse king Harald who falls deeply in love with and marries Maria, a local Christian queen. She dies soon afterwards, and in his despair, Harald returns to the pagan temple and asks a wizard to bring Maria back to him. The old man summons all the forces of the underworld. Thunder and lightening destroy the Christian church where she was buried. Harald dies in the catastrophe and is entombed in the pagan temple. Yet, afterwards, the two lovers leave their tombs and reunite each night. They ride their horses and make love until dawn, only to return to their separate crypts at the first rays of the sun.

The historical value of the poem lies in the reaction that it generated. Romanian nationalist commentators responded that one did not have to import foreign inspiration or rely in heraldic imagery alien to Romanian traditional culture. In 1898, the literary magazine *Familia* announced that its next edition would feature an analysis by Elena Niculiță-Voronca, challenging Eminescu's poem and introducing readers to the authentic Romanian folk tradition regarding vampires. The article, that appeared over five issues of the journal, included a small collection of short vampire stories, compiled by the author, and supplied the first formal analysis of the Romanian village vampire.

• Niculiță-Voronca, an amateur anthropologist, later expanded her interest in collecting local folklore, publishing several articles in *Șezătoarea, Ion Creangă*, and an extensive volume (1903) on Romanian traditional customs and beliefs. Pamfile quoted her approximately 130 times in his *Mitologie românească*. Niculiță-Voronca's work sparked renewed interest in authentic Romanian village folktales. Among the most important writers are:

• Artur Gorovei (*Credințe și superstiții ale poporului român*, 1915) was a folklorist, ethnographer, and editor of the first Romanian magazine of folklore, *Șezătoarea,* that appeared monthly. In recognition of his achievements in researching historic traditions, customs, rituals, and folktales, he was elected in 1940 as an honorary member of the Romanian Academy.

• Lazăr Șăineanu (*Basmele române în comparațiune cu legendele antice clasice și în legătură cu basmele poporeloru învecinate și ale tuturoru poporeloru romanice*, 1895). Șăineanu was a Romanian Jew who, despite his innovative studies of philology and linguistics, was refused full citizenship rights by the Romanian parliament and eventually emigrated to France. In addition to transcribing stories from oral tradition, he was a pioneer in comparative mythology, classifying folktales by type and context.

- Constantin Rădulescu-Codin (*Îngerul românului. Povești sau legende din popor,* 1913) and *Făt-Frumos, Povești,* 1913). A teacher and skilled collector of popular folklore, Rădulescu collected numerous stories and legends, a few of which concern vampires. His work was published in the series *Din Vieața Poporului Român,* organized by the Academia Română.

- Tudor Pamfile (*Mitologie Românească,* 2000, reprinting three volumes from 1916 and 1924). Trained as an officer in the Romanian Army, Pamfile was an enthusiastic ethnologist and editor of the small periodical *Ion Creangă,* about Romanian peasant art and literature. His main book on mythology contains the greatest variety of themes regarding Romanian vampires, impressive in its extent. His work reflects meticulous investigation and accurate rendition, but it does little to capture the narrative flow of the text. A few of his brief narratives published in *Ion Creangă,* plus two others from the Romanian Folklore Institute, can be found in English translation (McNally 1974).

- N.I. Dumitrașcu (*Strigoii în credințele, datinile și povestirile poporului roman,* 1929). This was the first attempt to collect, specifically, vampire stories. Dumitrașcu was a railway stationmaster and amateur folklorist who transcribed tales told by peasants in his region and published them in Pamfile's magazine and in a small brochure. A few of these stories were retold by Gabriel Stănescu and translated into English by Mac Ricketts (*The Man Who Tried to Cheat Death: Romanian Scary Stories,* 2000). For this volume, I intentionally did not reproduce those stories that already exist in English-language versions.

- Father Dumitru Furtună (1890–1965). A priest, teacher, and passionate collector of folklore, Furtună founded a theological seminary, a high school, and a theatre, and he hosted a literary society in his home. He published a few carefully researched articles about the Romanian village vampire in *Ion Creangă.* Fortuna died in poverty, for the communist regime confiscated his property and took away his pension.

- Otilia Hedeșan (*Strigoii,* 2011). A professor at Universitatea de Vest in Timisoara, she collected a number of vampire stores for her doctoral dissertation (*7 eseuri despre strigoi,* 1998). Hedeșan's focus, however, is not especially upon the content and meaning of the stories; rather they serve primarily as a convenient vehicle for her discussion regarding the nature of storytelling, its characteristic forms and structures.

Over the 20th century, vampires increasing became a theme of interest within popular culture. Not surprisingly, given Stoker's invention, curiosity led some commentators to the Romanian tradition. Failing to find Vlad Țepeș, they nevertheless did discover an important source of folk stories. A number of commentators have examined Romanian vampire myths—analytically distinguishing subtypes, inserting them into the broader discussion of comparative folklore, and interpreting their deeper symbolic structure. These analysts were not storytellers, and overwhelmingly, they relied for their data upon the few historical sources mentioned above. Among the most important are:

• Agnes Murgoci ("The Vampire in Romania," 1926). An English folklorist (née Kelly) married to a Romanian, Murgoci wrote a widely circulated article relying heavily on accounts published in Pamfile's periodical. The work helped contribute to the popular association of vampires with Romania, and it differentiated among various types of vampires and werewolves in the folk stories.

• Montague Summers (*The Vampire in Europe*, 1929). A British eccentric fascinated with the gothic and the occult, he wrote extensively about vampires in the attempt to show that the belief was still alive. His work reflects extensive comparative reading, and relies heavily on Murgoci for the section on Romania.

• Adrian Cremene (*La mythologie du vampire en Roumanie*, 1981). A French scholar interested in the impact that old beliefs have on modern society, he argued that the Romanian vampire dates from pre–Christian shamanistic practices and lives in popular consciousness as a reflection of the individual's psychological fear of death and fascination with immortality. Cremene, writing at the time of the Communist regime, was intent upon demonstrating that, despite official denials, vampire consciousness was inherent in the rituals, dances, and stories of ordinary village life.

• Jan Louis Perkowski ("The Romanian Folkloric Vampire," 1982/2006). An academic specializing in comparative folklore, he expanded the formal discussion of vampires to the Slavic world. Regarding Romania, he used the few vampire references extracted from Emil Petrovici's collection of local dialects and applied his analytical categories regarding vampire origins, activities, characteristics, and powers.

• Harry Senn (*Were-Wolf and Vampire in Romania*, 1982). An American anthropologist, Senn collected brief accounts of vampire stories during Fulbright-sponsored visits to Romania. He viewed the vampire story as a dimension of socialization, representing the outsider who is not fully integrated and, thus, is held responsible for the unexplained. He considered their endurance an expression of the failure of modernization and the attachment of villagers to an ancestral world where human beings and magical forces coexist in the normal cycle of nature.

Another source of inspiration for contemporary interest in Romanian vampires are literary works in which vampire themes were adopted by famous Romanian writers for their own artistic purposes. These include the fantastic stories of Petre Ispirescu (1984/1989), Romania's "Brothers Grimm," and the lurid short novel by Mircea Eliade, *Domnişoara Cristina* (1936), both which were required reading of my youth.

Finally, there are the stories told to me in childhood, especially by an elderly aunt whom I visited in her village of Bratca in Bihor County. I have a vivid memory of her narrative accounts, of the tone of her voice, and of the rapt attention she aroused. Quite possibly, this was the origin of my interest in the oral tradition of Romanian folklore.

* * *

There has been extensive historical scholarship regarding the real Wallachian ruler, Vlad Țepeș, much of which is based on medieval chronicles. Of Romanian scholars, Ion Bogdan (1896) and C. Karadja (1936) were among the first to study and publish about Vlad. Of the sources in English, especially valuable are the accounts by Florescu and McNally (1989), McNally & Florescu (1994), and by Treptow (2000).

Medieval accounts about Vlad include sources written in German, Russian, Latin, and Turkish. There is also record of a few letters and other documents written allegedly by Vlad or his aides. The oldest existing documents are four German manuscripts, copies of an original narrative (1462), now lost, that belonged to a Benedictine monastery in Lambach, in Austria of today. Inspired by three Catholic monks who, most likely, had met Vlad yet fled after incurring his anger for religious proselytizing, the narrative contains exaggerated accounts of his deeds. McNally has translated into English a copy of the original German manuscript, located at the Saint Gall monastery, Switzerland, and also the oldest surviving Russian manuscript about Dracula, from the Saltykov-Shchedrin Library in Saint Petersburg. Similarly prominent was Michael Beheim's sensational poem (1463) "The Story of a Bloodthirsty Madman Called Dracula of Wallachia," which was performed with great success at the court of Frederick III, the Holy Roman Emperor. The poem, now kept at the University of Heidelberg, was replete with gory details in which Vlad tortured his enemies, killed their families, and reveled in their blood. Accounts denigrating Vlad circulated widely, during the late Middle Ages, in oral and later in printed forms, constituting some of the first known horror stories in literature.

Within the Romanian tradition, Vlad, instead, is known as a heroic ruler, strict but fair, who defended his territory against the Turkish invaders from the East. In this form, celebratory accounts inspired nationalist poets and writers, for example, Mihail Eminescu, Ion Budai-Deleanu, and Petre Ispirescu. In general, these writers praised Vlad for his efforts at state building, courage as a warrior, and ethics in purging his nation of weaklings, cowards, thieves, and traitors. My concern in this volume, however, is with the older, less formal, narrative folk accounts.

Regarding Romanian folk stories about Vlad Țepeș, the main collection was compiled by Ion Stăvăruș (1978/1993). Many of the stories are reasonably well known within Romania. I have translated (rather than retold) them into English, maintaining as closely as possible the original Romanian prose style of the historic narratives and respecting the order in which Stăvăruș arranged them.

The present book puts the Romanian folk tales that circulated about vampires side-by-side with the Romanian folk tales about Vlad Țepeș, largely to prove that they do not, in fact, belong together. Yet, taken separately, each deserves recognition and respect.

Bibliography

Aarne, Antti Amatus. 1961. *The Types of the Folk Tale: A Classification and Bibliography*. Verzeichnis der Marchentypen (FF communications no. 3). Trans. into Eng. by Stith Thompson. Helsinki: Suomalainen Tiedeakatemia, 1961. 2nd revision.

Andreescu, Ştefan. 1976. *Vlad Ţepeş (Dracula): Între legendă şi adevăr istoric*. Bucureşti: Editura Minerva.

Baican, Elie. 1882. *Literatura populară sau palavre si anecdote*. Bucuresci: Tipografia academiei române.

Bălteanu, Valeriu. 2003. *Dicţionar de magie populară românească*. Bucureşti: Paidera.

Barber, Paul. 1998. "Forensic Pathology and the European Vampire." In Alan Dundes: 109–142.

Bîrlea, Ovidiu. 1979. *Studii de folclor*. Cluj-Napoca: Dacia.

Bizom, Teofil. 1913. "Vlad Ţepeş şi boierii." *Ion Creangă* 6: 180–1.

Bogdan, Alexandru. 1910. *M. Eminescu—Strigoii*. Sibiu: Tipografia Archidiecezana.

Bogdan, Ioan. 1896. *Vlad Ţepeş şi naraţiunile germane şi rusești asupra lui*. Bucuresti: Editura librăriei Socecu.

Borleanu, Elena Camelia. 2010. *Monografia lui Ion Creangă*. Craiova: Sitech.

Borleanu, Lucian, ed. n.d. *Legende Populare Românesti, toponimice şi istorice*. N.p.: Editura Lucman.

Bottigheimer, Ruth B., ed. 1986. *Fairly Tales and Society: Illusion, Allusion, and Paradigm*. Philadelphia: University of Pennsylvania Press.

Brandes-Latea, Ştefan, Cristina Zavoianu, Umberto Ferri. 2001. *Dracula, Mysteries of Transylvania*. Bucureşti: Universal Dalsi.

Budai-Deleanu, Ion. 1895/1897. *Ţiganiada sau Tabăra ţiganilor*. Rpt. 1998. Bucureşti: Garamond.

Buican, Denis. 1993. *Les Metamorphoses de Dracula. L'Histoire et la Legende*. Paris: Editions du Felin.

Canciovici, Mihai, ed. 1984. *Domnitori români în legende – Antologie de legende populare românești*. Bucureşti: Editura Sport-Turism.

Cândea, Ioan. 1894–95. "Strigoii." *Şezătoarea* 7: 133–4.

Caracostea, Dumitru. 1929. *Lenore. O problemă de literature comparată şi folklor*. Bucureşti: Atelierele grafice Cultura naţională.

Cartojan, Nicolae. 1929. *Cărţile populare în literatura românească*. Bucureşti: Editura Casei Şcoalelor.

Ciauşanu, Gh. F. 1914. *Superstiţiile poporului român în asemănare cu ale altor popoare vechi şi nouă*. Bucureşti: Socea-Sfetea.

Ciobanu, Radu Ştefan. 1979. *Pe urmele lui Vlad Ţepeş*. Bucureşti: Editura Sport-Turism.

Constantin-Dac, Dumitru. 2005. *Dracula, Voievod, Demon şi Vampir*. Bucureşti: Medro.

Cremene, Adrian. 1981. *La mythologie du vampire en Roumanie*. Monaco: Editions de Rocher.

Daicoviciu, Hadrian. 1968. *Dacii*. București: Editura pentru literatură.

Day, William Patrick. 2002. *Vampire Legends in Contemporary American Culture: What Becomes a Legend Most*. Lexington: University Press of Kentucky.

Djuvara, Neagu, and Radu Olteanu. 2003. *De la Vlad Țepeș la Dracula Vampirul*. București: Humanitas.

Dumitrașcu, N.I. 1915. "Fata și Strigoiul." *Ion Creangă* 4: 93–4.

_____. 1929. *Strigoii în credințele, datinile și povestirile poporului român*. București: Cultura Națională.

Dundes, Alan, ed. 1998. *The Vampire*. Madison: University of Wisconsin Press.

Eliade, Mircea. 1936. *Domnișoara Cristina*. București: Cultura Națională.

_____. 1974. *Death, Afterlife, and Eschatology*. New York: Harper & Row.

Eminescu, Mihai. 1884. *Poesii*. București: Editura Socecu.

_____. 1985. *Literatura Populară*. București: Editura Minerva.

Florescu, R. Radu, and Raymond T. McNally. 1989. *Dracula, Prince of Many Faces, His Life and His Times*. Boston: Little, Brown.

Folclor din Transilvania. 1962–85. *Texte alese din colecții inedite*. București: Editura pentru literatură.

Fundescu, I.C. 1896. *Basme, orații, păcălituri și ghicitori*. București: Tipo-litografia si fonderia de litere Dor P. Cucu.

Furtună, Dumitru. 1911, 1912, 1913. "De-ale strigoilor." *Ion Creangă* 7: 202–4; Nr. 1:11–2: 1913, Nr. 8: 237–8.

Gerard, Emily de Laszowska. 1888. *The Land Beyond the Forest*. New York: Harper & Brothers.

Gorovei, Artur. 1915. *Credințe și superstiții ale poporului român*. București: Editura Socec-Sfetea.

Hallab, Mary Y. 2009. *Vampire God: The Allure of the Undead in the Western Culture*. New York: SUNY Press.

Hașdeu, B.P. 1936. *Cărțile Poporane*. București: Editura Tipografiile Române Unite.

Hedeșan, Otilia. 2011. *Strigoii*. Ed. II-a. Cluj-Napoca: Dacia XXI, 2011.

Hertanu-Chiretu, Marinela. 2000. *Dracula, legendă și istoric*. Pitești: Paralela 45.

Ion Creangă, Revistă de limbă, literatură și artă populară. 1908–21. Bârlad: Tipografia și legătoria de cărți C.D. Lupașcu.

Ioneanu, George S. 1888. *Mică colecțiune de superstițiile poporului român*. Buzeu: Editura Librariei moderne A. Davidescu.

Ioniță, Maria. 1982. *Cartea vîlvelor*. Cluj-Napoca: Dacia, 1982.

_____. 1983. *Legende din Țara Moților*. București: Editura I. Creangă.

Ispirescu, Petre, ed. 1971. *Opere*. Bucuresti: Minerva.

_____. 1989. *Legendele sau basmele românilor*. Bucuresti: Minerva.

Iulian, Rodica. 2004. *Dracula sau triumful modern al vampirului*. București: Compania.

Jones, Stephen, ed. 1992. *Book of Vampires*. New York: Barnes and Noble.

Karadja, C. 1936. *Poema lui Michael Beheim despre cruciadele împotriva turcilor din anii 1443 si 1444*. Vălenii-de-Munte.

Leu, Corneliu. 1972. *Plîngerea lui Dracula*. București: Cartea Romanească.

Lupescu, M. 1909. "Păzitul Usturoiului." *Ion Creangă* 6: 155–57.

Marian, Simeon Fl. Marianu, S. Fl. 1892. *Înmormîntarea la români*. Bucuresci: Lito-tipografia Carol Göbl.

_____. Marian, S. Fl. 1893. *Vrăji, farmece și desfaceri*. Bucuresci.

_____. 1989. *Serbătorile la Români*. Bucuresci: Institutul de Arte Grafice Carol Göbl.

Marinca, Felicia. 1962. "O variantă a baladei Călătoria fratelui mort (Motivul Lenore)." *Limbă si Literatură* V: 72–75.

McNally, Raymond T., ed. 1974. *A Clutch of Vampires*. New York: Bell.

McNally, Raymond T., and Radu Florescu. 1994. *In Search of Dracula*. Boston: Houghton Mifflin.

Mesnil, Marianne, and Aisia Popova, eds. 1997. *Etnograful între şarpe şi balaur; Eseuri de mitologie balcanică*. Trans. to Romanian by Ioana Bot and Ana Mihailescu. Bucureşti: Editura Paideia.

_____. 1997. "*Vampirism si tradiţie orală în România, sursele populare ale unui mit cult*." Mesnil and Popova, 125–34.

Miller, Elizabeth. 2002. "Vampire Hunting in Transylvania." http://www.ucs.mun.ca/~emiller/transylvania.html (accessed April 21, 2012).

Mîrzan, Ion Alexandru. 2003. *Vampirii din Carpaţi*. Beiuş: Editura Buna Vestire.

Moisil, I. 1903. "Credinţi despre moroi şi strigoi." *Şezătoarea*, 1:15–6.

Moldovan, Elena-Elvira. n.d. "Eros si Thanatos in Domnisoara Cristina de Mircea Eliade." www.upm.ro/facultati_departamente/stiinte_litere/conferinte/situl_integrareeuropeana/Lucrari3/romana/Texte_lit.rom3_doctorat/39_Moldovan.pdf (accessed April 10, 2012).

Murgoci, Agnes. 1926. "The Vampire in Romania." *Folklore* 37: 320–349.

Muşlea, Ion, ed. 2003. *Arhiva de Folclor a Academiei Române, Studii, memorii ale întemeierii, raporturi de activitate, chestionare 1930–48*. Cluj: Editura Fundaţiei pentru Studii Europene.

_____. 1971. *Cercetări etnografice şi de folclor*. Vol. 1. Bucureşti: Editura Minerva.

Muşlea, Ion, and Ovidiu Bîrlea. 1970. *Tipologia Folklorului, Din răspunsurile la chestionarele lui B.P. Haşdeu*. Bucureşti: Minerva.

Niculiţă-Voronca, Elena. 1898. "Strigoii la Români." *Familia* No. 3:1; No. 4:39–40; No. 5:51–2; No. 6: 64–6; No. 7:76–78; No. 8:88–90.

_____. 1903. *Datinile şi credinţele poporului român*. Vol. I-II, 1903.

_____. 1913. "De când se felicită pe cel ce strănută." *Ion Creangă*. No. 2: 51.

_____. 1913. "Despre strigoi." *Ion Creangă* No. 3: 80; No. 4: 108; No. 5:139; No. 10: 305–6.

Oinas, Felix. 1998. "East European Vampires." In Alan Dundes, 47–56.

Pamfile, Ion. 1916/2000. *Duşmani şi prieteni ai omului* (1916), *Comorile* (1916), and *Pământul după credinţele poporului român* (1924, posthumous). Rpt. 2000 as *Mitologie românească*. Iordan Datcu, ed. Bucureşti: Editura Grai şi Suflet.

Pamfile, Tudor. 1916. Bucureşti: Ioradan Datcu Ed.

Pavelescu, Gheorghe. 1971. *Balade populare din sudul Transilvaniei*. Sibiu: Casa judeţeană a creaţiei populare.

Perkowski, Jan Louis. 1982/2006. "The Romanian Folkloric Vampire." *Eastern European Quarterly*, 16: 311–322, 1982. Rpt. in 2006. *Vampire Lore*, Bloomington IN: Slavica.

Pop, Ioan-Aurel, and Ioan Buzdugan, eds. 2006. *History of Romania: Compendium*. Cluj-Napoca: Romanian Cultural Institute.

Rădulescu-Codin, Constantin. 1913. *Îngerul românului, Poveşti şi legende din popor*. Bucureşti: Academia Română.

Riccardo, Martin V. 1983. *Vampires Unearthed: The Complete Multimedia Vampire & Dracula Bibliography*. New York: Garland.

Rickel, Laurence A. 1999. *The Vampire Lectures*. Minneapolis: University of Minnesota Press.

Rîpa, Isidor. 1976. *Balade şi legende maramureşene*. Bucureşti: Editura I. Creangă.

Rogoz, Georgina Viorica. 2004. *Istoria*

despre Dracula. Bucureşti: NOI Media Print.

Şăineanu, Lazăr. 1886. *Ielele, dînsele, vîntoasele, frumoasele, şoimanele, măiestrele, milostivele, zînele—Studiu de mitologie comparativă*. Bucuresci: Tipografia Acadmiei Române.

_____. 1895/1978. *Basmele române în comparaţiune cu legendele antice clasice şi în legătură cu basmele poporeloru învecinate şi ale tuturoru poporeloru romanice*. Bucuresci: Litotipografia Carol Göbl, 1895. Rpt. 1978 as *Basmele române*. Bucuresti: Minerva.

Sbiera, Ion. 1886. *Poveşti poporale româneşti din popor luate şi poporului date*. Cernăuţi.

Schmitt, Jean-Claude. 1998. *Strigoii—Viii şi morţii în societatea medievală*. Bucuresti: Meridiane.

Senn, Harry A. 1982. *Were-Wolf and Vampire in Romania*. Boulder, CO: Eastern European Monographs.

Sevastos, Elena. 1888. *Anecdote poporane*. Iaşi: Colecţia Saraga.

Şezătoarea, Revistă pentru literature şi tradiţiuni populare. 1892–1949. Folticeni: Librăria M. Saidman.

Stănescu, Gabriel. 2000. *The Man Who Tried to Cheat Death, Romanian Scary Stories*. Trans. Marc Linscott Rickets. Norcross: Criterion.

Stăvăruş, Ion. 1993. *Povestiri medievale despre Vlad Ţepeş—Draculea, Studiu critic şi antologie*, 2d ed. Bucureşti: Editura Univers.

Stoian, Emil. 1989. *Vlad I: Mit şi realitate istorică*. Bucureşti: Editura Albatros.

Stoicescu, Nicolae. 1976. *Vlad Ţepeş*. Bucureşti: Editura Academiei R.S.R.

Stoker, Bram. *Dracula*. Bantam Books: New York.

Summers, Montague. 2001. *The Vampire in Europe*. Rpt. as *The Vampire in Lore and Legend*. Mineola, NY: Dover.

Teodorescu, G. Dem. 1874. *Încercări critice asupra unoru credinţe, datine şi moravuri ale poporului românu*. Bucuresci: Tipografia Petrescu-Conduratu.

Treptow, Kurt W. 2000. *Vlad III Dracula, the Life and Times of the Historical Dracula*. Iasi: The Center for Romanian Studies.

Ugliş-Delapecica, Petre. 1968. *Poezii şi basme populare din Crişana şi Banat*. Bucureşti: Editura pentru literatură.

Vaz da Silva, Francisco. 2002. *Metamorphosis: The Dynamics of Symbolism in European Fairy Tales*. New York: Peter Lang.

Vulcanu, Iosifu, ed. 1865–1940. *Familia, foaie enciclopedică şi beletristică cu ilustraţiuni*. Oradea-mare si Pesta.

Vulcănescu, Romulus. 1987. *Mitologie Română*. Bucureşti: Editura Academiei R.S.R.

Wilkinson, William. 1820. *An Account of the Principalities of Wallachia and Moldavia, with Various Political Observations Relative to Them*. London: Longman.

Williamson, Milly. 2005. *The Lure of the Vampyre: Gender, Fiction and Fandom from Bram Stoker to Buffy*. Wallflower Press: London.

Zipes, Jack. 1994. *Fairy Tale as Myth, Myth as Fairy Tale*. Lexington: University Press of Kentucky.

Index